"Wee Beasties" is a term used in the medical and scientific fields to describe microscopic germs. Its use dates back to the 17th century when germs were first discovered.

This book has an accompanying song and they are used to encourage kids to wash their hands often to "beat the wee beasties" and prevent the spread of germs that cause viral and bacterial infections, especially in light of the global pandemic of COVID-19.

To thoroughly clean our hands, we need enough friction to generate suds with soap and water for at least 20 seconds, which is the duration of the accompanying song's chorus.
It can be downloaded at www.theknightbros.com

Join the Knights on the Round Rug for stories,
music, games and merchandise at
WWW.THEKNIGHTBROS.COM

The Knight Bros.

presents

WEE BEASTIES

Written & Illustrated by
Dr. David Knight

Music by
Bradford Knight

Song available for download at
w w w . t h e k n i g h t b r o s . c o m

On our fingies
Little germies,
Little squirmies,
Give us sneezies!

Soapy sudsies
Kill the germies,
Kill the squirmies,
On our fingies!

Germies, squirmies and wee beasties
Hate it when we wash our fingies!
Wash them hard and wash them long
As we sing this song!

We beat **beat**
we **beat** the **wee beasties!!**

We beat **beat**
we beat **wee beasties!!**

We beat **beat**
we **beat** the **wee beasties!!**

We beat **beat**
We beat **wee beasties!!**

Bd-bd-bd-bd-bd-bd-bd **Bd beat**

Bd-bd-bd-bd-bd-bd-bd Bd beat

After touching other thingies,
We must clean our little fingies!

If we touch our mouths or eyesies,
Germies just might crawl insidesies!

We sneeze into our elbows, yeah!

We won't sneeze in our hands, no way!

We sneeze into our elbows, yeah!

And wash our hands all day - Hooray!

We beat **beat**
we **beat** the **wee beasties!!**

We beat **beat**
We beat **wee beasties!!**

We beat **beat**
we **beat** the **wee beasties!!**

We beat **beat**
We beat **wee beasties!!**

Bd-bd-bd-bd-bd-bd-bd Bd beat

Bd-bd-bd-bd-bd-bd-bd Bd beat

Oh, I forgot to mention,
we can't see the wee beasties...

CPSIA information can be obtained at www.ICGtesting.com
Printed in the USA
BVIW121925291020
592146BV00012B/26

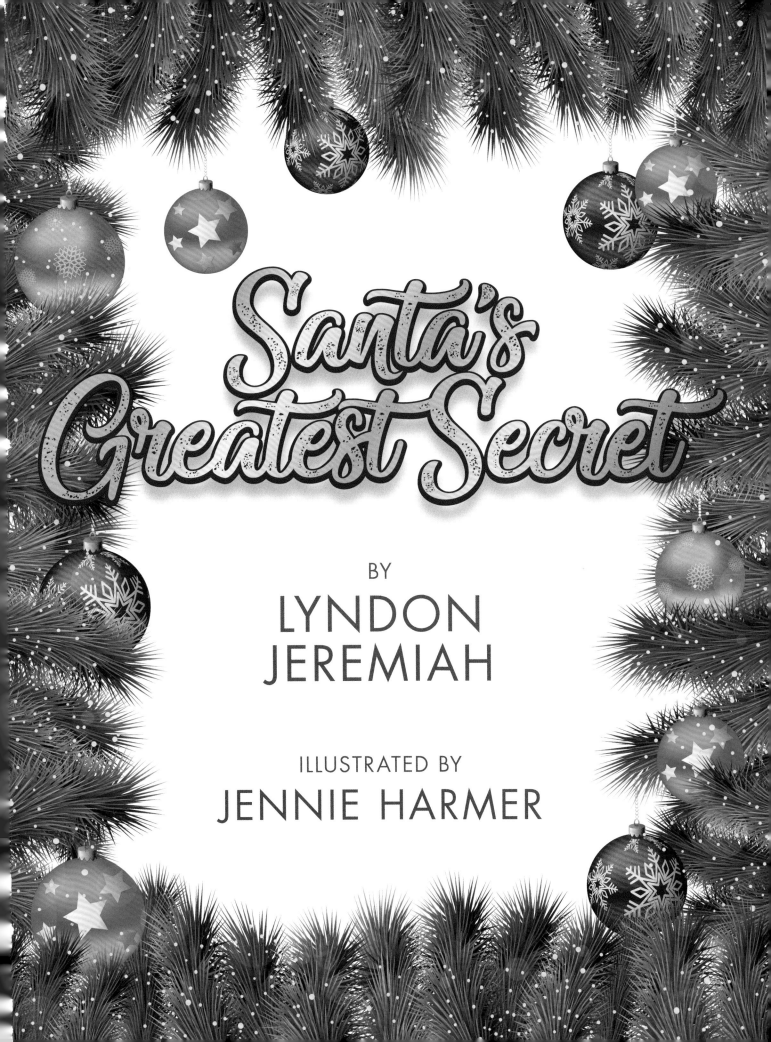

Santa's Greatest Secret

BY

LYNDON
JEREMIAH

ILLUSTRATED BY

JENNIE HARMER

First published in 2020 by Jeremiah Publishing 2020

ISBN: 978 1 8382713 0 5

A CIP record for this title is available from the British Library.

© Copyright Jeremiah Publishing 2020

Lyndon Jeremiah asserts his moral right under the Copyright, Designs and Patents Act, 1988 to be identified as author of this work.

Jennie Harmer asserts her moral right under the Copyright, Designs and Patents Act, 1988 to be identified as illustrator of this work.

Printed and bound in Wales at
Gomer Press, Llandysul, Ceredigion

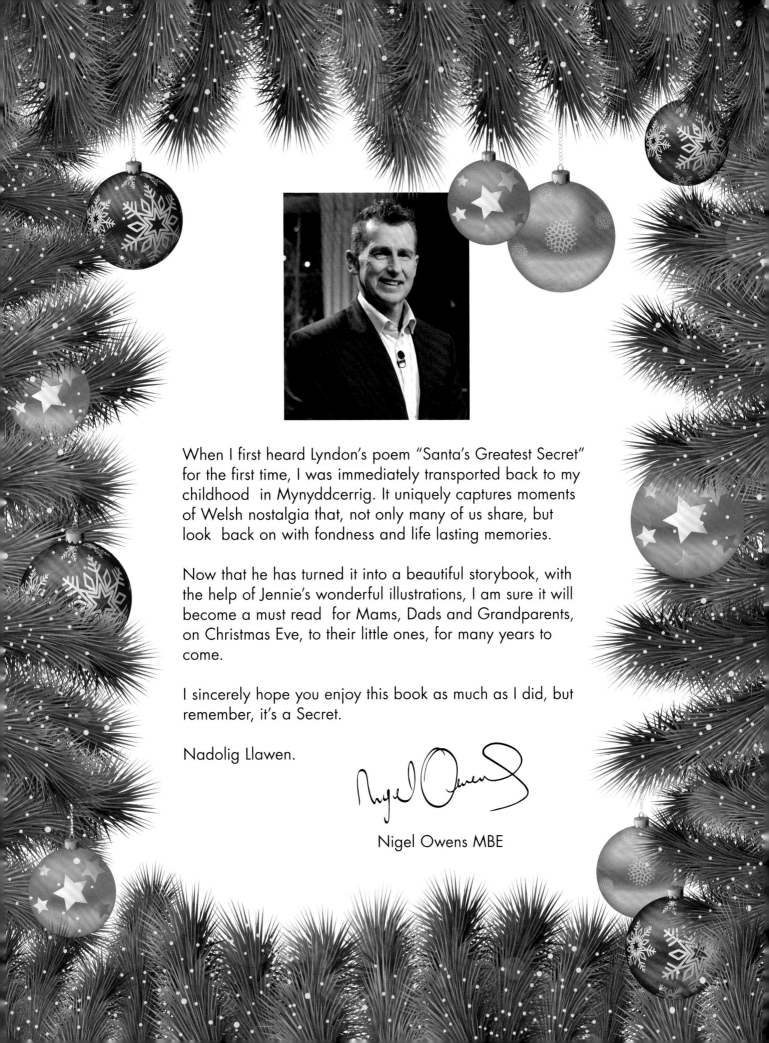

When I first heard Lyndon's poem "Santa's Greatest Secret" for the first time, I was immediately transported back to my childhood in Mynyddcerrig. It uniquely captures moments of Welsh nostalgia that, not only many of us share, but look back on with fondness and life lasting memories.

Now that he has turned it into a beautiful storybook, with the help of Jennie's wonderful illustrations, I am sure it will become a must read for Mams, Dads and Grandparents, on Christmas Eve, to their little ones, for many years to come.

I sincerely hope you enjoy this book as much as I did, but remember, it's a Secret.

Nadolig Llawen.

Nigel Owens MBE

To

....

From

....

Christmas

....

To the Children of Wales.
Young and old.
In countries wide and far.

Many miles away from here,
In a far and distant place.
Across the Crystal Mountains,
And through the Icy Wastes.

A mile from where your dreams are,
Turn left at Wonderland.
 You'll find a house that no one knows,
 And a very special man.

He's very large and jolly,
With a beard as white as snow.
Of course it's Father Christmas,
But there's something you
don't know.

When it turns December,
And the elves have made the toys.
He makes sure they're delivered,
To all the girls and boys.

04

It isn't always easy,
Some years it's very tough.
But always by the 26th
Santa has had enough.

He locks up all the workshops,
Puts the tools away.
Feeds the reindeer for the winter,
And gives the Elves their pay.

He packs his summer suitcase,
Loads up his other sleigh.
The one that won't be noticed,
On the motorway.

He heads off to his Homeland.
The place from which he hails.
It's always been a secret,
That Santa comes from Wales!

He was born in Aberpandy.
Where he ran and played all day.
It was here he learnt the secret,
How to give, not take away.

In the land where smiles are plenty,
He lived with Mam and Dad.
Santa told them of his worries,
And why he felt so sad.

"I think of other children,
It makes me feel so bad.
They haven't been so lucky,
To have the lovely life I've had."

As Santa he grew older,
A Miner he became.
Followed his Father's footsteps,
He worked hard just the same.

·PWLL ABERPANDY·

Descending the mine shaft,
It was always dark as night.
How he wished that everything
Was beautiful and white.

12

After work he liked to sing,
Around an open fire.
Singing was in Santa's blood,
That's why he joined the choir.

On Saturdays he liked to go,
Put on his weekend suit.
A big black sack upon his back,
Contained his rugby boots.

For Santa was a winger.
You should have seen him fly.
He waved to all the children,
Each time he scored a try.

15

His skill it was a mystery.
His team mates could not tell.
Why every time he passed the ball,
They heard a jingle bell.

His speed it was fantastic.
Santa ran at lightning pace.
He swerved and sold a dummy,
With a smile upon his face.

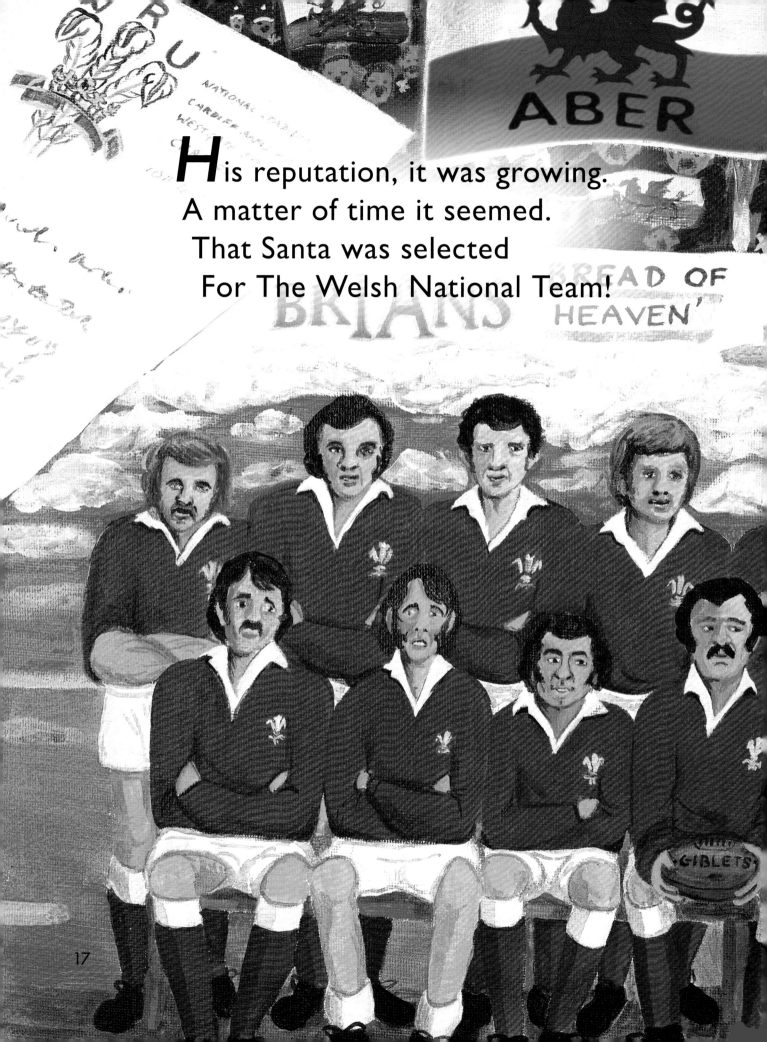

His reputation, it was growing.
A matter of time it seemed.
That Santa was selected
For The Welsh National Team!

At last he made his debut.
His friends had always said.
Santa, he was destined,
To wear the colour red.

He stood and sang the anthem.
His Mam and Dad were proud.
"Mae Hen Wlad Fy Nhadau"
Was never sung so loud.

But Santa left it all behind.
I think he always knew...

19

...that destiny was calling,
From where the North Wind Blew.

Santa now works for the World.
All countries wide and far.
Wales' greatest export,
A global Superstar.

But, being Welsh is not where you are from,
Or the colour of your skin.
It's the good you do for others,
And the love you have within.

22

So if you're lying in your bed,
Head full of Christmas tales.
Remember it's a secret.
Santa comes from *Wales!*

Acknowledgements

I would like to thank the following people for their assistance in the creation of this book.

Jennie Harmer
Nathan Shelton
Nigel Owens MBE
Rhian Mannings MBE
Chris Needs MBE
Gabe Cameron
Llinos Jones
Shannon Griffiths
Rob Chapman
Manon Cadwaladr
Siân Rees-Jones
Eirwen Thomas
Dilwyn Jones
Lloyd Davies
Peter Jones
Becki Estano
Pit Dafis

The Aberford, Barrowby
and East Garforth Railway

A Railway Conversation
for the
Model Railway Enthusiast

The Aberford, Barrowby and East Garforth Railway

A Railway Conversation
for the
Model Railway Enthusiast

Keith Crosby

The Pentland Press
Edinburgh – Cambridge – Durham – USA

© Keith Crosby, 1994

First published in 1994 by
The Pentland Press Ltd
1 Hutton Close
South Church
Bishop Auckland
Durham

British Library
Cataloguing-in-Publication Data

A catalogue record for this book
is available from the British Library

ISBN 1-85821-205-7

The names of persons and events described in this book are, to the best
of my knowledge, factual and are as accurate as memory can make them.

While every effort has been made to trace and acknowledge all copyright holders,
we would like to apologise should there have been any errors or omissions.

Cover photographs:

i. Hornby/Gresley D49/1 'Cheshire' pauses for instruction at East Garforth (East)
Signal Box.

ii. 'Cheshire' coasts through the western portals of Bramhope Tunnel with an
up-stopping passenger for Aberford Central.

Typeset by Carnegie Publishing, 18 Maynard St., Preston
Printed and bound by Antony Rowe Ltd., Chippenham

To 'the girl of my dreams', Alma, and our two sons, Melville and Robin.

Contents

Introduction

Bobby Thompson, North-Eastern comedian *par excellence*, was confiding to his audience, 'The wife calls down from the bedroom, "Bobby, the carrier bag handle's broke, can yer fix it?" "Well," says Bobby, "ah'm nae engineer." '

This just about sums me up, because 'ah'm nae engineer'; neither am I any great shakes as a comedian.

So, you might well ask, 'what's he doing writing a book about railways?'

Well, I'll let you into a secret – I have been asking myself the same question recently.

One normally expects an author to have a complete grasp of his subject before putting pen to paper, yet here am I rattling away at the keyboard of my little word processor; filling the screen with page after page of chatter, revelling in reminiscence completely lacking in technical depth.

In self-defence, I offer you one thing that I do have plenty of and that is imagination; imagination fed by reminiscence and a determination to simulate in model form something of what I have seen in 'real life', regardless of having had no engineering or mechanical training whatsoever.

As the following pages will reveal, I have spent a lifetime 'under the influence'; 'under the influence' of railways, real and model. Railways have always fascinated me, in both forms, and this has led me into the wonderful world of model railways whereby I have been fortunate enough, over the past thirty-five years, to have been able to recreate a simulation of my trackside memories. This simulation I have chosen to call 'The Aberford, Barrowby and East Garforth Railway'.

It is of the experiences and recall of memories concerned in its conception, construction and operation, that I would like to share with those of you who, like myself, are 'nae engineers' but nevertheless have a love of railways and would very much like to create a model railway of your own, but have only very basic modelling ability with which to begin.

If what I have set down in the following pages serves to give you food for thought and, subsequently, encourages you to 'set sail' on your own venture, then I shall consider my objective to have been achieved.

May your imagination ever prove fertile and uphold you until the end.

Keith Crosby,
Bishop Auckland
1993

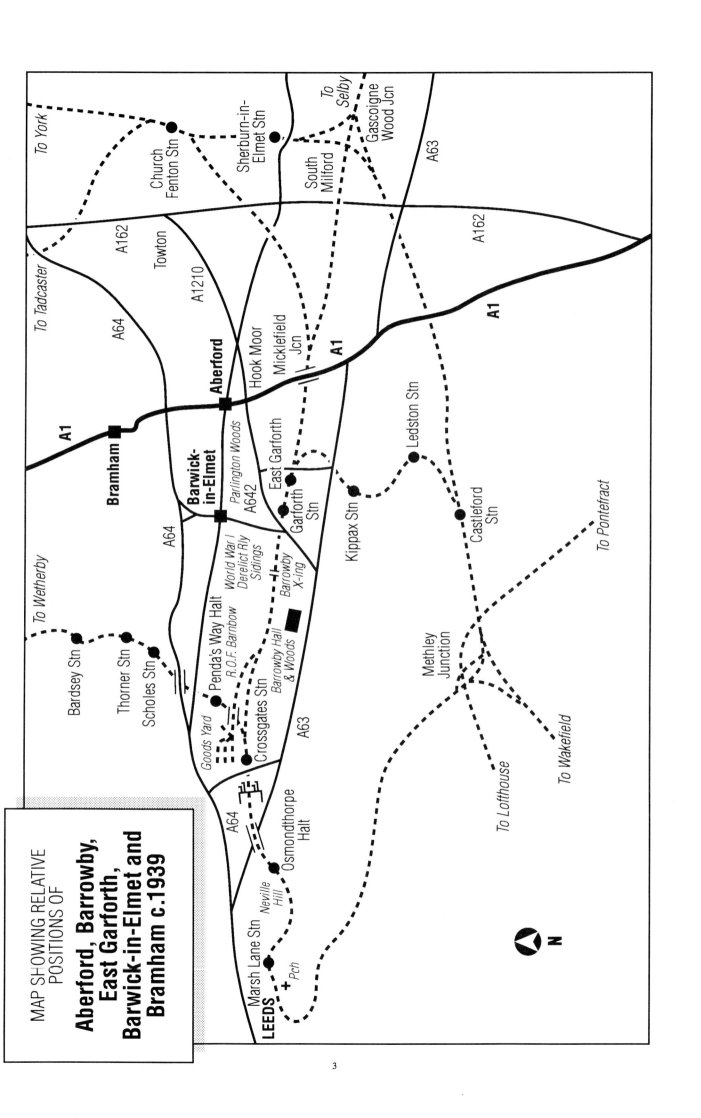

MAP SHOWING RELATIVE POSITIONS OF

Aberford, Barrowby, East Garforth, Barwick-in-Elmet and Bramham c.1939

To York

To Tadcaster

To Wetherby

Church Fenton Stn

Sherburn-in-Elmet Stn

To Selby

Gascoigne Wood Jcn

South Milford

A63

A162

Towton

A162

A1210

A64

Hook Moor

Micklefield

Jcn

A1

A1

Aberford

Bramham

A1

Ledston Stn

Parlington Woods

East Garforth

A642

Garforth Stn

Kippax Stn

Castleford Stn

Barwick-in-Elmet

A64

World War I Derelict Rly Sidings

R.O.F. Barnbow

Barrowby X-ing

Barrowby Hall & Woods

To Pontefract

Penda's Way Halt

Goods Yard

Crossgates Stn

A63

Methley Junction

To Lofthouse

To Wakefield

Bardsey Stn

Thorner Stn

Scholes Stn

A64

Osmondthorpe Halt

Neville Hill

Marsh Lane Stn

LEEDS

+ Pch

N

3

The Aberford, Barrowby
and East Garforth Railway

'Were it not for imagination, sir, a man would be as happy in the arms of a chambermaid as of a Duchess.' Boswell's *Life of Johnson*.

'In the beginning He created the railway and, seeing that it was good, He then created the world to go around it.' Me – with apologies.

Aberford, Barrowby, East Garforth, Barwick (pron. Barrick)-in-Elmet and Bramham (pron. Brammam), are small but real points on the map of the West Riding of Yorkshire. They are the pleasant–sounding names of equally pleasant villages a few miles east of Leeds, apart from Barrowby which is the name of a hall and its accompanying woods.

Other than Garforth, they share one thing in common – they have never been served by a railway. Never, that is, until I built a model railway system comprising two large stations and three small ones, going under the names of Stations 'A', 'B', 'C', 'D', and 'E', but which, somehow, did not sound exactly euphonious; they were lacking in mystery and excitement (you can say that again!)

I needed five 'proper' names – but which, what and where?

Then one day, as I was reflecting on some of the stamping grounds of my youth and the places my pals and I would go to on our bicycles, I remembered Aberford, Barrowby and East Garforth. These were real names, not made–up ones, and just what I wanted. So I added nearby Barwick-in-Elmet and Bramham to make up the five I required, and the rest was history – or something.

Here we have a utopia where steam and diesel motive power run happily side by side, drawing on the best of past and present with no one wittering about cost-effectiveness and economic justification, just so long as it works and looks good.

Here is a social, economic and railway-loving paradise, where roads are things to run our cars along and enjoy the rural scene; where conveniently placed lay-bys, at viewing vantage points, allow us to watch our trains go by whilst we picnic in peace and contentment, and the leeks get plenty of sunshine.

Here is where imagination is king; bound only by a reverence for tradition when planning for the future.

Early Memories

Consider, if you will, this aged scribe, born in 1928 who, from an early age, lived within sight of the Leeds to Selby railway line at various points between the city of Leeds (to whom we raise our hats of course) eastwards to the village of Garforth. It was a very busy line with a wide variety of traffic and locomotives.

His arrival on earth more or less coincided with the birth of what was to become his favourite of all locomotive classes – the LNER D49 4–4–0 Hunts and Shires, named after the many fox-hunts and counties 'occupied' by the LNER.

Those lustrous engines were our 'pacifics', bearing as they did many of the features of the Gresley 4–6–2's. We little boys could distinguish

Back to the 1930s and an almost brand-new Gresley D49/2 'Hunt', class no. 255 'The Braes of Derwent' leads a long train of varnished teak Gresley corridor coaches southwards of York.

an oncoming Hunt from a Shire by the formers' outside steam pipes to their cylinders.

They were brand new and fairly sparkled in their applegreen plus white–black–white lining and, to us, seemed very fast. We later heard that they were considered to be rough riders by the crews. At the Crossgates junction with the Wetherby line we could see them fairly rocking from side to side on the rails as they sped round the curve from Barnbow; we could actually see their driving wheels lift off the rails! Add to all this the pristine (in most cases) varnished teak Gresley corridor coaches and you had a sight to gladden the heart of every boy who wanted a Hornby Train set for Christmas.

I must have been born under a lucky star because my 1940 Christmas present was none other than the Hornby E220 special set, 'The Scarborough Flier' headed by D49 4–4–0 'The Bramham Moor'.

It came just in time because in a few short months supplies almost dried up because of the war. Anyway, it was the pride of my life as it ran hour after hour around the carpeted floor of my bedroom, under bed, dressing table and wardrobe – 20 circuits Leeds to Doncaster, 20 to Grantham and so on to King's Cross. Very little shunting

was carried out because I was too busy on my 'express runs' and, in any case, very few of us ever had more than one engine, except for Mr Edgar Kirk just down the road, who was a draughtsman and engineer by profession and who built his own gauge 'O' stock from scratch, even the wheels. At the time I knew him he had just built a V2 'Green Arrow'; oh, it was a beauty. He had his layout round the walls of the cellar of his terraced house, all very gloomy but so exciting. He it was who introduced me, by example, to model engineering, and whilst I shall never achieve his skills, he gave me something to dream about for the future.

Perhaps you might remember a Walt Disney film, *Cinderella*, I think it was, where there was a song entitled 'A Dream is a Wish your Heart Makes'? Well, the dream came true for me sure enough, but not for another 20 years or so, during which period an education had to be undergone, national service in 'the cream' of His Majesty's Services (RAF), a career in salesmanship established, marriage to the 'girl of my dreams', a home of my own and the birth of the first of my two sons.

As it was in the beginning

The year is 1960 and, at last, I have the opportunity to make a start; not in a cellar, but in a 24' × 12' garage with space inside large enough to house a Morris Minor 1000 and still leave plenty of room round the walls for a railway.

Because of family moves during the war years I had no model railway equipment left at all, so that when the time came to make my new start, Hornby Gauge 'O' electric was, sadly, no longer with us and Hornby Dublo had taken its place. So Hornby Dublo it had to be – 3-rail!

I don't think I had ever used a saw in my life before a friend introduced me to the delights of 2 × 1 timber, hardboard and panel pins – which were all the rage then – and, ere long, I had a 2' wide baseboard running round the walls of the lower half of the garage, supported by 2 × 2" verticals at a height of 3' 6". Dublo rail was laid to a double track main line with a four track through station, plus a few sidings for spare rolling stock.

I was reading the *Railway Modeller* regularly by now and had Edward Beal's handbook, plus John Ahern's on Landscape Modelling for reference, so I was in the process of picking up ideas on layout, electrics and scenery.

What nobody told me about was the noise of that wretched hardboard! It acted like the skin on a drum and I am sure those little trains made more noise than the real ones. Something had to be done to quieten things down: that something turned out to be insulation board and most of it is in position to this day. The whole caboosh was relaid and the hardboard set to one side because 'it might come in handy one day', which it did, but not as baseboard material.

Right, so we now had quieter running and I introduced cab control via ex-RAF bomb selector switches. My lovely cast-and-lithographed tin-plate stock commenced their many circuits and gave much pleasure.

At this stage I had to exercise a discipline that has stood me in good stead over the years, namely to select a railway group and stick to it despite all temptations. If you, dear reader, have read thus far, for which I thank you, you will not be surprised that the railway group I chose was the LNER as running between 1935 and 1939. There

was plenty of scope, but many a time I was tempted to stray such as when the Hornby Dublo 'Bristol Castle' came out.

I actually bought a 'Bristol Castle' but it spent more time back at Hornby's than it did on my layout; it just wouldn't pull! Eventually Hornby agreed to exchange it for a Class 20 diesel, which was a bit more successful.

Rolling stock was increasing considerably, and I was learning about scenery and making buildings. Also, G. W. Wrenn introduced flexible track and points. Now, I thought, here was my chance to go in for more realistic curves – still in 3-rail of course.

Well it was all right up to a point and I also acquired most of my H & M point motors at this time. Problems arose related to the climatic conditions prevailing in the garage, which were almost like operating out of doors: hot in summer, cold and damp in winter. It played havoc with the fibre sleeperage of the Wrenn track, so much so that, in the damp weather, they would expand and the rail gauge would do the same, so that trains dropped between the lines. I wouldn't have minded so much if there had not been so much of it, but it had to go.

By this time the layout had extended into the top half of the garage, through a hole kindly cold-chiselled for me through a brick abutment by my brother-in-law. The layout was also entering into the realms of 'split-level'; i.e. there was a 'high-level' terminus and a 'low-level' one. All very interesting scenery wise but problematical because of the gradients and lack of locomotive adhesion.

2-rail had now become established throughout the land and the big decision was made eventually to part-exchange what stock couldn't take or wasn't worth rewheeling, and track conversion to Peco was commenced. Luckily the Wrenn 3-rail track was on insulative sleepers so there was no electrical problem other than to disconnect the centre rails and decide which of the remaining two was to be the 'common return'. Of course, all the metal-based Hornby Dublo track had to be withdrawn from service completely. All right, so the radii of Hornby Dublo curves were too tight to look scale-like, but I was sorry to part with their electrically operated points because they were so beautifully made and the tiny solenoid operating mechanisms were a joy.

This comment applies to the Hornby Dublo electrically operated signals – which I still have not parted with, in fact I bought more as opportunity arose. Their bases are still in use but now have scratch-built lattice posts, signal arms and ladders mounted on them. As I said earlier, the solenoids are so tiny and the operating system so simple that one wonders why the boffins of today can't come up with something similar, instead of us having to use all these huge (by comparison) present-day point motors and/or relays.

Triang came up with the idea of Magnadhesion to help out with gradient problems, and it worked so long as you used steel track. But steel track, in my circumstances, tends to go rusty over the years and the rust becomes embedded into the rail surface with resultant drop in conductivity, so I have now settled for nickel silver and the more scale-width wheels of today seem to like it better.

Also, of course, we now have traction tyres to help with adhesion on the ready-to-runs. To me, it seems farcical to see the lightweight RTRs sauntering up gradients of 1 in 30 with no trouble at all, when kit-builts so heavy with extra lead in every conceivable nook and cranny that, to paraphrase Iain Rice (to whom we also raise our hats of course), all the lights in the county go dim. They struggle, they slip, strip gears and heat up motors just for the lack of a little 'rubberised assistance'.

I am sure that these heavyweights are responsible for breaking up so many of my fragile plastic-based Peco points. I don't know an awful lot about the technology of plastics, but Peco track seems to be made of a much more durable plastic than do the points. The sleepers, especially in the tie-rod area, just seem to crumble away and they are getting expensive nowadays.

Of the many aspects of railway modelling, making the best use of time looms very important. In my case I had the vision of a large continuous layout with considerable operational potential and, as we all become aware sooner or later, life on earth does not last indefinitely, so some short cuts have to be undertaken. I chose therefore, to settle for ready-made track.

During the 1960s I built a rake of six PC LNER Teak Gresley Corridors, which are still running perfectly. Thanks to LNER-inclined loco kit producers, I built 2 Wills J39 0–6–0s and a Gem D21 4–4–0 Triang Chassis, a Jameson hand-cut

D49 4–4–0, a K's GN Atlantic 4–4–2, a Nucast Q6 0–8–0 and Sentinel Railcar – and I am still trying to learn the art of meshing gears! So it can be seen that I was being kept busy adding to my LNER inventory, as well as extending the layout, through yet another hole in the wall, until eventually it ran round the entire area of the garage, complete with stations, scenery, signals etc. How much of this would have been achieved in the time if I had made my own track?

In the first rush of railway modelling I made a simple mistake, but one which was to turn to my considerable advantage later on.

Remember that I wanted a double track main line so that I could run two trains at the same time? I bought the usual Dublo transformer, two controllers and a packet or two of insulating tabs which fitted between the centre rail track connectors, where there was a crossover from one line to another, or where a track section started. Fine so far.

Then I wired the two controllers to the outputs of the transformer and thence the tracks, switched on and started running my two trains. Again, fine so far. Fine that is until I wanted to reverse one train whilst the other one was going forward, and up came the little buttons of the circuit breakers! I puzzled and puzzled to no avail, so hot-footed it off to my principal supplier of the day, lovely old Tom Applegarth of Durham City, long since departed this mortal coil, God rest his soul.

He it was who told me about things like double-wound transformers and the like and exchanged one of my controllers, which wasn't one of the rectified sort, for one that was, and presto, I was away. Locos now backed and forwarded independently of each other and points and signals clicked away in satisfactory manner. It would seem that for each train to run independently, it must be controlled by a controller having its own individual a.c. power input which it then rectifies into the necessary d.c. voltage, completely unshared by any other controller.

The early 1960s were the days when Cab Control was being discussed at great length in the modelling press.

They were also the days when one could get quite a lot of ex-government equipment, left over from war time days. We seemed to be very fond of ex-RAF bomb selector switches, each of which had 16 on-and-off switches grouped in 4s on a

Controller 'By-pass' Switches

Allowing Mainline Controllers (C1 & C2) to Take Over Controller 3 (Sidings) Sections

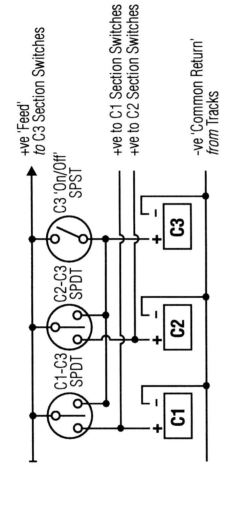

+ve 'Feed' *to* C3 Section Switches

+ve to C1 Section Switches
+ve to C2 Section Switches

-ve 'Common Return' *from* Tracks

C3 'On/Off' SPST

C2-C3 SPDT

C1-C3 SPDT

Circuit Diagram of Controller 'By-pass' Switches

Explanatory Notes

1. Object – to facilitate easier/smoother exits from, and entries to, the mainlines from the 'sidings', i.e. sections normally under the control of Controller 3. This is, in effect, an adaptation of 'cab control'.

2. Method – to provide the power outputs of Controllers 1 & 2 (Up & Down Mainline controllers) with a 2-way switched connection to the output wire to the sections controlled by Controller 3, in advance of its section switches, thus introducing a 'Bypass' alternative to the use of Controller 3.

N.B. Negative terminals of all controllers are connected together, to form a 'Common Return' to all controllers. See diagram.

3. Operating Procedure – e.g. when drawing a train out of a station loop (a C3 section), onto the Down Mainline (C2 section):

   (a) Ensure that all C3 section switches are 'off', other than the ones needed for the manoeuvre. Otherwise trains other than the required one will also move.

   (b) Switch off C3 and switch 'in' the C2-C3 switch.

   (c) Using Controller 2 – take train out on to Down Mainline and proceed.

   (d) When train clear of C3 sections, switch 'out' C2-C3 switch.

   (e) C3 sections are now free again to be operated by Controller 3.

4. When switching 'in' Controllers 1 or 2 to Controller 3 sections, Controller 3 must be switched off to avoid 'crossed polarities' e.g. C1 set for forward when C3 set for reverse.

Polarity Changeover Switches for Reversing Loops

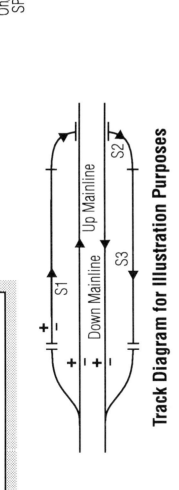

Track Diagram for Illustration Purposes

DPDT Polarity Changeover Switch

Section Switches
On/Off
SPST

To S1   To S2   To S3

To L.H. Rails

To R.H. Rails

C1

Explanatory Notes

1. Object – to take a locomotive round a reversing loop, thus changing its direction, and out on to the 'opposite' mainline without having to stop to match polarities when reaching the mainline. See diagram for details.

2. Method – to provide a DPDT polarity changeover switch between Controller 3 (or C1/C2 via 'Bypass switches') and the section switches for the reversing loop, (sections S1, S2 & S3 in the diagram).

   (a) Let the section switches S1, S2 & S3 be wired independently of the remainder of Controller 3 section switches, so as to allow their polarity to be changed.

   (b) Let the output wires from switches S1, S2 & S3 be connected to the LH running rail of the reversing loop.

   (c) Disconnect the existing 'common return' wire from the running rails and replace with a new one coming from the output of the changeover switch. Let this new wire be connected to the RH running rail of the reversing loop.

   (d) Let there be an insulated rail joint in both running rails at each end of the reversing loop, thus making the loop electrically independent of the remainder of the layout.

3. Operating procedure (refer to track diagram):

   (a) Bring train into S1 from the Up Mainline, using the C1-C3 'bypass' device, and stop when clear of the point/turnout.

   (b) Switch 'out' C1-C3 and switch 'in' C2-C3 'bypass', and 'changeover' the polarity switch. The polarity of sections S1, S2 & S3 now 'matches' the polarity of the Down Mainline.

   (c) The train can now be driven round the reversing loop, and out on to the Down Mainline without a pause or hesitation (don't forget to change the Down Mainline entry point after the manoeuvre).

   (d) Finally, switch 'out' the C2-C3 'bypass' and change the polarity changeover switch back to 'normal'.

Circuit Diagram of 'Retarding Resistor'

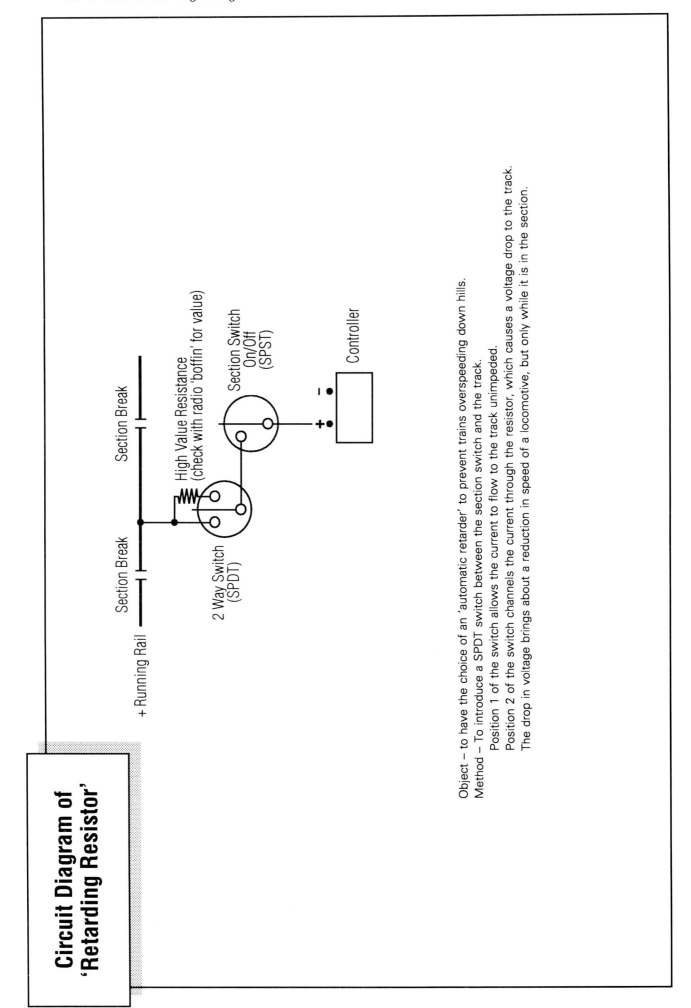

+ Running Rail

Section Break

Section Break

High Value Resistance
(check with radio 'boffin' for value)

Section Switch
On/Off
(SPST)

2 Way Switch
(SPDT)

Controller

Object – to have the choice of an 'automatic retarder' to prevent trains overspeeding down hills.
Method – To introduce a SPDT switch between the section switch and the track.
Position 1 of the switch allows the current to flow to the track unimpeded.
Position 2 of the switch channels the current through the resistor, which causes a voltage drop to the track.
The drop in voltage brings about a reduction in speed of a locomotive, but only while it is in the section.

neat panel. With three of these items you had enough to switch your track sections using any, or all, of your three controllers. The idea was that each and every controller could power every section, so long as you kept a clear head and remembered which controller was controlling what.

After a year or two I was able to rationalise the idea somewhat; for example, I soon realised that running three trains at a time was as much as I could comfortably manage. In any case the layout had an up main line and a down main line and why complicate things by making their controls interchangeable? Thus the up and the down main lines each have their own controller, whilst a third controls all movements off the main line, such as sidings and loops. This saves on the number of section switches required.

Up main line is under the control of controller No. 1. Down main line controller 2 and 'sidings' controller 3.

This is all right as far as it goes, but one soon comes up against the matter of matching controller outputs when you leave a 'siding' for the main line (or vice versa). If you are not careful you will get a momentary surge of power when half of the loco is on the main line and the other half still on the 'siding'. Not dangerous, but not exactly conductive to smooth running.

I have found a way out of this situation by using a SPDT changeover switch between the main output wire of controller 1 and that of controller 3, and similarly one between controller 2 and controller 3.

By labelling one switch position 'Direct' and the other 'Bypass', or some such term (it doesn't matter so long as you understand what you mean) you have a facility for using the main line controller to, say, take a train out of a 'siding' on to the main line using the main line controller only and bypassing controller 3, and again, vice versa.

It is important to have controller 3 switched off at this time, and all other sections under its control – except the ones you require for the manoeuvre, otherwise you will have unwanted loco movements elsewhere and also crossed polarities creating short circuits.

A further adaptation, on my layout anyway, is where an Up main line train comes into the Aberford Central station loop (i.e. controller 1 bypassing controller 3) and then has to gain the Down main line, controller 2, via one of the reversing loops.

The procedure is as follows:

Stop the train at the station loop (using controller 1). Switch off controller 1 and return the by pass switch to 'Direct'.

Switch controller 2s bypass switch to 'Siding' and, here's the clever bit if you can understand it, reverse the polarity of the reversing loop to the polarity of the Down main line by means of a conveniently sited DPDT changeover switch, and take the train sedately out of the station, through the reverse loop and out on to the Down main line without a hesitation, protest, surge, or short.

When the movement is completed and the train is merrily chugging away along the Down main line, return controller 2 bypass switch to 'Direct', change back the polarity DPDT switch to 'Normal', and there you have it.

As an aside at this stage, older modellers such as myself will remember that in 3-rail days one did not have to bother about changing polarity on reverse loops; the current was fed to the centre rail and returned via the outer rails (or was it the other way round?) and this remained the same regardless of the direction of the locomotive. Forward or reverse was according to the position of the controller, whichever track the loco was on (remember the power went into the outside rails and returned through the centre rail). This was one of the few advantages of the 3-rail over 2-rail as far as I could see, apart from not having to bother about insulated wheels. Also you could, if you wish, organise an illuminated track occupation diagram without resorting to the use of relays. I was just starting to do this when I went 2-rail.

However, by this time, so much was being demanded of the poor old Hornby Dublo transformer, as the layout grew in complexity, that one became aware every time one threw a passing contact point switch or operated an electric uncoupler, that all the locomotives in use would momentarily slow down. (These were the days before capacitor dischargers and diode matrices.) A change in power units was indicated and I chose the H & M variable transformer transistorised controllers because they claimed to offer certain advantages, but I am unable to remember what they were. They did have an increased power output, and that stopped trains slowing down when points were switched.

What these controllers did not offer was constant speed up hills and down dales. To overcome overspeeding on downward gradients I inserted a track section break at the top of the gradient and another at the bottom. The section feed wire was fed into a two-way switch (SPDT), the outputs of which led to the track (a) through a fairly high-value resistance or (b) direct. This saved a certain amount of controller-operating when I just wanted to leave the main line trains running whilst I got on with some work elsewhere on the layout. It was not a perfect solution but it is still there when required even with the later sophisticated Compspeed Closed Loop Feedback controllers. It is usually an indication of a motor past its best when it still tends to run away downhill despite the retarding effects of the feedback.

The H & M controllers all failed eventually, usually as a result of the power transistors overheating, and that was when I changed over to Compspeed, but even those don't last forever. Nevertheless they are, for me, the best yet, especially the Compspeed W model with its simulated coasting, braking and acceleration facilities. No good for coreless motors though; I melted the little gold wire brushes on the only one I tried and said 'never again at that price'. Surely, if these coreless motors are really the answer to every maiden's prayer, it should not be beyond the ingenuity of manufacturers to make them resistant to the pulse power of the feedback controllers. After all, man has only to think of something to be able to do it.

By now, if there is one such, even the most sympathetic reader must have realised that I am no engineer; a model-maker yes but engineer no.

Nowhere in railway modelling are my shortcomings in this respect more in evidence than when it comes to motor transmissions. Surely no one can have stripped more brass gearwheels that I have?

Thank the Lord for Iain Rice I say; someone who can talk my novice's language, and at last I think I am getting somewhere.

Imagine all these years of modelling and no one has really gone into print on the subject before, in such close detail.

I have always been a lone worker because the amount of free time I have had always seemed too limited to make it possible to join a club — even if they would let me in (not all clubs have a 'strangers welcome' policy, you know). This is perhaps why I have had to work on a trial and

1990. Perseverance compensated chassis for Nu-cast Gresley V3 2-6-2 Tank locomotive. A lovely mover. (Photo KC)

error basis all this time. For instance, a loco kit will take me about 3 months, start to finish, but I reckon on about a further three years before it will be running properly. I am not blaming manufacturers for this, just my own inadequacy, but I get there in the end.

I love working with metal and I have become quite skilled at soldering but it has all been self-taught.

Having said that, I do ask around when I want to know something. Model railway shows often have stands for the EM society, and their members have been most helpful and I am grateful to them. I notice the tools and materials they use, and when I see something that I think I ought to have, then off I go to Eileen's Emporium stand, make my purchase, return home and learn how to use it.

How about this: my last two locos were built with compensated chassis! I saw the EM boys doing it first. Their smooth running and perfect current collection are a joy — and in much less time than my normal three years of struggle.

My next project is going to be 'hinging' coupling rods on my 6- and 8-wheel kit-builts. Do you notice how even the RTR models have them now? I think it says a lot for progress on the part of the British outline manufacturers. I am full of admiration for the engineering that goes into Hornby, Bachmann and Lima these days.

One is always meeting up with the prophets-of-doom fraternity moaning that things aren't as good as they used to be and that quality has gone down the pan etc., but not so in the railway modelling arena. In my opinion, quality has never been better and whilst prices continue to rise on the one hand there seems to be corresponding improvement on almost every facet of our modelling world. Things are getting better, chaps!

Again I think of Iain Rice doing battle with the kit manufacturers, in the most positive way imaginable – actually showing them how to improve their products – and they, the manufacturers, seem to be taking notice quite happily, which augurs well for the future. I think this situation is referred to as 'consumer orientation'.

Mention has been made to extensions of the layout, but before I go any further may I highlight the fact that there was never a preconceived layout plan in my mind, other than the double track main line.

The garage is really two buildings joined together with the intervening wall removed, apart from side abutments to give strength. The previous occupier of the house had two cars which he could park end-to-end in the space. It almost seems as though destiny was working with me in mind, even before I knew it. Let's face it, it has been the most perfect accommodation for a railway in relation to my financial circumstances (i.e., not rolling in the crispies).

However, like all things in this mortal life, nothing is absolutely perfect. The 'old' part of the garage was originally the wash-house or whatever and adjoins the house at the same level close to the back door.

A compromise was made with the 'new' part in that the level of the back street is about 15″ above that of the back door, so the floor of the 'new' part slopes down towards the 'old' part.

I labour this point because it accounts for subsequent peculiarities of the layout to do with heights above the floor of the tracks.

When I commenced operations I just used the 'old' part, at the lower level, with a track height of about 3′ 6″ above the floor. Then came the hole through the (southern) abutment to gain access to the 'new' part. The result was that by the time I reached the garage doors the track height was down to about 2′ 6″.

Well, that wasn't too bad I suppose, and I got to work wood-butchering (my relatives' expression, not mine) 2 × 2″ inch timber supports for 2 × 1 framework topped with ½″ insulation board track baseboards. Note well that I had taken advice and used screws and glue for the framework, but I wish my advisors had told me to grease the

screws first to make them easier to move if need be.

A bane of my existence at this time was drilling holes into brickwork for wall plugs. Just my luck because hammer drills were not to come onto the market (at affordable Black & Decker prices) for a year or two yet, and much of the wretched brickwork is what the locals here call 'blue' brick. It was like drilling into cast iron and very drill-blunting. A couple of holes, a great deal of sweat, and a new drill bit was needed. Masonry drills seemed to be very expensive at the time, but fortune was to smile on me a year or two later when I became friendly with a plumber who gave me so many masonry drills that I still have many of them twenty years later, plus of course a hammer drill which I had, by this later time, bought for myself. It was a justifiable expense from a household point of view because it extended my usefulness to the household in my secondary capacity as shelf-putter-up and general DIY dogsbody.

Where was I? Oh yes, track heights. This first incursion into the 'new' part of the garage produced a considerable terminus and marshalling area together with motive power department and turntable, in a space of approximately 12′ × 2′ 6″. This extended the operational facilities no end and it was intriguing to see the trains disappear (or appear) through the hole in the wall.

I sought at this time to create an imposing tunnel portal at this position and came across a good photograph of the northern portal of the Bramhope (pron. Bramope) Tunnel on the Harrogate to Leeds line via Arthington, which I duly constructed and, even though I say it myself, made a nice job of it (see cover photo).

So now I had an up-and-over continuous main line, on two levels, in the 'old' part, including what was becoming quite a large through station to become known initially as Station B (the terminus was known as Station A) and which was on the second, upper level approached and quitted by gradients. The trouble was running-round trains ready for the return to the Station A terminus; it took time and was fiddly, also there was no turntable.

With my mental theodolite in hand I put on my surveying boots and discovered that with some rather tight 30″ curves I had room, just, for a 'reversing loop' diverting to the left, away from the down main line exit of Station B, up a rather steep and tortuous incline in order to cross over the main lines, then down again to re-enter Station B on the Up side, thence to the Station A terminus, all without having to run round the trains any more.

This reversing loop is still in position, supported by the most enormous and overscale simulated-masonry viaduct that you ever did see, and which now goes by the name of Brussleton Summit 1,370′ (suggested by the erstwhile Stainmore Summit betwixt Barnard Castle and Kirkby Stephen). Before I had a new roof fitted to the 'old' part of the garage, Brussleton Summit actually had real snow fall on it in winter, via gaps in the slate roof.

This area of the layout is along the lower end of the garage, which is also (from the other side) the upper end of the house. Isn't is strange how things can be two different things at the same time? Anyway, this area is all underneath the great Brussleton Fell (named after the old rope-hauled railway incline approaching Shildon, Co. Durham, eastwards from Witton Park on the old S & D R).

Immediately after passing the Brussleton Summit sign, the single track tunnels through the fell to emerge at the platform end of Barwick-in-Elmet station.

Barwick-in-Elmet station serves four purposes. (1) It provides the trains with somewhere to stop and take on water after their arduous climb. (2) It has a bay in which short-length stopping passenger trains can reverse and await their next place in the operating schedule, 'the old J72 quietly simmering away on a hot summer's day until the time comes for its return to the main line junction', you know the sort of thing. (3) It houses two other sidings and a goods shed serving the local pork and pie factory, plus pens for the piggies. (4) It makes a very attractive-looking corner piece to the south-eastern-most corner of the layout, which in my opinion is reason enough. Don't forget it is pronounced Barrick not Bar-wick!

I suppose the next extension marked the beginning of the layout as it is today, namely the chiselling of another hole through the wall on the opposite abutment to the one previously described, and the creation of a baseboard 12″ wide as far as the garage doors in the 'new' part of the garage. Trackwork was to be doubled with run-round facility at the terminus, but this idea did not last very long before I devised a 10′ 'lifting

Wills/Triang/Gresley J38 0-6-0 No. 1443 rests in loco-spur at Barrowby
Main Colliery, in the lee of the overscale Brussleton Viaduct. (Photo KC)

Nu-cast Worsdell J21 0-6-0 No. 996 'Simmers in the bay' platform at Barwick-in-Elmet. (Photo KC)

section' to take the tracks across the garage doors and meet up with Station A at the other side. This lifting section, whilst heavy, was 'liftable' if you got hold of it at its balancing point, which I had to do each evening so as to move it out of the way to get the car in. I made use of some ex-War Dept. multi-pin plugs and sockets to provide track and point power with a special 'back feed' arrangement to stop trains running into the void if the lifting section was lifted.

It was at this stage that my shortcomings as a surveyor came to light again, because the track height of the new spur along the north wall was about 3" higher than the Station A area along the south wall, due to the hole in the wall being cut too high, although it didn't seem so at the time.

I just had to make the best of it and it has remained so ever since.

Now I really did have a main line run worth talking about, something approaching 60', but this was just the beginning.

Station A now became a through station with terminus facilities on both Up and Down sides, with 5 storage sidings on the up side and a single track terminus leading off the Down main line, which also had 4 storage sidings to reverse trains into, plus the existing MPD.

It became obvious that a headshunt was required on the Up side and that was how the third line appeared on the lifting section. It was needed for incoming trains, which were terminating, to pull forward and then reverse into the storage sidings.

Then another brilliant idea came into my head – how about a second reversing loop; a line to take trains forward from the Up side of Station A, across the lifting section using what was the previous headshunt line, then burrow south-eastwards under the Up and Down main lines and Station B to join up with the Down main line where it comes out into the open at the east end of Bramhope Tunnel?

This was to be 'the last of my territorial claims in Europe' and was the makings of the layout as it is today, adding immensely to the operating facilities because one can now reverse trains in both directors at will.

It also gave operations plausible starting and finishing points – in both directions, even though they were only 12" apart. For example, a train that has terminated on the Up side of Station A can set off via the 'new' reverse loop, to gain the Down main line and eventually complete its journey at the dead-end terminus on the Down side

Mainline/Worsdell J72 0-6-0T calls at the old 'Spotters' Halt' with a pair of Triang Clerestories.
Note limited 'sky' effects – also bicycle underneath baseboard. (Photo KC)

of Station A. Similarly, a train can set off from the Down side terminus, gain the Up main line via the double set of crossovers at the west end of Station A, cross the lifting section, travel along the 'new' spur through the hole in the wall, up the hill to Station B and thence down again either to pass through Station A or terminate on the Up side, and reverse into the storage sidings.

I created a small country station on the 'new' spur and called it 'Spotter's Halt'. It was beautiful with a small stream executed in polyurethane varnish, plus reeds and cows and things. It remained like this for a number of years before I took it all up, made new fibreboard baseboards and frames, and created a new country village and station with a loop on the Down line plus headshunt and a siding. Remember of course that the track of the Up to Down line reversing loop passes behind all this but is hidden by the scenery. Also I introduced a crossover between Down and Up lines on the east end for the occasional reversal, from Down to Up line, of the 3-car DMU and the Sentinel railcar. This station was then re-named 'East Garforth' – about three years before British Rail actually created their East Garforth Halt on the Leeds/Selby line. I swear there

was no collusion. It provided a very pleasant point of interest and the siding has become a goods yard-cum-refuge for the local pick-up goods train. It is all fully signalled with working upper-quadrant semaphores controlled through a diode matrix, all very impressive.

There is a space of about 24″ below the east end of the East Garforth where the reversing loop comes out 'into the open' after having burrowed beneath the main lines. This is the site of the tiny Bramham station halt. The line then enters another tunnel to burrow under Station B on its way to gain the Down main line at Brussleton Junction.

I might as well tell you now, although I was going to save it until later, that it all seemed a bit impersonal calling stations simply A, B, and C etc., but the question was – what to call them?

This is where I called upon my youthful stamping grounds of Aberford, Barrowby, East Garforth, Bramham and Barwick-in-Elmet. Apart from East Garforth, there never was a railway at these places in real life, but we are not dealing with real life, are we? (Seems real enough to me when I am running it.) They are all real places within spitting distance of the A1 dual carriage-

Barrowby Main Colliery and coal loading facilities. (Photo KC)

Barrowby Main Colliery shown in relation to Barrowby Station and Town Centre. (Photo KC)

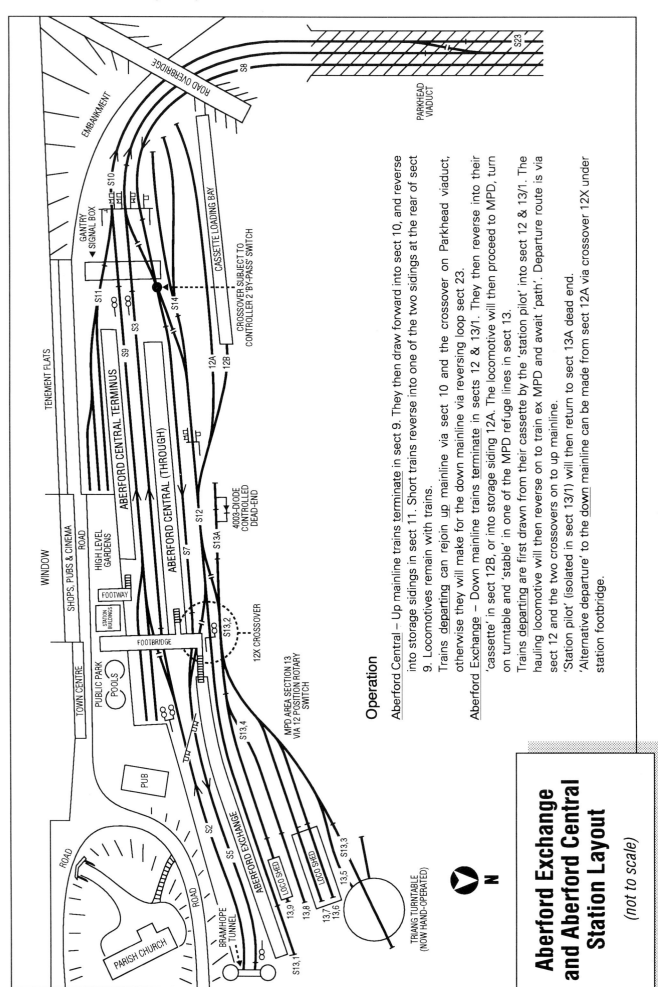

Operation

Aberford Central – Up mainline trains terminate in sect 9. They then draw forward into sect 10, and reverse into storage sidings in sect 11. Short trains reverse into one of the two sidings at the rear of sect 9. Locomotives remain with trains.

Trains departing can rejoin up mainline via sect 10 and the crossover on Parkhead viaduct, otherwise they will make for the down mainline via reversing loop sect 23.

Aberford Exchange – Down mainline trains terminate in sects 12 & 13/1. They then reverse into their 'cassette' in sect 12B, or into storage siding 12A. The locomotive will then proceed to MPD, turn on turntable and 'stable' in one of the MPD refuge lines in sect 13.

Trains departing are first drawn from their cassette by the 'station pilot' into sect 12 & 13/1. The hauling locomotive will then reverse on to train ex MPD and await path'. Departure route is via sect 12 and the two crossovers on to up mainline.

'Station pilot' (isolated in sect 13/1) will then return to sect 13A dead end.

'Alternative departure' to the down mainline can be made from sect 12A via crossover 12X under station footbridge.

Aberford Exchange and Aberford Central Station Layout

(not to scale)

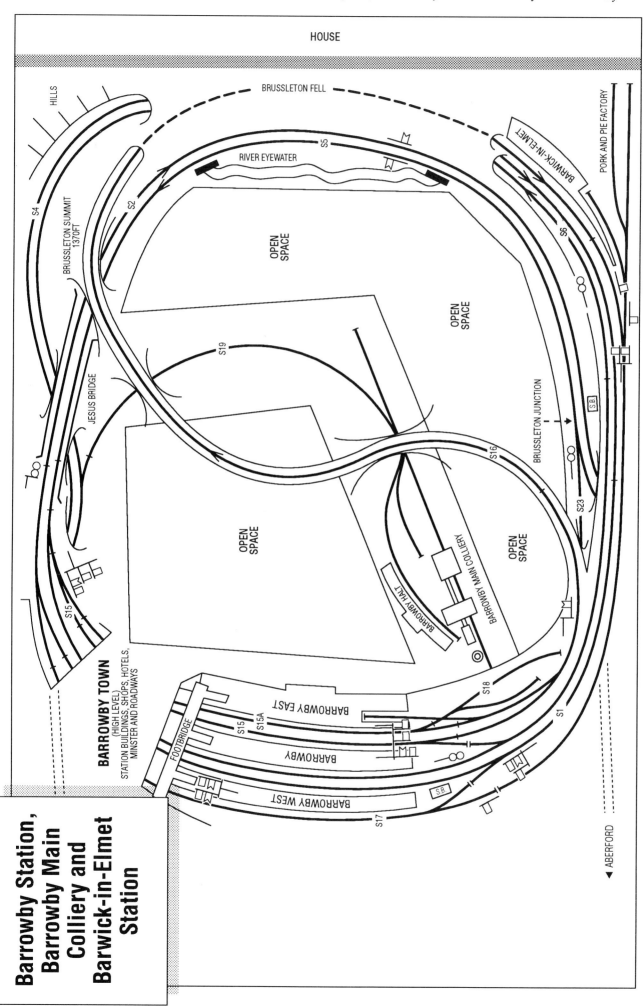

HOUSE

BRUSSLETON FELL

HILLS

S4

S5

RIVER EYEWATER

BRUSSLETON SUMMIT 1370FT

S2

BARWICK-IN-ELMET

PORK AND PIE FACTORY

OPEN SPACE

OPEN SPACE

S19

JESUS BRIDGE

S6

S.B.

BRUSSLETON JUNCTION

S16

S23

OPEN SPACE

S15

OPEN SPACE

BARROWBY HALL

BARROWBY MAIN COLLIERY

BARROWBY TOWN
(HIGH LEVEL)
STATION BUILDINGS, SHOPS, HOTELS, MINSTER AND ROADWAYS

FOOTBRIDGE

S18

BARROWBY EAST

S15 S15A

BARROWBY

S15 S15A

S1

BARROWBY WEST

S.B.

S17

ABERFORD

Barrowby Station, Barrowby Main Colliery and Barwick-in-Elmet Station

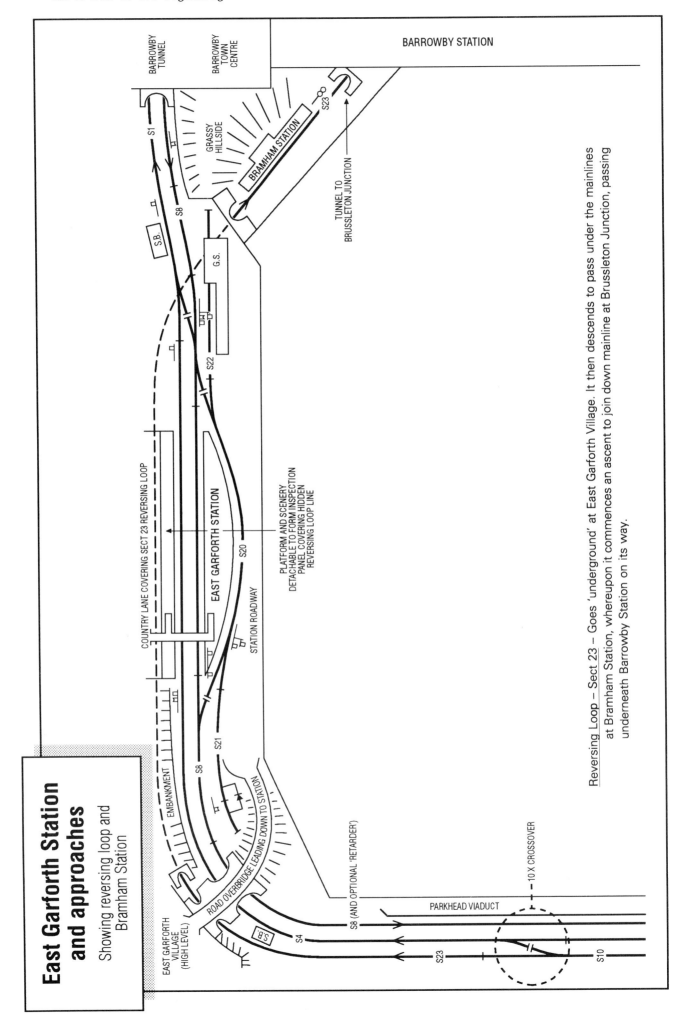

East Garforth Station and approaches

Showing reversing loop and Bramham Station

BARROWBY STATION

BARROWBY TUNNEL

BARROWBY TOWN CENTRE

GRASSY HILLSIDE

BRAMHAM STATION

S1

S8

S.B.

G.S.

S22

S23

TUNNEL TO BRUSSLETON JUNCTION

COUNTRY LANE COVERING SECT 23 REVERSING LOOP

EAST GARFORTH STATION

PLATFORM AND SCENERY DETACHABLE TO FORM INSPECTION PANEL COVERING HIDDEN REVERSING LOOP LINE

S20

STATION ROADWAY

EMBANKMENT

S8

S21

ROAD OVERBRIDGE LEADING DOWN TO STATION

EAST GARFORTH VILLAGE (HIGH LEVEL)

S.B.

S4

S8 (AND OPTIONAL 'RETARDER')

PARKHEAD VIADUCT

10 X CROSSOVER

S23

S10

Reversing Loop – Sect 23 – Goes 'underground' at East Garforth Village. It then descends to pass under the mainlines at Bramham Station, whereupon it commences an ascent to join down mainline at Brussleton Junction, passing underneath Barrowby Station on its way.

way, although that thoroughfare was simply called the A1 in those pre- and early post-World War II days.

The last of my track-laying ventures was to create Barrowby Main colliery, approached by reversal from the Down main line at 'datum' level below Barrowby Station.

This was a melancholy venture in two ways. First, I don't really have a clue about the detail of a real colliery and, secondly, everything had to be made and painted mucky. It put years on me after all my efforts to try and beautify the layout with pretty scenery. Nevertheless, it has a winding house with those prominent winding wheels – formed from a pair of old Ks 6′ 8″ driving wheels with tyres removed, plus a boiler house, an overhead coal conveyor leading from the washing plant to the wagon loader and, most important of all, a tall chimney with a lightning conductor. So far none of my visitors has picked me up on the detail, so may I conclude that I got away with it? The area also serves as storage siding for the coal train of 14 assorted Dublo, Lima and Mainline wagons, some dating back to my first ever purchase of a 3-rail Hornby Dublo goods train set back in 1954, i.e. lithographed tinplate.

So there you have it dear reader, 'as it was in the beginning'. As I said earlier, very little of the layout was planned in advance other than in the broadest sense, like wanting a double track continuous main line.

What has happened since has, in a manner of speaking, suggested itself with the passing of time, and growing familiarity with the operating potential of what had already been achieved has led to the various additions and extensions to increase that operating potential.

I have been steeped in LNER atmosphere all my life and have always lived in close proximity to it. I have known the people who worked on it, I have known the locomotives and the rolling stock, the architecture, the signals, the lineside fittings.

What I have done primarily is to create a model railway system with an LNER flavour. Secondly I have developed a layout rich in operational interest that never ceases to challenge and certainly never becomes boring.

Having said that, I must concede that the track layout could just as easily be LMS, SR or GWR. In fact a friend of mine who is 'into' German railways is busying himself adapting my layout plan in terms of 'right hand drive'.

It has been conceived as a one-man operated layout, with a central control panel and an operating schedule, which is rather like a timetable but without the restrictions of time. It is really quite demanding and requires a lot of concentration, but I am rather expecting that, one of these days, a computer boffin will come along and put the whole thing onto a disk with the object of being able to 'play trains' without actually having any. Perish the thought!

So, venture with me into the next phase – 'As it is now'.

As It Is Now

Time of writing 1993, and as late film director Sam Goldwyn is once reported to have said, 'We have passed a lot of water under the bridge since we first started.'

A dedicatory quotation at the beginning of a book on gardening I once read goes as follows:

A garden should be rather small, else you'll have no fun at all.

I sometimes wonder if this quotation should not be applied to model railway layouts.

Certainly the Aberford, Barrowby and East Garforth affair has now assumed mammoth proportions, tending at times to run me rather than me run it.

Faults, and the solving of them, seem to be the name of the game. I am unable to see how it can be otherwise when I think of the mass complex of mechanisms and electrics that are the consist of a layout.

Often do I stagger to bed at one o'clock in the morning after a three- or four-hour trouble-shooting session, during which time not a vehicle has moved.

Of course, fault-finding is not the only reason for non-rolling of wagons. On a one-man-band affair like mine, new models have to be built or scenery improved, and who has to do it? Me!

I like to have the company of a steadily moving pair of trains running round the main line whilst I am working on a project, but it seems to be sod's umpteenth law that, when you are at the most delicate part of whatever it is you are doing, one of the trains will derail and, regardless of the fact that the two trains have been running perfectly for ages, the moment you go to attend to the derailment, or whatever, the other one will come off at the opposite end of the layout.

To this end I have composed myself a slogan and nailed it in a prominent place. It goes as follows:

Interest begets patience, and patience plus bad language begets endurance.

I often wonder where I get all the words from. Must be the left-overs of a mis-spent youth.

Anyway, back to the prologue, now where did we get to?

Oh yes, 1993, and 3-rail is long since gone, along with the old Wrenn flexi-track. RTR models now take one's breath away with wonderful photographic detail impressed on their plastic; so much so that if I was to live another 100 years I could never make a model to equal them in appearance, notwithstanding the availability of etched metal kits.

The object of our study, the Aberford, Barrowby and East Garforth Railway, hasn't had a change to its track layout in nearly 10 years, other than to replace broken points and worn out tracks, and yet it continues to challenge and excite, from an operational viewpoint, so I must have achieved something.

As my sons, two in number since 1970, grew up, it was gratifying to see them being interested by the railway scene, So much so that my elder son has been a volunteer on the North Yorkshire Moors Railway for about 5 years, as a loco fitter.

To encourage their interest in the layout, I was happy to 'bend' my self-imposed LNER 1935 – 1939 restraint to the extent that present-day rolling stock and diesel locomotives are now running side by side with steam. The only proviso being that they must have run on North-Eastern metals in real life (whatever that is). Mind you, I have had to draw the line, for the time being at least, on the introduction of 'the electrics' if only because the clearances in some of the tunnels are minimal.

I must say that, when it comes to operating 'the schedule', diesel-hauled trains make life very much easier because of their reliability – even in model form.

My only regret is that the boys' interest in the layout is rather passive; they like to go in for an hour or so every now and again to run 'the schedule', but show no inclination to make anything, and, on a rather sad note, my wife – 'the girl of my dreams' referred to on page v – died a month after I retired in 1988, so I am now a full-time housewife with no more time to spend on the layout that I had before I retired, except late at

'Spotters' Halt' becoming 'East Garforth'. (Photo KC)

night after supper, hence the reference to creeping off to bed at 1 a.m. quite regularly. It would never have been condoned previously!

However with the introduction by Bachmann, earlier this year, of their LNER green 2–6–2 V2, and my purchase of one, I am able to say that, at long last, I have reached the completion of my pre-determined loco stud.

I am now in the fortunate situation of being able to call on NER Worsdells, Ravens, a GN Ivat Atlantic and the gorgeous Gresleys, a very satisfying and representative collection of 28 steam locomotive power, to which can be added, with no apologies, 17 diesel power units. They all run happily together, or separately, depending on which of us is operating at the time.

Reference to the loco and rolling stock inventory will, perhaps, explain why I don't go in for much shunting; there is simply too much to do keeping the main lines occupied and preparing for the next move on 'the schedule'.

Thank goodness I thought of running to a schedule early on in my 'career' when everyone else seemed to be talking about timetables and getting clocks re-geared to run to scale time, whatever that is.

A schedule is, I suppose, rather like a timetable except that it does without the time element. It has the advantage over a timetable when, say,

East Garforth Station taking shape – also Bramham Halt. (Don't look under baseboards) (Photo KC)

East Garforth completed – January 1982. Showing Jameson/Gresley D49/2 No. 274 'The Craven'. (Photo KC)

running repairs have to be carried out to track, vehicles or wiring, or even when a decision has been made to build something. The schedule is simply suspended and everything stays as it is until the time comes to recommence running.

In 'real life' train movements must balance out, otherwise impossible situations will arise where all the stock is at one end of the system, and there is insufficient at the other end.

The Schedule

Preparing an Operating Schedule

Planning a schedule takes quite a time, and a clear head, because quite a number of operational considerations must be decided upon before even a start on its writing, or printing, can be made. For example, assuming that 'the schedule' is to represent a normal working day, it will need to commence with:

1. The outlying early-morning commuter trains conveying passengers to the main line stations, either to go to work at that place or connect with the main line train taking them onwards to some more distant destination.

2. Consideration will have to be given to preparing the early, long-distance main line passenger trains and drawing them from the sidings to the terminus, well in advance of departure time, to allow for 'loading'.

3. Other classes of trains will have to be prepared and despatched along the main lines in advance, or in the rear, of the express passenger trains; such as newspaper trains, pick-up goods trains to and from the branches, suburban passenger trains to the branches and freight trains of all descriptions requiring a path in the 'schedule' in both outward and inward directions.

4. This advance planning procedure will need to be continued until the 'end of the day' is arrived at and the local passenger trains have returned to their country stations, ready for the start of the next day.

On my layout, at the 'end of the day', all trains originating at Aberford Central will have moved over to Aberford Exchange, and those originating at Aberford Exchange will have moved, vice versa, to Aberford Central.

I refer to all these activities under the heading of 'Schedule A'. In order words, all trains will have reversed their positions at the end of Schedule A, and this will be where the next part of the considerations will commence – and this next stage in the procedure will be referred to as 'Schedule B' which, in effect, will return all trains to their original starting points, ready to start 'Schedule A' again.

Are you with me so far? If there are any questions, kindly address them to me on the back of a £10 note, c/o the publisher.

When you are working out your first 'schedule' it will naturally be supremely influenced by the amount of rolling stock you have, and the design and nature of your layout.

I would imagine that, after a while, most layouts will have developed a starting point and a finishing point, so that there will be a 'going out' and a 'coming in' facility. The number of trains involved, as I said above, will depend on how much rolling stock you have, so it is just a matter of getting it all organised.

One of the objects of all these considerations is to get 'the schedule' down in print, either hand- or typewritten or even, perhaps, displayed on a TV screen. Let's face it, you cannot expect to keep it all in your head. If you are like me you will have a memory like a sieve, and you will surely appreciate the importance of recording it somehow.

This brings us to the question of how to record it in words. For instance, how would you consider recording the following instruction?

'Place the 6-coach PC Gresley Corridors in the carriage siding, then draw the Station Pilot loco out of the Motive Power Dept and attach to the coaches. Then draw the coaches into Aberford Exchange Terminus and hold the Station Pilot at the buffer stops. Then draw the main line locomotive out of the Motive Power Dept and reverse on to the coaches. Wait there until the place in the schedule comes to take it out on the Main Line.'

Specimens of Train Description Chart and Operating Schedules A and B

Codes used:

= Train-Carrying cassette

Prep E# = fit cassette for train E to loading spur in sect 12

E# to 12 Hold = Station Pilot to draw train E from cassette to Aberford Exchange departure platform.

J to # = Train J to reverse into empty cassette in sect 12 loading spur

<——— UP = Up main line

———> DOWN = Down main line

Hold = Train to wait where it is until next path in schedule

RSP = Return Station Pilot to its siding (13A)

A to continue = Train A to continue its journey on main line

+ = Completion of journey e.g., D to 16A +

Train Description and Location Chart

Train		Commence A	Commence B
A	Pullman	11A	Cassette
B	LNER 6-Corridor P.C.	Cassette	11A
C	4-Clerestory	9A	Cassette
D	2-Clerestory	16A	9A
E	5-Coach Non-Corridor	Not Used	Cassette
F	LNER 5-Corridor (Kirk)	Cassette	Cassette
G	Parcels	Cassette	11C
H	Steam Railcar	15C	15C
I	3-car DMU	Cassette	Not used
J	H.S.T. (Blue Set)	Cassette	9B
K	Fitted Freight	11B	Cassette
L	Pick-up Goods	Cassette	12A
M	Tankers	11C	21
N	Bogie Bolsters	Not Used	14
P	Coal Train	19	Not Used
Q	H.S.T. Exec Livery	Cassette	11B
R	5-Coach Trans-Pennine	Not Used	Cassette
S	7-Coach 'Coronation'	Cassette	Cassette
T	6-Coach 'Royal Scotsman'	Cassette	Cassette
	(Substitute Train – for Preservation Specials)		

Schedule A

1	H to 15A Hold (prep G#)
2	D to 17 and ML———>Up
3	H to ML <———Down
4	G# to 12A Hold (prep J#)
5	H to E Garforth 20 Hold
6	G to ML <———Down via 12X
7	J# to 12A Hold (prep B#)
8	G to 17 via 15A Hold
9	J to MI <———Down via 12X
10	D to 9 Hold
11	G to ML ———>Up
12	B# to 12 Hold (prep L#)
13	D to 9B +
14	J to 15A Hold
15	K to ML <———Down (from 11B) via 23
16	G to 9 Hold
17	B to ML ———>Up RSP
18	G to 11B +
19	L# to 12A (prep I#)
20	J to 17 Hold
21	I# to 12 Hold (prep # for A)
22	K to 15A Hold
23	H to 15C (via 20 & 15B) +
24	L to ML <———Down via 12X
25	B to 9 Hold
26	J to ML ———>Up
27	K to 17 Hold
28	L to 15A Hold
29	A to ML <———Down via 23
30	B to 11A +
31	C to 9 Hold
32	L to leave coals in 15B & re-attach to Guards Van in 15A Hold
33	A to Hold Barrowby ML <———Down
34	L to E Garforth 20 & 21 +
35	B'by Pilot to shunt Coal into 18+
36	C to 15B (from 9) via 23 Hold
36A	D to 9A Hold
37	A to continue ML <———Down
38	J to 9 Hold
39	K to ML ———>Up
40	J to 9B +
41	H to 16A (from 15C)
42	K to 9 Hold
43	I to ML ———>Up
44	A to 12 Hold
45	K to ML <———Down Via 23
46	A to # + (prep # for Q
47	C to 17 Hold
48	Q# to 12 Hold (prep # for K)
49	I reverse into E Garforth 20 Hold
50	C to 9 via ML ———>Up Hold
51	Q to ML ———>Up RSP
52	K to 12 Hold

53	C to ML <———Down via 23
54	K to # + & (prep F# to 12-Hold)
55	Prep # for C
56	C to Hold Barrowby ML<———Down
57	M to 15A via 23 (from 11C) Hold
58	C to continue ML <———Down
59	Q to Hold Barrowby ML———>Up
60	F to 17 via ML———>Up RSP
61	Q to continue ML ———>Up
62	C to 12 Hold
63	P to ML <———Down (from 19)
64	C to # + (prep S# to 12 Hold)
65	Prep # for I
66	Q to 9 Hold
67	S to ML ———>Up RSP
68	P to Hold ML <———Down (Barrowby)
69	M to 12(ex15A) via ML <———Down Hold
70	P to continue ML <———Down
71	M to 12A +
72	P to 15A Hold
73	I to ML <———Down from 20
74	Q to 11C +
75	S to 9 Hold
76	F to ML ———>Up
77	P to 17
78	I to 15A
79	M to 15B via 12X Hold
80	S to ML <———Down via 23
81	F to Hold Barrowby ML ———>Up
82	P to 9 via ML ———>Up
83	F to continue ML ———>Up
84	M to 17 Hold
85	S to Hold Barrowby ML <———Down
86	I to 12 from 15A Hold
87	S to continue ML <———Down
88	I to # (Prep # for S)
89	B'by Pilot shunt Coals to 15B
90	S to 12 Hold
91	L to 15A (from 20) Hold
92	P to ML <———Down via 23
93	F to 9 Hold
94	M to ML ———>Up
95	S to # + (prep # for F)
96	L reassemble Coal & Vans in 15A
97	P to 19 +
98	F to ML <———Down via 23
99	H to 17 (from 16A) Hold
100	F to 12 Hold
101	L to ML <———Down (from 15A)
102	F to # + (prep # for E)
103	H to 15C (from 17) +
104	L to 12 and 12A +
105	M to 9 and ML <———Down via 23
106	to 20 & 21 +

Schedule B

1	H to 17 (from 15C) Hold (prep E#)		60	R to continue ML <———Down
2	D to 9 Hold		61	K to 9 Hold
3	H to ML ———>Up		62	H to 17 (from 20) via ML ———>Up Hold
4	D to ML <———Down via 23		63	Q to ML ———>Up (ex 11B) via 10X
5	E# to 12 Hold (prep A#)		64	K to 11B +
6	H to reverse to E Garforth 20 Hold		65	H to 15C (from 17) +
7	E to ML ———>Up RSP		66	R to 12 Hold
8	A# to 12 Hold (prep R#)		67	G to ML <———Down (ex 11C) via 23
9	D to 15B Hold		68	R to # + (prep S#)
10	L to ML <———Down via 12X		69	S# to 12 Hold (prep # for G)
11	E to 17 Hold		70	G to Hold Barrowby ML <———Down
12	A to ML ———>Up RSP		71	M to 15A (ex 12A) via 12X Hold
13	R# to 12 Hold (prep J#)		72	G to continue ML <———Down
14	J to 9 (from 9B) Hold		73	Q to 9 Hold
15	D to 16A +		74	S to ML ———>Up RSP
16	L to 15A Hold		75	G to 12 Hold
17	J to ML <———Down via 23		76	Q to ML <———Down via 23
18	L to leave vans in 15B and return to 15A Hold		77	G to # + (prep C#)
19	A to Hold Barrowby ML ———>Up		78	M to 17 (from 15A) Hold
20	E to 9 (from 17 Hold		79	B'by Pilot to leave Vans in 15B
21	H to 17 (from 20) Hold		80	Q to Hold Barrowby ML <———Down
22	A to continue ML ———>Up		81	L to 15A (from 21 & ML <———Down) Hold
23	E to 9B +		82	Q to continue ML <———Down
24	A to 9 Hold		83	C# to 12 Hold (prep # for Q)
25	R to ML ———>Up RSP		84	S to 9 Hold
26	J to Hold Barrowby ML <———Down		85	C to ML ———>Up RSP
27	M to Aberford 7 (from 21) Hold		86	L to Assemble Vans (15B–15A) Hold
28	L to E Garforth 21 (from 15A) +		87	Q to 12 Hold
29	M to 15A Hold		88	S to ML <———Down via 23
30	J to continue ML <———Down		89	Q to # (prep F#)
31	H to 15C (from 17) +		90	ML <———Down
32	J to 12 Hold		91	C to 9 Hold
33	N to assemble & to ML <———Down via 12X		92	M to ML ———>Up (from 17)
34	J to # + (prep K#)		93	F# to 12 Hold (prep # for S)
35	N to Hold Barrowby		94	C to 9A +
36	M to 12 & 12A (from 15A) +		95	M to 9 Hold
37	N to continue ML <———Down		96	F to ML ———>Up RSP
38	B'by Pilot to Shunt Vans into18 +		97	L to 17 (from 15A) Hold
39	N to 15A Hold		98	M to 11C +
40	B to ML <———Down via 23		99	F to Hold Barrowby ML ———>Up
41	K# to 12 Hold (prep # for B)		100	L to 9 Hold
42	A to 11A +		101	F to continue ML ———>Up
43	R to 9 Hold		102	S to 12 Hold
44	K to ML ———>Up RSP		103	L to ML <———Down via 23
45	N to 17 Hold		104	S to # + prep # for L)
46	B to Hold Barrowby ML <———Down		105	E to 9 (from 9B) Hold
47	R to 15A (from 9) via 23 Hold		106	L to 12 Hold
48	B to continue ML <———Down		107	E to ML <———Down via 23
49	K to Hold Barrowby ML ———>Up		108	L to # + (prep # for E)
50	N to 9 (from 17) Hold		109	H to 17 (from 15C) Hold
51	K to continue ML ———>Up		110	F to 9 Hold
52	B to 12 Hold		111	H to ML ———>Up (from 17)
53	N to ML <———Down via 23		112	E to 12 Hold
54	B to # + (Prep # for R)		113	F to ML <———Down via 23
55	N to 12 & 14 +		114	E to # + (prep # for F)
56	R to ML <———Down (from 15A)		115	H to 9 Hold
57	H to 15A (from 15C Hold		116	F to 12 Hold
58	R to Hold Barrowby ML <———Down		117	H to 15C via 23 & ML <———Down +
59	H to 20 Hold		118	F to # + (prep G#)

It is very explicit and, I think, very easy to understand; what could possibly go wrong?

As far as I can see, nothing can go wrong and when you have come to the end of writing your instructions in like manner for 'Schedule A' and 'Schedule B' you will have the most comprehensive set of instructions ever.

Printing Out The Schedule

The next consideration then is, how and where are you going to display these instructions? You must have somewhere accessible to place them and I have visions of a book the size of a bible being required for a layout of the size of mine!

I suggest, therefore, that you consider working out some abbreviations and a form of easy-to-understand shorthand; in other words, a code, so as to get the physical size of the thing reduced to manageable proportions.

Looking again at the example I gave earlier, let us see if I can explain a way of reducing it to shorthand.

Most of my trains are in 'rakes', not exactly permanently coupled but something like that, and these 'rakes' are stored away from the tracks in what I like to call 'cassettes' – long narrow boxes with track inside. In place of one of the cartridge sidings at Aberford Exchange, I now have a turnout (i.e. a point) leading to a short spur on a ledge at the side of the layout. I place a train-loaded 'cassette' onto this ledge and connect it to the spur. The Station Pilot then draws the train out of the 'cassette' and along to the terminus track of the station, to be followed by the main line locomotive from MPD.

This particular train, shall we say, is designated 'Train B' in the 'schedule' and a cassette is designated by a # sign. The electrical section number of the Aberford Exchange Terminus line is number 12.

Right then, erewigo:
1. 'Prep. #B', meaning, connect cassette for train B to spur.
2. 'B to 12 hold', meaning Station Pilot draw train to terminus, main line loco to attach and wait.

When the time comes to depart on the 'Up' Main Line, this will be the code:
3. 'B to ML———>UP. RSP. Prep. #E', meaning Train B to 'Up' Main Line, return Station

Pilot to MPD, remove Train B Cassette and replace with cassette for Train E (the next one in the schedule).

The time will come when your train has completed its scheduled 'tour of the tracks' and is safely tucked up, out of harm's way, in a siding somewhere. I find it useful to indicate 'end of journey' with a + sign, then I know it is not merely being held somewhere until its next 'path' is free for it to continue. So to give an example, Tanker Train (Train M) is to reverse from Aberford Exchange Terminus section 12 into the refuge siding 12A. The 'code' will look like this:

M to 12A (from 12) + – and that's it! Nice and short.

So then, you have decided where you want to start. Good.

Making a List of Trains

Now, I suggest, you need to list your 'trains', by which I mean the rolling stock which, when assembled, will form a train going from somewhere to somewhere else and which will require a 'path' in the 'schedule'.

I chose to list my 'trains' alphabetically, e.g.:
Train A – 6-coach Pullman
Train B – 6-coach PC Gresley Corridors
Train C – 4-coach Clerestories
and so on. I have almost used up the alphabet, but I don't expect I shall be adding many more now.

When you have made this list, print it on to a nice card and keep it handy for referring to because you will need it often. I also find it interesting to put a date on, to see how long it lasts before it needs updating.

Perhaps it might also be a good idea, at this stage, to number all electrical track sections. This will help with the 'code', for example, instead of having to refer to 'the furthermost siding at the far side of Station X', all you need to do is quote the section number.

When you have completed 'the schedule', you will find it useful to add an extra entry on your 'list of trains', namely, an indication as to the location of each train at the commencement of Schedule A and Schedule B. It will serve as an extra check that you have got things in the right place.

Finding a 'Path' For a Train

This is the mind-boggling bit, because you need to keep in mind – or on bits of paper – where your rolling stock is at the time you are planning your next move, so as to avoid planning an impossible, or unworkable, or conflicting move.

Knowing something about the workings of the average mind, you are going to do this anyway – make mistakes I mean. Use your favourite means of keeping a clear head, be it in liquid or solid form. I am going to suggest that you handwrite your intended plans on paper first and remember to keep a bottle of Tipp-ex nearby because you are going to need it!

In my own case I limited myself to one sheet of A4 paper each for Schedule A and Schedule B, so as to keep the physical size within reasonable bounds. When the planning is completed and checked, and checked again, then I commit it to my word processor which allows me 54 lines per page and, using the previously discussed method of coding, an A4 sheet allows me two vertical columns of about 30 letters width, so that works out at about 108 train movements, and that's plenty. There are times when I am busy with other things – such as writing this letter to the gentiles – when it takes maybe three months to complete a schedule, so there.

If you have to handwrite, don't forget that you, and maybe others, will have to read it easily and comfortably. So, best writing chaps, with good clear ink or ballpoint, that can be seen from at least 3 feet away.

Let us now assume that you have decided the route and purpose of your first train.

It will need to be assembled, provided with a locomotive to haul it and then proceed on its journey.

Now is the time, not for all good men to come to the aid of the party, but to decide what is to be the consist and route of your second train.

Will the first train get in the way of it, and if so, which will have priority – the first or the second? Of course if you are lucky enough to have a double track main line, train No. 2 can travel in the opposite direction to train No. 1 by using the other main line tracks. If you are 'single track' you may need some form of overtaking

loop to allow one to pass the other, or whatever. On the other hand, you may decide to keep it simple and just have one train 'in steam' at a time. Nonetheless, it will all need to be written down in sequence, making sure that nothing is already occupying the bit of track you are going to need. If there is, then organise your schedule to allow it to be moved somewhere else – or don't have it there in the first place. You should always arrange to 'hold' your train somewhere until the path ahead is clear. In fact you can do anything, all you need to do is plan it in advance, then write it into your schedule.

The rest of your schedule planning will proceed along similar lines, until you reach the point where everything that has to go has gone, and all journeys are completed, i.e., end of Schedule A.

This is your ideal time to fill in the locations of your trains, on your 'List of Trains' (refer to previous page), as being their location, at the commencement of Schedule B.

Now you need to 'turn over the page' and start planning Schedule B; getting everything back to where it was at the commencement of Schedule A, in the same orderly and tangle-free manner.

As I said earlier, the way you go about planning will necessarily be influenced by your layout, your rolling stock, and your particular interest in railway operation.

As the months and years roll on, you will accumulate more and more stock and, I'll bet my bottom dollar on it, your layout will change here and there. New operating possibilities will suggest themselves to you, which may or may not call for a radical re-thinking of your schedule. So never think of it as being finished.

Planning by Objectives

'Planning by objectives' was a popular business philosophy in the days before I retired and it can be very useful to us in our world of railway modelling.

Basically it has to do with knowing what you want, i.e., your 'objectives', and then 'planning' how you are going to go about getting them.

So, whatever happens, please do not regard your schedules as inviolable; expect to have to change them from time to time, and have your 'objectives' clearly in your mind when the time comes. It is quite amazing how much easier it is to achieve something when you know what it is that you want to achieve.

Try and apply this to the rest of your modelling activities; it will save you a lot of time, effort and money. Keep asking yourself what it is you are trying to do, and then seek ways to do it.

Creating an operating schedule, surely, is a prime case of planning by objectives.

You have decided that you want to do something more than just 'run a train set'.

You have taken the trouble to analyse how you want to operate your layout.

You have considered your layout design and your rolling stock, and have decided on a plan of action to make the best possible use of both.

You have committed your plan to paper and have created a schedule.

Well done, O thoughtful one.

I forecast that you are about to enter (one of) the most creative and imaginative aspects of railway modelling; one which will present you with many challenges but will give you much pleasure at the same time.

Operating a Schedule

Together, we have considered the merits of creating a schedule and how to create one. I think it might now be advantageous to consider the schedule in operation.

I suppose that the first job to be done, once the schedule is 'finalised' – a wrong word, because it will never really be finalised – will be, physically, to place the rolling stock where it should be, according to the 'List of Trains' location entries. This will take a bit of time, but should only need doing once, and when everything is in its rightful place then it is 'all systems go'! Switch on the controllers, power the sections, points and signals and carry out 'move' No. 1 of Schedule A.

By now the old brain cells will be in a highly activated state as they 'scan' the schedule, with thoughts going through them like: 'Have I switched on the right sections?' 'Are the points set?' 'Which controller am I using?' and so on.

This is as it should be, because you are in sole charge of an intricate procedure – I never said it would be simple did I?

Well, with your first train is in its place and ready for the off, place your hand on the controller and, when you are satisfied with your scan of the schedule, make your move to set your first train in motion.

'And good luck to all who sail in her.'

Relax for a short time and just observe the object of your delight taking its first hesitant steps.

Are all the wheels on the rails? Are all vehicles securely coupled? Is the locomotive coping with the load?

If the answer is yes, then consider the next entry on the schedule and carry it out.

I hope I am not labouring all this too much for you because, whilst you have expended an awful lot of effort creating a schedule, you are now about to develop a method of operating it.

A large part of this method will be to do with observation.

Part of your attention will be focused on the sequence of the schedule, but another part will concern itself with the well-being of the train(s) in motion.

Trains tend to 'divide', i.e., become uncoupled, when you least expect it. This is why I was always keen on having a guard's van at the back – like a full stop at the end of a sentence. The alternative is to put one of those nice little scale loco lamps on the last vehicle, so that when you see a train come past you without a lamp, or a guard's van at the end, you know something is amiss.

One aspect of operating a schedule is that you are unconsciously aiming at getting to the end of it without a mishap. So far it has never happened on my layout, but I keep on hoping.

What happens is that you begin to notice problems occurring on a regular basis, so you take steps to put them right. It might mean shutting down the system for a time whilst you realign a length of track, or improve the reliability of some couplings or somesuch. This is to the good and, if you keep your cool, your constant attention to overcoming shortcomings of all kinds will enhance your operations and bring nearer the day when you will get through the end of a schedule 'without let or hindrance'.

I don't think there is much more I can say on the subject at this stage; repeated use will suggest further refinements and fine tuning to you.

Now let's have another look at the layout.

The Layout

Baseboards

After over thirty years some of my fibre insulation board has been knocked about more than somewhat. Changes of layout, holes to pass wires through, holes dug for Peco point motors, all have had their effect. I dread the day when I shall have to take up, say, Aberford Central and Exchange, to replace insulation board with this Sundeala stuff I keep hearing about. It takes just a matter of an hour or two to uplift a complex section of track work and its accompanying wiring, but for every hour taken to uplift it takes a month to put it all back again in working order.

I used Weyroc, or somesuch Ryvita-like stuff, when I built the East Garforth extension. It is solid and durable and, even in the semi-outdoor conditions of my garage, has shown no signs of warping. It is only when you want to put in track pins that you realise its major shortcoming from a modeller's point of view – how very hard it is. Every pinhole has to be drilled using small-diameter drills, which break so easily and you don't get many to the £1. I have had to resort to shaping household pins into a sort of spade, on a carborundum stone, and using them in my mini-drill.

One material I very much hesitate to use in my prevailing climactic conditions is plywood. I have never known wood like it for attracting the dreaded worm. Only the other day I had hastily to dispose of a 40-year-old table, used as a supplementary bench. It had become badly infested, almost overnight. The legs and supports were fine, it was just the 12-ply formica worktop that the little burrowers had a taste for. I wouldn't have minded, but there it was, happening right under my nose. I wonder where they will strike next?

Weathering The Rolling Stock

Because of the much-mentioned climate in my modelling domain, I actually have to clean my stock – not weather it! Nature and dust do the weathering for me.

Also as previously mentioned, I have Hornby Dublo lithographed tinplate vehicles, bought in 1953, still merrily running around the tracks. I keep them for sentimental reasons but their original paintwork is still there under all the grime.

Everyone I suppose, has problems with dust and the only answer that I can see is my old faithful Black & Decker 'metal-mickey' vacuum cleaner (vertical cylinder job). It is always ready to hand and is a necessary tool. It doesn't do to let the cobwebs take over completely.

I have a method of cleaning locomotives and the occasional coach which has proved effective over the years, and it is what engine cleaners use in real life – oil and paraffin.

I mix the two together in about equal parts and apply it with a soft half-inch brush; not so liberally as to flood the model. The soft brush treatment allows me to get into tiny crevices and around the tiny details without breaking them off. The resultant shine is quite real-looking, even on plastic. In fact it becomes hard to distinguish between metal and plastic.

Perhaps I lied just a little when I said that I do not weather my stock.

Being a bit of a photographer, I know something about highlights. A highlight is usually one of the brightest parts of a picture and the eye of the beholder makes straight for it.

On model locomotives the brightest part seems to be the valve gear – and the eye has difficulty getting away from it. In 'real life' whoever sees mirror-bright valve gear? Go on, have a look at some when you next get the opportunity. The real thing is a gungy sort of browny-greyey-black.

So what does your aged scribe do? He paints his valve gear and coupling rods with thinned-down satin black. He does the same, with even-more-thinned-down satin black, to the brilliant white-black-white lining of his beloved LNER green locos and their lettering and numbering transfers. Then, and only then, does the super-structure of the locomotive become the eye's natural focusing point.

I don't think it is just my overworked imagination, but the locos seem to look so much larger as a result of this visual toning-down process.

Another part of the 'illusion-creating' process is to paint the wheels right to the very edge, and get rid of the 'shiny tyre'.

To me, the big trouble with the appearance of so many of today's preserved locomotives is their glittering valve gear and shiny tyres. In the steam days of yore, that sort of appearance lasted for the first couple of hours out of the paint shop. You could always see the valve gear but it didn't 'shout' at you. The bodywork was the part you really looked at, all nicely polished – with an oily rag!

Electrics and Route Selection

To me, electrics are to do with joining wires to things to make them work. One wire takes the electricity to a thing and another brings it back; what goes on in between is still a bit of a mystery to me. I have read, and continue to read, books about it and also people tell me things, but it doesn't seem to sink in. How do you spell thick?

What I do know is that, to be able to get the most out of a layout, it needs to be broken down into sections and those sections need: (a) to be insulated from one another and (b) each of the sections needs power putting into it, preferably via a switch.

So a wire goes from one of the terminals of the controller, let's call it the 'output' terminal, to a switch and from there to one of the rails in the chosen section (the left one, facing forwards). A second wire will then be connected to the other rail of that section and returned to the other terminal of the controller, let's call that the 'return' terminal.

In the early pages of this tome I mentioned using ex-RAF bomb selector switches for my sections. They never let me down, and I never heard any wartime aircrew complain about them either. As the years went by, the easternmost extremities of our far-flung empire started to market a variety of mini switches, suitable for making our own individual switch panels. I became aware of their presence amongst us at the time when I had just installed a heavy-duty capacitor-discharge unit for the multi-operation of points and signals.

Also at this same time, there appeared a series of articles in the *Railway Modeller* about diode switching and diode matrices. I bought a few of those little black things with a wire sticking out of each end and did a bit of experimenting.

The first use I put some to was to provide an automatic stop at the end of two sidings; very clever. The engine would stop and go no further when it reached the isolated end bit, so the buffer stops were safe and there was no longer any danger of the locos ending up on the floor. Turn the controller to reverse, and, surprise surprise, the little old engine would reverse out. This was great. Could I, therefore, apply these things to the mini-forest of new lattice post signals that I had just constructed, on Hornby Dublo electrically operated signal bases, for use at the newly constructed East Garforth station?

Well, after a mind-bending planning period, similar to the schedule planning extravaganza, I came up with a cat's cradle of interconnected wiring, in and out of diodes, rotary switches and push-buttons, with which I was able to operate all the signals and points at East Garforth.

I called the system 'Route Selection', which used a 6-position, 12-pole, rotary switch and three push-button 'press for on' switches. These are (note the change to the present tense, because they are still very much in use) six 'routes' that can be selected by the rotary switch, of which the first 'route' is to set all points and signals to 'mainline clear'. The remainder are for access to the station loop, crossover and sidings.

The clever bit is the use of three push-buttons to activate the points and signals as follows:

Button (1) All signals to danger i.e., 'On', regardless of position of the rotary switch route selector.

Button (2) Signals to clear i.e., 'Off' for route selected.

Button (3) Points to change in accordance with route selected.

N.B., to clear all points i.e., reset to main line, the route selector is turned to route No. 1 and push-button No. 3 is pressed.

'Wiring Up' The Route Selectors

Now let me see if I can explain how the affair is 'wired up'; and please note straightaway that I 'feed' 24 volts a.c. into the capacitor-discharge unit. In other words, I am not making use of microvolts or any of that sort of state-of-the-art electronic wizardry.

Please remember also that the purpose of one of the output terminals of the capacitor-discharge unit is to 'feed' current to the switches and thence to the point and signal 'motors' whilst the purpose of the other terminal is to allow the current to 'return' to the capacitor-discharge unit (CDU).

Because all the return wires are going to the same terminal, they can all be soldered to one 'common return' wire, thus effecting a saving on wire and complexity.

For each of the six positions of the rotary switch route-selector there are two 'poles', or output terminals.

The first of each pair of the 'poles' is connected, via a diode matrix, to the appropriate 'off' (clear) terminals of the *signal* motors to be activated for the route selected.

The second 'pole' is connected, via another diode matrix, to the appropriate terminals of the *point* motors requiring to be activated for the route selected.

Power *to* the terminals of the rotary switch comes via push-button No. 2 for the *signals*, and via push-button No. 3 for the *points*.

Power *to* the push-buttons comes from the capacitor-discharge unit.

You need a clear head when planning how to line up and connect the diodes (just like I do as I try and put all this into words), remembering that they only pass current one way – hence their use as 'solid-state' switches. Their presence enables you to 'route' the current to where you want it to go, and avoid sending current where you don't want it to go, hence the need for a 'matrix board'. A matrix board acts as a sort of distribution panel for the current, usually coming in the form of a sheet of paxolin with lots of individual lines of copper adhering to it and which can be

purchased from radio spares shops, such as Tandy, under the reference 'circuit board'.

A piece of this paxolin board, cut to whatever size is necessary to ensure an adequate number of copper lines, thus acts as a distribution panel for the circuits required, and it is to this first matrix board that the wires leading to the signal and point motor terminals are physically connected.

So, just for example, supposing Route No. 6 needs to feed point motor terminals Nos. 7B, 8B and 9B ('B' standing for 'turnout' position as opposed to 'main line' which is referred to as 'A') – there is a copper-line terminal on the matrix board for every 'B' point motor terminal but, in my case at East Garforth, just one matrix terminal for all 'A' point motor terminals is required, because all the 'A' point motors act together in unison. So, all the feed wires to the 'A' point motors are physically, and electrically, joined together at this juncture.

Similarly, there will be terminals for every 'B' signal solenoid terminal (the 'Off'/Clear position) and just one for all the 'A' signal ('On'/Danger position) terminals.

Now then, to get back to the example:

The 'other ends' of the matrix board terminals for 7B 8B and 9B point motors, are connected to the No. 6 output terminal of the rotary route-selector switch, *via a diode*, which will allow current to pass through it to the matrix board and thence to the point motor terminal – but not from the point motor terminal back to the rotary switch.

This is very important, because you have to make sure your diode is 'facing' the right way – remembering that a diode is a semi-conductor, rather like a valve, which only passes current from negative to positive but not from positive to negative, or is it the other way round?

Anyway it doesn't matter, in effect, because if current isn't being passed in the direction you want it to go then you have got the diode the wrong way round, so you simply reverse it!

Actually there is often a little ring printed at one end of the diode which indicates the 'positive' end.

Testing the Circuit

To test that all this is working, select route No. 1 on the rotary switch and press push-button No. 3.

This should set points 7, 8 and 9 to the 'A'

East Garforth Station Circuit Diagram

Detailing Route Selection Switching using Diode Matrix Distribution Panels

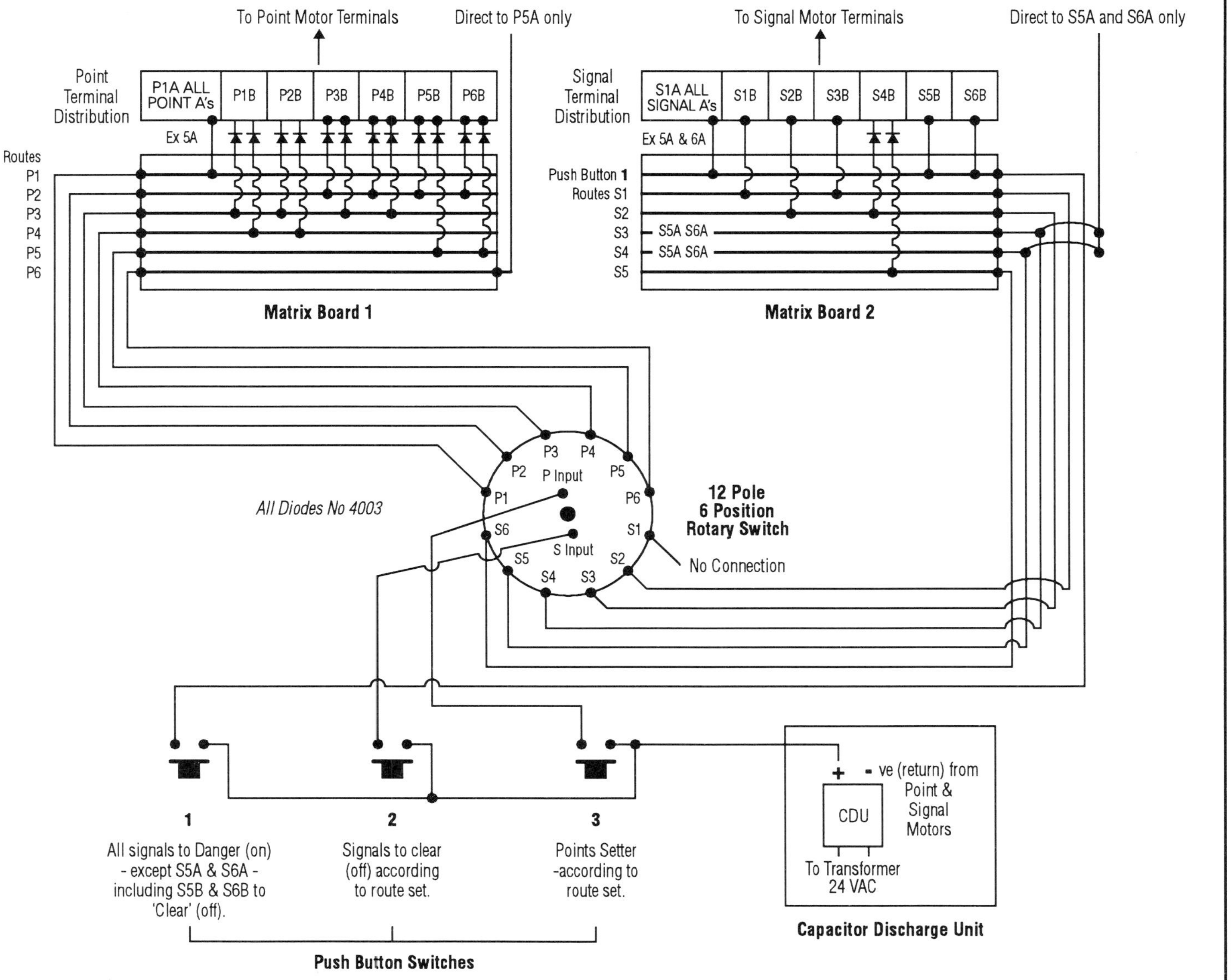
To Point Motor Terminals
Direct to P5A only
To Signal Motor Terminals
Direct to S5A and S6A only
Point Terminal Distribution
P1A ALL POINT A's
P1B
P2B
P3B
P4B
P5B
P6B
Ex 5A
Routes
P1
P2
P3
P4
P5
P6
Matrix Board 1
Signal Terminal Distribution
S1A ALL SIGNAL A's
S1B
S2B
S3B
S4B
S5B
S6B
Ex 5A & 6A
Push Button 1
Routes S1
S2
S3
S4
S5
S5A S6A
S5A S6A
Matrix Board 2
All Diodes No 4003
P1
P2
P3
P4
P5
P6
P Input
S Input
S1
S2
S3
S4
S5
S6
12 Pole
6 Position
Rotary Switch
No Connection
1
All signals to Danger (on) - except S5A & S6A - including S5B & S6B to 'Clear' (off).
2
Signals to clear (off) according to route set.
3
Points Setter -according to route set.
Push Button Switches
+
- ve (return) from Point & Signal Motors
CDU
To Transformer 24 VAC
Capacitor Discharge Unit

Explanations

P = Points, S = Signals, * = Diodes ('arrow' shows direction of current flow)

e.g. P1A – Point No 1 set for 'straight'
P1B – Point No 1 set for 'turnout'
S1A – Signal No 1 set for 'on' (danger)
S1B – Signal No 1 set for 'off' (clear)

* – Point & signal distribution can utilise cable connectors.

N.B. (1) Point Movement P5A (Route P6) is occasionally used to allow a loco to enter sect 21. The point's 'normal' position is P5B.

(2) Signal movements S5A & S6A are only required when routes P3 & P4 are selected.

(3) Route P1, in effect, sets all points to 'straight' or mainline (except point P5A)

(4) Push-button switch No 1 is used to re-set all signals to 'on' (danger) before selecting another route.

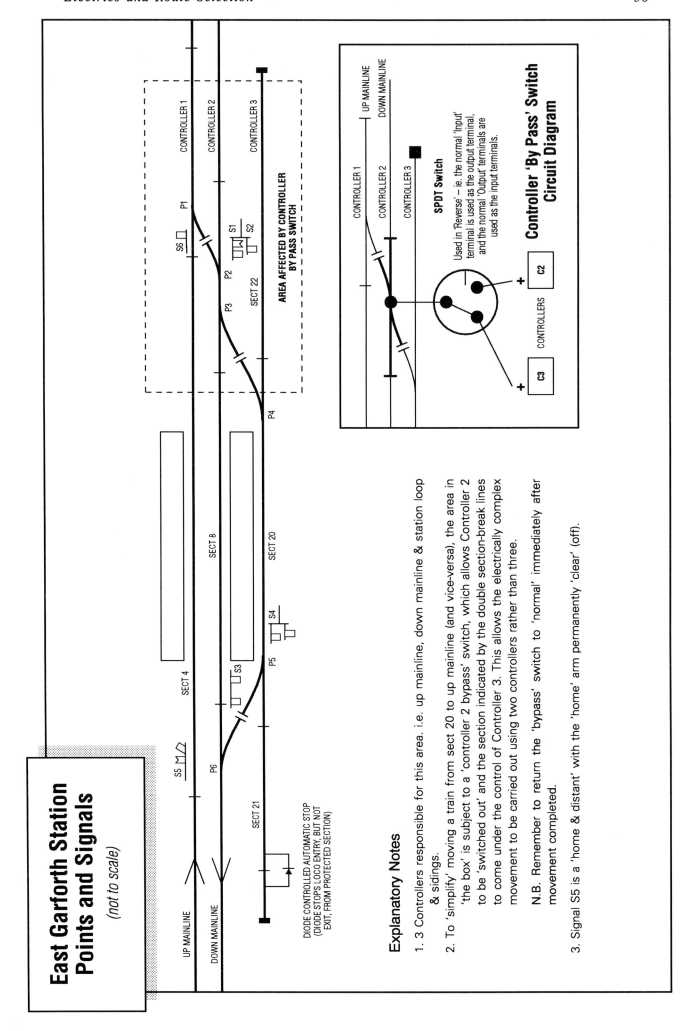

East Garforth Station Points and Signals
(not to scale)

UP MAINLINE

DOWN MAINLINE

DIODE CONTROLLED AUTOMATIC STOP
(DIODE STOPS LOCO ENTRY, BUT NOT EXIT, FROM PROTECTED SECTION)

SECT 21

SECT 4

SECT 8

SECT 20

SECT 22

S5

P6

P5

S3

S4

P1

P2

P3

P4

S6

S1

S2

CONTROLLER 1

CONTROLLER 2

CONTROLLER 3

AREA AFFECTED BY CONTROLLER
BY PASS SWITCH

Explanatory Notes

1. 3 Controllers responsible for this area. i.e. up mainline, down mainline & station loop & sidings.

2. To 'simplify' moving a train from sect 20 to up mainline (and vice-versa), the area in 'the box' is subject to a 'controller 2 bypass' switch, which allows Controller 2 to be 'switched out' and the section indicated by the double section-break lines to come under the control of Controller 3. This allows the electrically complex movement to be carried out using two controllers rather than three.

N.B. Remember to return the 'bypass' switch to 'normal' immediately after movement completed.

3. Signal S5 is a 'home & distant' with the 'home' arm permanently 'clear' (off).

Controller 'By Pass' Switch Circuit Diagram

UP MAINLINE

DOWN MAINLINE

CONTROLLER 1

CONTROLLER 2

CONTROLLER 3

SPDT Switch

Used in 'Reverse' – ie. the normal 'Input' terminal is used as the output terminal, and the normal 'Output' terminals are used as the input terminals.

C3

C2

CONTROLLERS

+

+

(main line) position, (because all 'A' terminals are connected together to act in unison, remember?)

If, say, points 7 and 8 change to 'A' and point No. 9 goes to 'B' then you have probably connected the wires to the wrong terminals of point No. 9, so reverse the connections to point No. 9 and check again. Hopefully that will now have put things right.

Now comes the real test:

Turn the rotary switch to route No. 6 and press push-button No. 3 again. Points 7, 8 and 9 should now change to the 'B' position.

If any of them didn't change to 'B' then check to see if the diode to that particular point motor terminal is the wrong way round. If it is, then reverse it.

If all went as planned, then you are in business and can set about repeating the process for all the other routes.

You will maybe have noticed, by now, that there are a number of wires from the various rotary switch outputs sharing the same terminals on the matrix board, and you are asking yourself, maybe, why they don't 'cross circuits' with one another.

The answer to the question lies with the diodes, and the phenomenon that they only pass current one way.

Because all rotary switch output wires are connected to the matrix board through diodes (facing the correct way), there can be no feedback or cross-circuiting between feed wires, because the current is only being allowed to flow *from* the rotary switch *to* the matrix board.

A 'Mini' Matrix Board

To avoid connecting a lot of wires to the small individual *output terminals of the rotary switches*, you may find it a help to create a 'mini' (or intermediate) matrix board, for the purpose of:

(1) attaching a single incoming wire from the rotary switch terminal and,

(2) distributing it amongst the copper lines, from which will go individual wires to the copper lines of the 'main' matrix board, having first been soldered to their respective diode.

The number of copper lines required on the 'mini' board will be dictated by the number of point/signal motors needing to be activated for the particular route required.

I then turned to the second set of the rotary switch output 'poles' and connected them as above, but this time to the signals.

Other Ways of Using 'Route Selection'

Now all the above was fine, because I had, at East Garforth, a nice, neat and not-too-big station area which just lent itself perfectly to Route Selection.

At other major parts of the layout, such as Barrowby and Aberford, a different approach was made to Route Selection because of the relative complexity of the trackwork, and the fact that I hadn't at that time got a full set of electrically operated signals – they were 'yet to come'.

What sufficed at the time then, and what has proved itself capable of adaptation since, was Rotary Switch Route Selection just for the points.

The rotary switches are each activated by 2 push-button switches, one labelled –A for Main line, the other labelled –B for turnout, and are powered from the same ubiquitous capacitor-discharge unit.

There are 2 rotary switches for Barrowby – 1 for the 'down' side and 1 for the 'up'.

Similarly for Aberford – 1 for Aberford Central and 1 for Aberford Exchange.

There is also a 'mini' selector, but not a rotary one, for Barwick-in-Elmet, just using 'stud-contact' superimposed on to a small schematic track diagram and an 'electric pencil'

Where colour light signals are in use I wire them via the relevant point motor adaptor switches or, as in the case of the 'old' H & M motors, the alternative switch contacts.

Where I have subsequently introduced electrically operated semaphore signals, I have inserted 'mini' (I must have a thing about mini's) push-button control switches in the rotary switch track display diagram, referred to in detail later.

From experience, I have found that, for some reason or other, operating two or three points simultaneously plus signals proves too much even for the heavy-duty capacitor-discharge unit, so it is more reliable to separate their switching. It does mean, however, that some semaphore signal movements are cosmetic in that they are not interlocked with the points.

Never mind though, they look good.

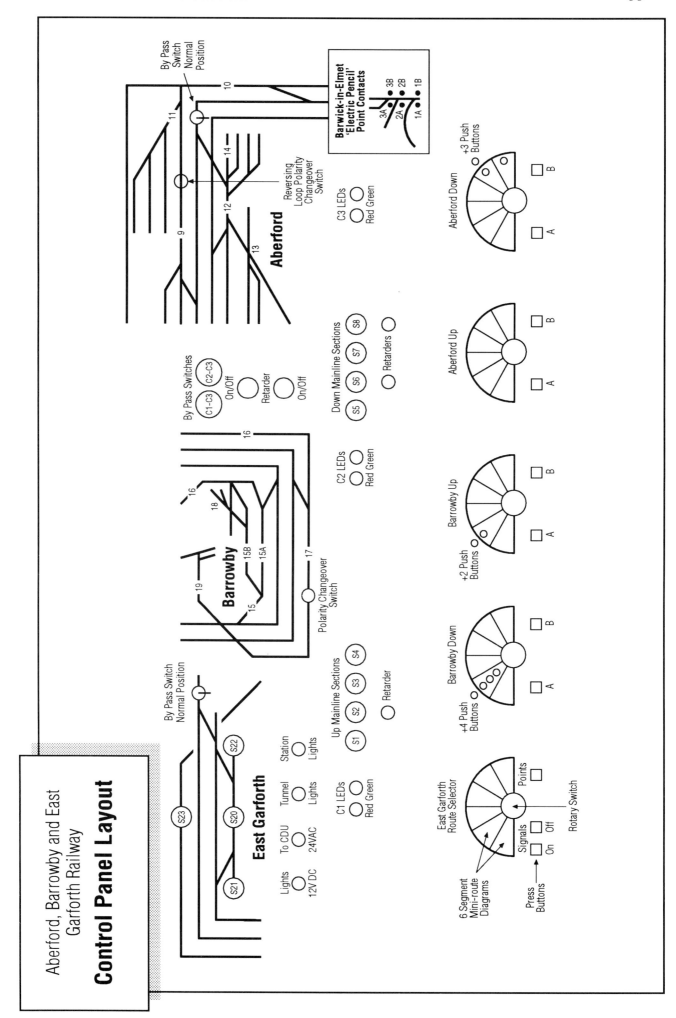

Aberford, Barrowby and East Garforth Railway

Control Panel Layout

Creating A Control Panel

It may be logical at this stage, I think, to consider where on earth we are going to put all these electrical gubbinses.

Which takes us back to 'planning by objectives' in that we know we have to put the stuff somewhere (the objective), so we must plan the 'where', 'why' and 'how', in that order.

Where?

In my case, I needed a strategically placed control panel where I could see most, if not all, of the layout. This has proved to be adjacent to the 'up' side of Barrowby, roughly in the centre of the garage.

Then I decided that a nice piece of ⅛″ perspex, about 30″ × 12″ and painted matt black, would serve as the display panel.

How?

Rotary Route Selector Switch Sub-Panels

Along the lower third of the control panel I drilled holes to take the 'stems' of the 5 rotary route selector switches.

Above each hole I created a semi-circular display panel of 3″ radius, divided into 6 segments, each of which carries a small schematic diagram of the route concerned, in line with the various switch positions. These small diagrams are necessary, because they serve to remind me which points are to be activated by the various route selector switch positions.

The display panels are coloured differently, to act as a further visual reminder which station area they control, e.g., East Garforth is coloured blue, the two Barrowby ones are red for the Up main line and green for the Down main line and, similarly, the two Aberford ones are in red and green.

I 'draw' the track diagrams in white paint, using my old-fashioned school pen nib and holder. This makes them easy to read, with my tired old eyes, from two or three feet away.

Beneath each panel are drilled ½″ holes to take the fairly large size push-button switches.

The upper two-thirds of the Control Panel are occupied with schematic track diagrams, positioned roughly above the areas covered by the route selectors. I used ⅛″ white adhesive carlining strip to represent the tracks.

Along the strips are drilled yet more holes, this time to take the 'mini' track-section switches. The strips also carry the section numbers.

Central Control Console and 'lap counters' – situated on west side of Barrowby Station. (Photo KC)

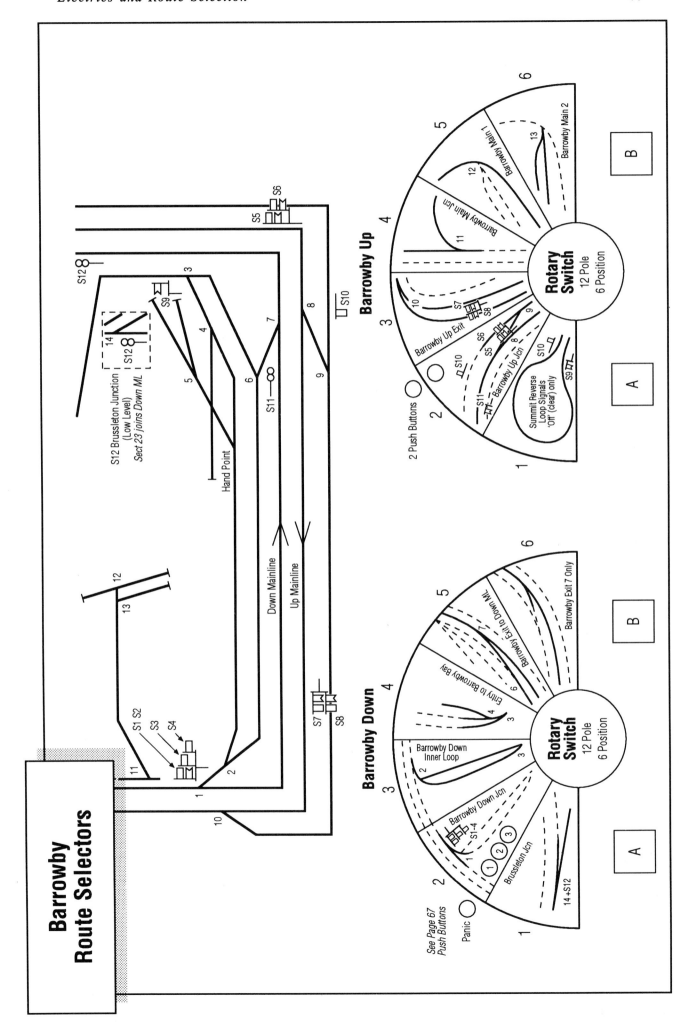

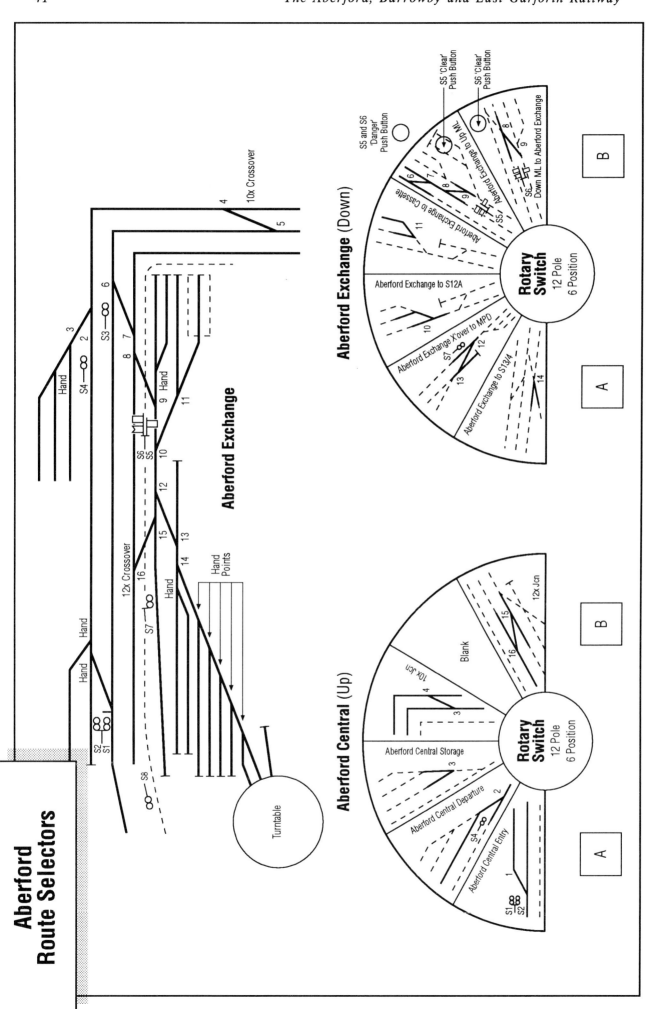

Aberford Route Selectors

Aberford Exchange (Down)

Rotary Switch
12 Pole
6 Position

S5 and S6 'Danger' Push Button

S5 'Clear' Push Button

S6 'Clear' Push Button

Down ML to Aberford Exchange

Aberford Exchange to Up ML

Aberford Exchange to Cassette

Aberford Exchange to S12A

Aberford Exchange X'over to MPD

Aberford Exchange to S13/4

B

A

Aberford Central (Up)

Rotary Switch
12 Pole
6 Position

12x Jcn

Blank

10x Jcn

Aberford Central Storage

Aberford Central Departure

Aberford Central Entry

B

A

Aberford Exchange

Hand

Hand

Hand

Hand

Hand

Hand

10x Crossover

12x Crossover

Hand Points

Turntable

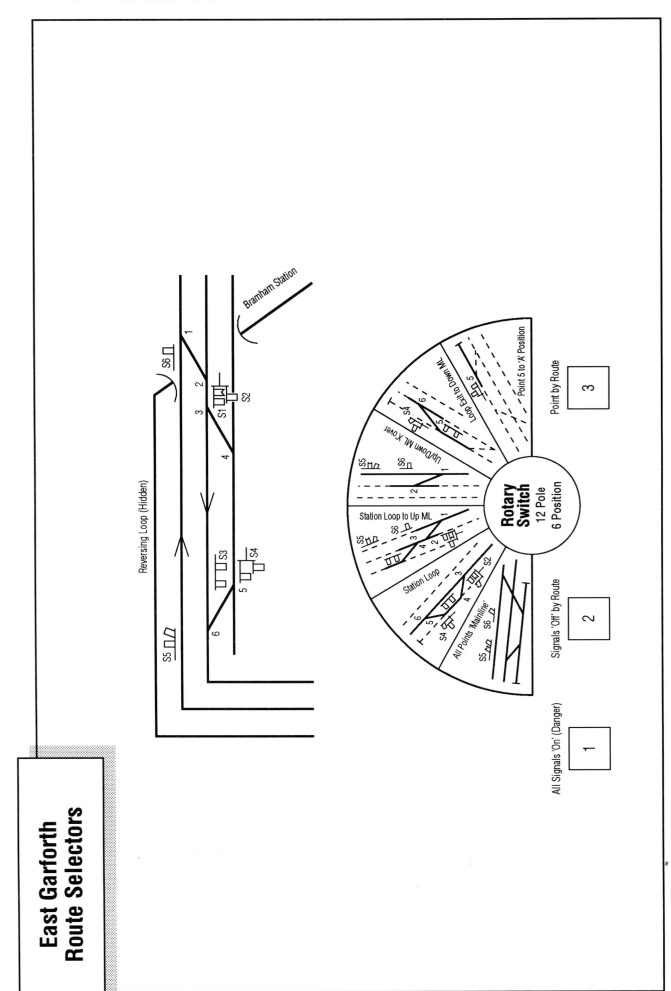

East Garforth Route Selectors

Bramham Station

Reversing Loop (Hidden)

S6

S1 S2

S3 S4

S5

Rotary Switch
12 Pole
6 Position

Station Loop to Up ML

Up/Down ML X over

Loop Exit to Down ML

Point 5 to 'A' Position

Station Loop

All Points 'Mainline'

All Signals 'On' (Danger)

1

Signals 'Off' by Route

2

Point by Route

3

There are quite a number of important control switches placed across the top third of the panel. Just in case they might prove of interest, they are:

1. Capacitor-Discharge Unit SPST in/out of circuit, plus LED indicator light.
2. 12-volt DC SPST on/off auxiliary supply to station lights and colour light signals.
3. Controller 1 to controller 3 sections, SPDT 'bypass' switch.
4. Controller 2 to controller 3 sections, SPDT 'bypass' switch.
5. Controller 3 to controller 3 sections, SPST on/off.
6. Aberford Central to Down main line reverse loop, DPDT polarity changeover.
7. Aberford Exchange to Up main line crossover, SPDT 'bypass' switch (to isolate Controller 2 from Down main line in vicinity of crossover).
8. East Garforth (East), station loop to Up main line crossover, SPDT 'bypass' switch (to isolate Controller 2 from Down main line in vicinity of crossover).
9. Track-resistor downhill section 2 Up main line, Brussleton Fell, SPDT.
10. Track-resistor, in/out of circuit, downhill section 6 Down main line, Brussleton Tunnel, SPDT.
11. Track-resistor, in/out of circuit, downhill section 8 Down main line, Parkhead Viaduct, SPDT.

Finally, to complete the 'peppering' of my cherished control panel with drill holes, there are red and green LED polarity indicators for each controller. These are connected, via current-limiting resistors, to allow the green LED to light when the controller it represents is set for forward, and red for reverse. I find this a most useful memory aid.

The completed control panel 'sits' on ¾" shelving board 4' long by 4" wide.

Another shelf, of the same size, is situated below and carries the capacitor-discharge unit plus the three track controllers.

The various mains input transformers have been built into small, ventilated boxes which are screwed underneath the lower shelf.

The whole is supported at each end by verticals of the same heavy board as the shelves and stands about 3' 6" above the floor.

A frightening maze of wires emanates from the control console, or at least it would be frightening if, at the initial planning stage, I had not seen the advantage of labelling every, yes every, individual wire.

I know all about the advantages of 'colour coding' wires, but as the years go by and new circuits are introduced it is almost impossible to match old and new by colour. One often gets the opportunity to purchase a 'job lot' of wire at a not-to-be-sniffed-at price, hence my abandonment of colour-coding throughout.

I use 3" lengths of coloured adhesive tape, preferably white or yellow, and write the destination of the wire on it before wrapping it round the wire in the form of a name tag, or label. This forethought saves time-wasting wire-chasing when a wire comes adrift, as it does occasionally.

It also helps to write notes and diagrams about your circuits, to refer to in years to come when you have completely forgotten how you did it.

It needs considerable self-discipline to write things down and file them carefully for future reference, when you would much rather be running a goods train or making a new loco, but it pays handsome dividends in later years. I know from experience.

Soldering Wire Connections

It never ceases to surprise me how many of my acquaintances fight shy of soldering, and I am not just talking about railway modellers. I look on it as something that has to be done, so I must be able to do it. There are many who can do it much better than I can, and the last thing I want to do is to set myself up as some sort of expert.

We have just been considering the construction of a control panel, with all its wires and switches. How on earth can one do it without soldering?

This is one area of the modeller's art that has been very well covered, and there is nothing that I can add to the vast fund of knowledge on, and the documentation of, the subject. Again I take pleasure in mentioning the name of Iain Rice and recommend anyone who has any misgivings on the subject to invest in his book on etched kit construction, like as what I did.

For most of my modelling life I have had three electric soldering irons: a real hefty 60-watt one, a ubiquitous 25-watt one and a low-power fine-bit 15-watt used mainly for low melt soldering.

Principal Needs When Soldering Wire Connections

1. For soldering the terminals of most small-scale switches I find my first need is the 25-watt iron. Any higher wattage might end up melting the plastic of the switches before the solder takes hold.
2. An extension lead, preferably with two output sockets so that you can plug in an inspection lamp as well as the iron.
3. A wire stripper and cutter.
4. Piece of medium grade emery *cloth*, about 3″ × 1″.
5. Tin lid of Fluxite soldering paste.
6. Coil of resin-cored solder, lightweight grade.
7. Length of heavy-gauge plastic-covered single core wire, to form into a hanging-hook to mould round the handle of the soldering iron, and thus be able to hang it up on some convenient projection, rather than laying it down somewhere unsafe.
8. Jam jar containing a bunch of steel wool – to clean the bit of the iron regularly and whilst it is hot.
9. Pair of sharp-nosed pliers.
10. Small screwdriver.
11. Large handkerchief for when the fumes of the flux make you sneeze!

Having assembled all the above items within hand's reach, plug in the iron and hang it somewhere safe, then take the first piece of wire and strip off half an inch of the insulated covering. Now place the coil of solder somewhere near the piece of wire. Wipe the tip of the (hot) iron on the steel wool in the jam jar. Offer the wire to the solder with one hand, and with the other hand bring the iron to the solder, melt some onto the bit and apply quickly to the wire so as to 'tin' it. The wire may already be tinned, but this will make sure.

Next, go to the switch terminal required, wipe the iron on the wire wool then offer the solder to the terminal and 'tin' it with the iron.

Lastly, offer the tinned end of the wire to the tinned terminal and apply the tip of the iron to melt them together. Move the iron away and allow about 5 seconds for the solder to cool and harden; if you can blow on the joint that will help cool it that much quicker. Try not to let the iron dwell too long on the terminal for fear of overheating the plastic of the switch.

Holding soldered items in the points of the pliers can help dissipate some of the heat, where space allows you to do so.

All this can be very fiddly because the terminals can be (a) quite small and (b) quite close together. This is where extra light from the inspection lamp can come in handy, because it is so easy in cramped conditions to melt the insulation covering of adjacent wires, especially if they can't be seen very clearly, and this will lead to short circuits.

Practice makes perfect, so they say, and by the time you have wired up your control panel you certainly will have had plenty of practice.

Keep wiping the soldering iron bit on the wire wool to prevent the resin flux burning on – that's the brown stuff in the middle of the soldering wire often referred to as the 'core', as in 'cored' solder. Cored solder seems to be the best kind of solder to use for making electrical connections, because it is nowhere near as corrosive as, say, the liquid acid fluxes used when soldering sheet metals.

So off you go, invest in a 25-watter and practise on some spare bits of wire until you get the hang of it. Remember, it is something that has to be done, so persevere.

In conclusion, hearken back to the heading of this section – something to do with soldering wire connections. Other applications of the solderer's art will be discussed later.

That's a fairly hefty part of the Aberford, Barrowby and East Garforth Railway we've got under our belt. Perhaps the time is now opportune to consider the trackwork and lineside fittings.

The Track

Having read thus far you will probably be thinking, 'What can be said about Peco track? If you are rich you buy it in boxes of 25-yard lengths, cut off the long bits on curves and join it together with fishplates.' A wee bit simplistic perhaps, though true enough, but what a lot else goes along with it.

I regard Peco track as an 'enabler'; it saves me a lot of time and enables me to get on with other things.

I find that there is a sort of art in laying it

which comes with time and experience, so if I retail a few of the latter then someone, somewhere, might benefit.

Track Underlays

My pre-retirement days were spent selling my company's products to the retail and wholesale trade. Part of the job was to encourage feature displays of our products and, to this end, I supplied display materials to 'crown' the displays.

I don't think I could be accused of being disloyal if I was to say that, usually, I was supplied with far more than my clients could possibly use, so what was I to do with the surplus? Give it to the refuse collector? Take it to the council amenity tip? Parcel it up and send it back to the company – at huge expense considering most of it would be time-expired within two months?

Consider also that most of this material was printed on the most beautiful cardboard, in various thicknesses.

I'll tell you what: the local authority saw very little of it because it was 'treasure trove' to me as a railway modeller, with the company's blessing I might add (but not in writing). So, if you will take my tip, gain the acquaintance of a friendly supermarket manager, and ask to be allowed to relieve him of his unwanted show material.

Some of the 3′ × 2′ sheets of ⅛″ board cost the earth if you ever have to buy them!

I think by now you will have got the message – cardboard is lovely and is there for the asking. It is lovely to use, straightforward to cut, easy to prepare and will (I think, but am not yet in a position to confirm) last a lifetime.

Now you are asking questions again. 'What has this got to do with track underlays?' some of you are saying, right? Well, I'll tell you, so carry on reading.

Peco track simply laid on to a baseboard seems to lack something, even when it is disguised with the ballast effect. Real-life track rests on a bed of stone ballast anything up to 12″ deep.

Cutting ⅛″ card underlays will provide that extra height. However, before it is laid, the card needs to be 'treated'.

Cardboard, as it comes, is susceptible to dampness and will reduce to a soggy, useless mess very quickly unless 'treated'. This is where my youthful days of yore as an aero-modeller came in handy, because I used to use a cellulose preparation called 'Balsa Sanding Sealer' on balsa block to give a 'key' for the paint to stick to.

DJH/Raven A8 4-6-2 T No. 1501 prepares to depart from Aberford Exchange with Train C. (Photo KC)

'Not only, but also', this sanding sealer stuff rendered balsa wood waterproof. Well, says I, if it waterproofs wood then it should also do the same to cardboard – and it jolly well does; I can prove it all over my layout!

Again, 'not only, but also', it not only gives a first-class 'key' to the paint but, also, woodworms don't like it.

A tin of the stuff can be let down to nearly six times its volume with cheap thinners, of the type car sprayers use to clean their spray guns. Thus thinned it goes quite a long way and dries hard within minutes. In fact, the thinner it is, the better it soaks into the card, and I have found it superior, for our purpose, to any other form of preservative.

So lay your length of track, lightly, and cut your untreated cardboard to ⅛″ or so proud of either side of the sleepers. Then remove the card, treat with the thinned-down sanding sealer, and let it dry and harden. Finally, spray, or brush paint to a suitable track base colour. I tend to use grey primer or matt black. When dry, place under the Peco trackage, and insert the track pins.

Adapt this procedure to points and crossovers, remembering to leave gaps where you have 'dug' holes for the Peco point motors.

I do not recommend gluing down the underlays to the baseboard. Should you, however, in your wisdom and after much forethought, decide to 'ballast' your track and underlays, there will be adhesive enough floating around anyway.

I don't know about you, but whenever I have – in the past – gone to the trouble of gluing down ballast and track, it only seemed to be a matter of days before I had to lift it for some reason, and what a job it was! So now I do not glue down my track at all.

Pinning Down the Track

It will save a lot of trouble later if you will discipline yourself to drill track pin holes in the sleepers before you lay them. To this end, my personal method, offered merely for guidance, is to drill every fourth sleeper, unless using a whole yard length in which case, about 12″ from each end, merely drill every eighth sleeper.

As I remove the 'chairs' from the last two sleepers at each end of a piece of track, to allow for insertion or easy removal of rail joiners, I commence counting every fourth sleeper from the first sleeper with 'chairs' on.

I am in possession of a Tipp-ex 'pen' with which I 'dot' each drill hole. This is a marvellous visual aid in dark places and can always be painted out later.

For a drill I use an ordinary household pin, with the head cut off, and shaped to a screw-driver-like end on the carborundum stone. It takes about a minute of time and is very cost-effective.

For 'track pins' I literally use pins, – little ½″ steel stationery pins. When pinning down the track, tamp the pin down as far as it will go and then, with one of those clever 'track pin lifter' gadgets, raise the pin until the head is about 1mm above the sleeper. This will allow the track to 'float' just a little, which has an effect on rolling stock similar to springing. Certainly do not pin down the track tightly. Track needs to give a little, as in the real thing.

Another 'discipline', whilst a track length is on the bench, is to file or grind off a little of the flange on the lower face of the end of the rails themselves. This eases the fitting of new, and tight, rail joiners. But, of course, you already knew about that. Whilst you are at it then, why not round off the upper face of each rail end, just enough so that when you run your finger over it (ouch!) there is no sharp edge? The wheels of your locomotives and rolling stock will appreciate this 'rail joint smoother'.

Points, also, can be treated similarly to good effect, especially the 'wing rails' and the ends of 'frogs' which always seem to me to be very sharp.

A final observation is to do with track cutting and concerns cutting in the exact place that you want. I am thinking, in particular, of cutting the 'long bit' off the inside rail of a curve, or when you reach the place where you want to join up with a length of previously laid rail.

I take it for granted that you will be leaving gaps, at rail joints, to allow for track expansion in summer and contraction in winter.

When you have made your decision, exactly, where you want to make your cut, try using the tip of a sharp knife to 'mark the spot' on the rail surface. This will show up quite nicely when you take the length of track to your place of cutting.

I have tried many ways of cutting track, but I always fall back on my old trusted Eclipse Piercing Saw, because it cuts exactly where I want it to, and leaves no feathery edges. Also I keep an old 6″ length of 2 × 2″ timber on which to place the track and which will lift it off the bench just enough to give the saw that little bit of extra clearance.

All that needs to be done, after the cutting, is to round off the rail ends and remove some of the lower flange to facilitate fitting the fishplates. How about that for alliteration?

Track Alignment

Try and lay two or three feet of track – straight. Almost impossible to do so without a kink, so you have to look along it – preferably at track height to iron out the kinks. That is the easy bit, so what about the curves?

Might I suggest a further investment, namely a set of metal Tracksetter Templates for, say, 3′ and 4′ radius? They really are a boon to getting curves without 'flat spots'.

Mind you, I do like to 'lead in' to my curves with what are called in real life 'transition curves'. What this means is that, for the comfort of passengers and the well-being of rolling stock, it is better that track does not suddenly change from straight to curved. To this end it is usually possible to commence a curve very gradually until it reaches the radius required, so in practice, it might mean starting the curve somewhat earlier.

A similar procedure is also desirable at the exit from the curve.

It doesn't really matter if you lose some of your 'straights' because really, they are not the exciting things one might imagine them to be, in the modelling scene.

My personal opinion is that curves add to the visual sense-of-movement and create extra interest.

Track Levelling and Super-Elevating Curved Tracks

Derailment of rolling stock occurs frequently, I think you will find, even on the best of layouts, and for a variety of causes. If however, you happen to notice vehicles regularly coming adrift at the same location, then I think you might be well advised to suspect that the fault lies with the track rather than the vehicle.

To this end, a number of quick tests can be made, as follows:
1. Test the gauge with your track gauge.
2. Is there a 'kink' in the track, or a previously unnoticed 'tight spot' in a curve?
3. Is there a broken rail joint or a rail joiner moved out of position?
4. Is there a 'dog's-leg' rail joint, especially on a curve, where there is a tendency for rail ends to spring towards the outside of the curve?
5. Has the track developed an adverse camber or a 'twist' from side to side?

Regarding the heading of this section, by track levelling I am not referring to gradients but, rather to 'unintended undulations'. F'rinstance, there might be an unwanted and previously undetected 'foreign body' underneath the track, such as a piece of grit or stray piece of wire, causing the track to rise a little at that point – or the baseboard might have a lump in it or even a sag.

Sometimes it is not easy to detect these 'undulations' without the aid of a small, and I mean small, spirit-level. I have a very useful plastic-cased affair about 3″ × 1″, with a level along the long side and one on the short side. I move this very slowly along the suspect bit of the track and watch for the beginnings of a change in the position of the bubble. With practice this has become a most useful tool for me and has shown up track irregularities that are very difficult to see in the normal way, yet were resulting in frequent derailments.

Connected with track levelling is the deliberate 'un-levelling' of track, from side to side, known as 'super-elevating'.

In real life, our roadways and railways are 'super-elevated' on corners, known to modellers as 'curves', so as to raise the 'outside' edge of the corner, or curve, above that of the 'inside' edge. Sometimes, the word 'camber' is used instead of 'super-elevate.'

The purpose of this is, so I am told, to help resist the forces that make moving bodies want to go off in a straight line, or at a tangent to corners that are on the level or on 'the flat'. The effect of raising the outside edge of the curve is to make the vehicles 'lean into' the curve and thus 'bias' them in favour of the curve. This adds to our safety on the roads, and, on the railways, enables rolling stock not only to corner more safely and comfortably but also faster.

I think I have now reached the point I am trying to make; let's see. The deliberate super-elevating of model railway track on curves not only looks good, but also enables the rolling stock to go round 'em easier, more assuredly and with an increase in adhesion for locomotives. To this end therefore, the placing of 1 millimetre (now I've gone metric again) thickness strips of 'treated' card or wood, underneath the 'outside' edge of the sleepers on a curve, will give the super-elevation required for most circumstances. Where there are 'reverse curves', as in an S-bend where the curves are first one way and then the opposite or 'reverse way', let the last 6″ of the first bend and the first 6″ of the 'reverse' bend become level before 'changing sides' of the super-elevation strips. If you fail to do this, and suddenly 'change sides' of the strips, then there will be a danger of rolling stock trying to 'twist' and becoming derailed.

Test the evenness of the super-elevation by means of the aforementioned spirit-level; trying to keep the bubble in the same place throughout.

My experience is that track tends to twist from side to side anyway, even straight track, for a variety of reasons, and this must be watched for by regularly going over the tracks with the spirit-level.

One hears a lot these days of the advantages of 'compensating' one's rolling stock and locomotives. This refers to methods of allowing axles and/or their bearings to rise and fall a little so as to allow them to compensate for slight track irregularities. A few of the vehicles that I have compensated have more than proved their worth in this respect and, as time goes on, I shall endeavour to add to their number.

In the meantime, however, all that we have been discussing about track levelling and super-elevating still holds good.

I would go so far as to say they are all complimentary to each other, bringing nothing but good in the establishment of a smooth-running model railway system.

'Go thou, and do likewise.'

In conclusion, may I be permitted a word of apology to those readers who make their own track and who have seen no reference to the art in my writings.

The reason is, as you may well have deduced,

Mainline/Worsdell J72 0-6-0 T No. 509 shunts pick-up goals at East Garforth.
Note signals (working) now in position. 1986. (Photo KC)

that I have never made any, and I am only retailing here my own actual experiences. You see, I am not very good at many things and only moderately good at others. In other words, I am mediocre.

The fact that I get there in the end is no recommendation, but may be a consolation.

In a similar vein, to those who model in the finescales such as EM and P4 etc., please forgive this old peasant from the lower classes for not mentioning, so far, your exquisites. What we now know as 'finescale' was but a tiny little cloud above a distant horizon all those hundreds of years ago, when I made my investment in '00' gauge. It was for craftsmen and artists, both of which I was not.

My investment was not only in hard cash but in time, and it is time that is now beginning to run short.

I am sure that I would never have lived to complete a system the size of mine, despite its many shortcomings, if I had adopted finescale, even had it been available in those early days.

As it is, regardless of shortcomings, I have a most absorbing and interesting model railway system, albeit a little 'coarse' (like some of my language) by finescale standards, but it works well and it looks good so, if you will pardon the expression, I am going to stay with it.

Scenery and Buildings

'And having made the railway, he then made the world to go round it.'

I guess that more or less sums up my attitude towards scenery. It is the stuff that goes round the railway, to disguise or fill in the gaps where I can't put any more track.

Before you go off in a huff, let me hasten to qualify by saying that, regardless of the basic reason for scenery being, as I see it, to fill in gaps, it is the scenery, perhaps even more than the rolling stock, that can create the big 'suspension of disbelief' (not my words, but I love the sound of them) in the eyes of the beholder.

In the 'early' days of the layout, all seemed to be baseboard-making, tracklaying and wiring. I knew where I wanted the track to go and made baseboards accordingly. Only occasionally was I able to see a 'scenic opportunity' first and make the baseboard to fit in with it afterwards.

By 'baseboards' I really mean something like 'track supports' because quite large areas are what I have heard called 'open frame', especially where there are gradients involved.

Right, then; the 'track supports' were in position and the track laid, wired and tested. All looked very basic and certainly not much of a scenic masterpiece; rather like a building site when the buildings are completed but not landscaped.

This is when some standing back and thinking had to take place, a process that refused to be hurried.

Obvious areas like stations and sidings were left out of the deliberations for the time being; it was the 'countryside' areas that had to be thought about first.

F'rinstance, something that suggested itself at the lower end of the garage was a stream coming into the scene from under a small rail overbridge, flowing alongside the track for a couple of feet or so before winding away out of sight under another small overbridge. I had seen such a scene on the East Coast main line near Grantshouse, alongside the diminutive river Eyewater, just north of Berwick. So that was one scene fixed in my mind.

In fact, the lower end area of the garage presented me with quite a problem because of the complexity of tracks at different levels.

First was 'the stream', then the gradient carrying the main up and down lines from Brussleton Junction up to Barrowby. Behind that was the gradient carrying the main lines down to Barrowby Main (colliery) Junction running next to the end wall of the garage.

Finally, and literally to 'crown' it all, was the reverse-loop line to Barwick-in-Elmet, now known as 'Brussleton Summit' and which was above all the rest.

My solution was to create one massive 'fell', now known as Brussleton Fell, rising to 2′ above the 'stream' which was at 'datum level'.

I decided that the rising gradient, carrying the main line from Brussleton Junction to Barrowby, would be 'out in the open', and the falling gradient to Barrowby Main Junction along with the high-level Brussleton Summit line would be 'out of sight' amongst the innards of 'the Fell'.

This is where huge quantities of cardboard, Evostik and staples were consumed to form contours of a rugged 'fellside'.

The routine was something like building the fuselage of a flying model aeroplane in the old balsa wood days.

The cardboard contours would be the 'formers' and they would be linked to each other with miscellaneous lengths of card, the 'longerons' about 1″ wide, then Evostuck and stapled together. The whole was then covered with one thickness of newspaper, Evostuck to the 'formers' and 'longerons'.

On to this 'base' was 'clagged' (north-eastern expression for soggy mess) two or three thicknesses of Polycelled newspaper, which was then left to dry. This produced the 'ground surface' of 'the fell'.

The next job was to take some 'cork bark' and thin it by cutting off most of the back surface. This left me with a very much thinner but far more pliable simulation of 'rock facing', which I proceeded to glue along the lower face of 'the Fell'. This was to give the impression that the course of the railway had had to be blasted out of the rock. I also glued left-over scraps at various other parts on the 'fell-side', to look like rocky outcrops.

All the remaining surface of 'the Fell' was covered with Modroc plaster bandage, suitably moistened with a 2″ paint brush and water.

The last act at this stage in the game was to 'paint' the rock faces with thin Polyfilla.

Whilst all this was drying, I made four tunnel portals to tidy up the entries and exits of the various tracks where they went into and out of 'the Fell'.

Then came the best part – the colours.

The 'fell-side' was again Polycelled and green grass scatter stuff liberally sprinkled on, the surplus carefully vacuum-cleaned off later.

The 'rock faces' were painted odd mixtures of grey, brown, black, white and green, until it looked right.

Lots of little bushes and saplings were 'planted', made out of old-fashioned loofahs from the chemist, Dylon-dyed chartreuse in a pan of boiling water.

The idea of these loofahs is first to soak them in water until they fully expand, then cut out the centre core – which makes useful poplar trees and the like. The remaining outer part can then be cut to simulate the 'silhouette' of a row of trees, and little tiny ½″ triangles can be cut and teased-out to form shrubs. Obtain a couple for yourself and use your imagination. I am sure you will be amazed at the versatility of the loofah.

Of course, much use is also made of lichen and other tree- and bush-like materials. Just recently I have been teaching myself to make trees, using twisted wire for trunks and branches, with lichen and Heki foliage matting. They look quite good, and, no doubt, will get better as I become more proficient.

Sorry about the digression, but it seemed relevant at the time.

What to do with Corners

As many modellers have mentioned in their writings, corners are important areas to be considered, if only for the reason that most rooms have at least four of them.

Because of the abutments in the centre of my garage, I have had eight corners to deal with, so I now offer a list f'rinstancing what I did with them:
1. SE corner – is the site of Barwick-in-Elmet station and Pork and Pie Factory sidings.

Pastorale – East Garforth Village, junction of Station Road with Main Street. (Photo KC)

2. E side of South Abutment – has a country lane and cottage with garage and gardens.

3. W side of South Abutment – has a large parish church and churchyard raised up on a 'commanding promontory' overlooking Aberford.

4. SW corner – is in the form of a grassy slope with a road bridge coming out of the angle of the corner and crossing the railway just short of the W side of Aberford.

5. NW corner – carries the village of East Garforth, raised well above the railway. Here is yet another road bridge over the railway emanating from the angle of the corner, which serves as the road link with East Garforth station.

6 and 7.   On all three faces of the North Abutment are formed, in semi-relief, the buildings of the 'city' of Barrowby. They are quite imposing structures utilising the excellent Superquick Regency Buildings and Shopping Arcade kits, modified somewhat. In the background can be seen the west front of 'the Minster' which bears a striking resemblance to that of York. All this stands on a plinth above and across the railway, with roadways, and a 'Station Road' leading down to Barrowby Station building – the large Superquick kit one.

8. NE corner – mostly comprises hilly scenery surrounding the northern entries to Brussleton Fell. It is designed to lead the eye 'out of the picture' and create an impression of great distance.

Buildings

Duly considering what I have written about Brussleton Fell and the treatment of corners, I realise that, as far as scenery goes, I have dealt with most of the layout except the stations.

It is a moot point, as I see it, whether stations come under the heading of scenery or buildings. After all, you don't have a station if there are no buildings. Even a simple platform is a building of sorts. I mean, we don't go in for earthmounds for trains to stop at; they have to be finished off somehow.

I propose therefore, for the purpose of this dissertation, to regard stations as buildings, so there.

Platforms

Remembering at all times that it is the British railway scene that we are modelling, it should surprise no one if, under the heading of buildings, I place platforms first in order of picking.

Longshot of East Garforth Village Corner, with up 'Coronation' passing under Station Road bridge, hauled by Hornby/Gresley A4 4-6-2 No. 4489 'Dominion of Canada'. 1993. (Photo KC)

The up 'Coronation' leaving Barrowby behind 'Dominion of Canada'. (Photo KC)

In Britain, railway platforms are to assist people to get on to, and get off of, trains.

Refrain from asking me why. I wasn't there when the decision was made. All I know is that carriage doors are a long way off the ground. Perhaps steps had not been invented in the 1820s.

The other purpose of platforms seems to be to enable people to get from the world without, to the trains within.

Sometimes, platforms form an island between two railway tracks, and have to be approached and quitted by means of a footbridge or a subway. These same footbridges or subways will, in turn, connect with (a) another platform or (b) the world without.

Having said all that, if you happen to work on the railway, you will be allowed to descend from a platform and walk across the tracks in order to gain access to a pre-determined place or structure, that is if an oncoming train does not hinder your progress.

Now we begin to hint at public safety, because railway trains and people are commodities to be kept a 'safe distance' apart, unless the former are stationary or the latter are contained within the former.

Also, people get very cross when struck by moving trains and their relatives tend to claim expensive amounts of money from the railway companies in the form of compensation. Perhaps this explains why platforms are shaped the way they are.

What are these shapes?

Shapes of Platforms

Most railway platforms that I know tend to be long, rather than flat surfaces, hereinafter referred to as 'topfaces'. There is nothing 'fixed' about their horizontal dimensions because they are made to fit a particular location.

However, there does seem to be some measure of agreement that their width, side to side, should not be less than 8′, and considerably more if they are adjacent to a high-speed through line.

They are raised up from the ground, roughly to a level just below that of an opened carriage door.

They are usually held up by, at least, a wall about 3′ high, hereinafter referred to as a 'riser', often made of bricks and set back from the platform edge by about a foot.

Aberford Central Station – a study in platforms. (Photo KC)

Very often they end in what is called a 'ramp', which is the term used to describe the way the ends of platforms slope down to the ground. This is a very useful means of gaining access to platforms from ground level by railway personnel; especially if they are pushing things like barrows.

Note that, during World War II, platform edges were white-painted, hopefully to help people see where they (the platform edges) were in the blackout. This practice is still in use at some stations.

These, then, are what I have in mind when I refer to 'shapes' of platforms.

Platform 'Furniture'

Under this heading are what can be regarded as normal fittings to be seen on most platforms, and does not include litter or anything else dropped casually. I do include the following:

Station lamps, seats, luggage trolleys empty and full, station name boards, litter bins, chocolate and cigarette vending machines, weighing machines, waiting rooms with ladies and gents 'facilities', platform number signs, direction boards, advertising billboards, fire-precaution buckets of sand and water, milk churns, fish

boxes (phew!), boxes of merchandise, bicycles, water cranes and starting signals.

And that is just for starters! All I say is, please leave room for the passengers when making yours.

Making Platforms

All my platforms, with one exception, are made of ⅛″ card and Evostik – 'topface', 'risers', and interior cross-bracing.

Supposing, then, we are going to make an 'island' platform. The first part of it will be the most important, and this will be the 'topface'.

The Platform 'Topface'

The first task, then, is to make a template, on newspaper, of the position of the nearest rail of the tracks on either side of where the platform is going to be.

Most likely, one sheet will not be enough, so you will need a second, perhaps even a third. Anyway, lay the first sheet of newspaper across the tracks at the position where the beginning of the first of the ramps is going to be, say the left one.

Without moving the sheet, carefully make an impression of the nearest rail of one of the tracks, by rubbing your finger over the paper along with length of the rail. Then do the same for the nearest rail of the other track.

If a second sheet is needed, carefully place it so as slightly to overlap the first one, and, with a pencil, mark where the track impressions of the first sheet line up with the second sheet. Whilst you are at it, make a mark on the first sheet to correspond with the commencement of the second sheet, because the ends of the sheets will have to be cut in such a way that they will match up with one another, allowing for the slight overlap – say ½″. Now make impressions of the rails on sheet two in the same way as for sheet one.

Repeat this again if a third sheet is needed, and, when satisfied that you have 'got it right', number the sheets 1,2,3 etc., and, with a pair of scissors, cut them along the impression lines rubbed on earlier.

Finally, create a slight 'taper' to the 'ramps' by narrowing the ends about 5mm on each edge. this gives a nice 'lead in' to the platforms.

You should have by now, in total, an accurate set of templates of the area between the two tracks, so place the sheets back into position between the tracks to confirm. If all is well, carefully join the sheets together with sellotape or glue of some sort.

Of course, you will have realised that this template is going to be too wide for the actual 'topface' of the platform, so here comes the clever bit.

With the template in position, select your longest item of rolling stock, a coach for example, and place it on one of the tracks. Holding a pencil or marker pen vertically against the front end of the coach and, with the pencil or pen touching the paper template, slowly move the coach along the track, from one end of the template to the other, making sure your pencil or pen is marking the template. Repeat this procedure for the other track.

Now you will have an accurate marking on the template of where the actual edges of the platforms are going to be, allowing for 'overhang' of coaches where there is a curved platform edge involved. Cut the template, yet again, along this line.

The next state in the proceedings is to offer the template to a nice large sheet of ⅛″ cardboard (remember the friendly local supermarket manager?) and mark out edges of the template on the board with a pencil.

If the sheet of board is not large enough, then make a mark on the template where the end of the first piece came to, and move the template to another part of the board to mark out the second piece, and so on until you have marked out enough card to cover the template. Unlike the joints on the template, which overlapped, the ends of the card will be butt-jointed and reinforced from underneath.

The time has now come to cut the board, and this is where a nice new blade in the Stanley knife will come in handy, because you are going to have to do the cutting freehand, unless you are lucky enough to have dead straight platform edges, in which case use a steel rule as a guide.

Taking a deep breath, make a 'light' cut, right along the first line, and then the second. Don't try to cut through in one, just in case you slip. Use the first light cut as a guide to repeated cuts until you are through. This way, you will end up with nice crisp edges to your lengths of card. When all the lengths are cut, try them for size between the tracks. Mark out any tight spots with a pencil and cut them to fit – don't sandpaper them, otherwise you will risk your crisp edges.

When satisfied, 'treat' the pieces of card with sanding sealer and wait until they harden. Always remember to treat the edges as well as the main surfaces. This also applies if you have to do any more trimming; re-treat the new edge. It is all part of the sealing process, leaving no room for dampness to get in.

Before setting aside the pieces of your 'topface' now completed, it just remains to mark, on the underside of the card, where the 'ramps' are to commence and to make two light cuts about 2mm apart from side to side of the platform.

With the tip of the Stanley knife, remove the narrow sliver of card between the cuts. This will enable you to bend down the ramp, when the time comes, without disfiguring the 'topface'.

The next step to be considered is the wall or 'riser' which lifts the 'topface' above the ground level, so read on.

Platform Walls or Risers

This should be fairly simple, but as usual, there is something that has to be done first. In this case a decision has to be made, namely:

How high, above ground level, do you want your platform 'topface' to be? Personally, I like mine to be on a level with the footsteps under the carriage doors. This is a 'variable' measurement which depends on: (a) The height of the railhead above 'ground level', which is influenced by track underlays, ballast and sleeper thickness. (b) The height of your under-door footsteps.

So the thing to do is to take a measurement from ground level to your under-door footsteps, then deduct the thickness of the platform 'topface' plus a further 2mm for 'topface' covering (to be discussed in a minute). This will leave you with a measurement of the height of the platform wall or 'riser', somewhere between 20 and 25mm, I think you will find.

With a bit of luck, and because the platform we are making is an 'island' platform, the height of the walls will be the same on both sides of the platform. This is not always the case, because with some types of platforms for example, the near edge may have to blend with some scenery and may even be supported by it, in which case, only one platform wall will be required.

Taking the longest sheet of card that you can find, mark out strips to the width of your earlier measurement for the height of the walls, and cut enough of them to support both sides of the 'topface'. If you will take my advice you will mark out sufficient strips to allow for the walls to be of two thicknesses of card. Mark those strips that will be fitted under the 'ramps' in such a way as to allow about 3 inches for the slope of the 'ramp'. These 'end strips' should be cut about ½″ short of the end of the ramps to allow the 'topface' to come down snugly to ground level.

Whilst in the cutting mode, cut a number of strips about 1″ × 3″ which will be used in such a way as to bring the various 'topfaces' together, by Evosticking them across the joints from underneath.

When all the strips have been cut, and before gluing them together, the card will need to be sealed with sanding sealer and left to harden for about 30 minutes.

Now is the time to Evostik the two wall thicknesses together, but before doing so observe that the card itself will have a 'front' face and a 'back' face. By gluing a 'front' face to a 'back' face you will overcome any tendency in the card to warp.

Having glued the two wall thicknesses together, now is time to consider 'facing' them with stone or brick, or whatever.

When you have made your decision, make sure you have enough plasticard, or whatever, to do the job, because these walls can consume quite a lot of material.

Some of my platforms are faced in plasticard and others in embossed card, But I always use Evostik as the adhesive because it is quick and it is certain.

Now, I suggest, it is time to lay out the 'topfaces' on a nice big flat surface, bottom side uppermost, and glue the previously cut pieces of 1″ × 3″ strip across the joints, If you happen to have a stapler, use staples as well and bend over the ends.

When these have set, turn the 'topface' over and offer it to the space between the tracks to make certain it fits nicely where you want it. If it does, then now is the time to return the 'topface' to the bench, turn it over again, and commence gluing the 'walls' to the underside of the 'topface', remembering to allow about ¼″ 'overhang' for the platform edges. It may be necessary to use a pin or two temporarily to hold down the 'topface' to the slopes of the 'ramps'. The pins can be removed later when the glue has set.

Finally, cut some more card strips the same width as the platform walls and glue them to the underside of the 'topface' in a zig-zag pattern from side to side between the walls. This will give added strength to the 'topface' and resist any tendency for it to sag.

With a bit of luck the construction of your island platform is now completed. The only thing left to do is put the 'surface' on the 'topface'.

Finishing Touches

This is a debatable item and subject to personal choice, so I will try not to be controversial. I will just say that what has worked well for me over the years has been to Polycell the 'topface', cover it with newspaper and paint it.

I first cut newspaper to size, dry, allowing

¼″ overhang to cover the platform edges, then apply a liberal coating of Polycell to the 'topface' and carefully lay on the newspaper, trying to arrange for joints to be as close as possible without overlapping.

When all is firm and dry, a coat of matt dark grey paint is applied and the platform edges painted white.

Using newspaper as a surfacer may seem the ultimate in penny-pinching, but it has worked for me and has the advantage, albeit slight, of being slightly rough in texture.

Using Hardboard Instead of Card

The Up main line platform at Barrowby happens to be right underneath the one part of the garage roof that is subject to a slight water leak in wet weather. After 25 years of the platform getting wet I decided to remake it, using hardboard and my trusty jigsaw.

The measuring procedure was the same as for card, but I had a nice long piece of hardboard going spare and was able to cut out the 'topface' in one, and the walls only needed to be one thickness. I used the rough side of the board as the platform surface and as the front surface of the walls. I used sanding sealer to coat all surfaces, even underneath cross-bracing. The lot was Evostuck together, using panel pins to secure the 'ramps'.

The walls were painted a dusky red which, from the normal viewing distance, passes nicely for weathered brick.

The platform surface looks gratifyingly rough when painted matt dark grey with white edging.

When I tell you that the platform is curved, you can imagine that it was somewhat of a trial of skills and patience making it out from the paper templates.

I am glad that I carried out the experiment and the 'topface' doesn't look too thick. If I ever have to remake any of the other platforms I may well repeat the idea, but this is not to be construed as doing away with card for other buildings. It will depend on the circumstances.

The main object behind going to so much detail about making the island platform from card, has been to describe a method of constructing buildings that has been tried and tested all over my system, and which has stood up to the rigours of temperature and humidity variation for over 30 years.

For me it has been a cheap and plentiful source of material, it is easy to cut and, when sealed, takes paint well and is almost impervious to damp.

Summary

1. Try to make the acquaintance of a supermarket manager and ask to 'relieve' him of unwanted items of display material, especially the large 3′ × 2′ sheets. It doesn't matter about the printing because that will be covered over in the course of construction.
2. Make great use of Balsa Sanding Sealer, to seal against humidity and dampness, and also give an excellent 'key' to paint. Endeavour to find a supply source of cellulose thinners as supplied for brush and spraygun cleaning, which are quite adequate for our purpose and very much cheaper.
3. When gluing two thicknesses of card to each other, try to place similar 'faces' together so as to resist any tendency to warping.
4. Keep a sharpening-stone handy to 'freshen up' the edges of your cutting knives.
5. Remember to 'rebate the insides' of corners, i.e., two light cuts about ⅛″ apart and remove the sliver with the knife tip.
6. Don't be afraid of using newspaper to 'surface' large areas of card. Just make sure that there are no air bubbles – rather like wallpapering.
7. Woodworkers' 'white' adhesive (Resin W) may well be preferable to the Polycell type for fixing brick papers and the like to card.

Experience with sanding sealer will suggest many additional uses. For instance, a sheet of notepaper, when 'sealed', takes paint perfectly and can substitute for thin plasticard.

Before assembling Superquick Building Kits, seal them first. They may darken a little but they will almost last forever, and may I recommend using Evostik instead of sellotape to stick the glazing in place; sellotape tends to come unstuck after 20 years or so.

Also you may well find the small tubes of Evostik much more manageable for our purposes because of their small nozzles. Keep a small jar handy to keep the tube upright when not in use, this will save you money. Don't roll up the bottom of the tube as you use it, but rather gently squeeze it flat and then it will always fit into the jar. Make use of a 1″ panel pin as a 'nozzle stopper' when the tube is not in use.

Adhesives can run away with an awful lot of money unless you are careful with them, so accept a 'discipline' with them by keeping them stoppered when not in use and, in the case of tube adhesives, always but always keep them upright - do not let them lie flat. This is particularly relevant when using 'super glues' which seem to go solid on one so quickly. No matter how hard I try, they always seem to beat me before the container is empty.

That then is all I propose to say about my methods of constructing buildings, for the time being anyway. Everyone I have ever met has his or her own method and object in mind, many of them far better than mine.

I must confess that buildings, to me, are rather like an extension of the scenery and my 'object' in mind, for most of it, is to 'suggest' or 'give an impression' of the real thing, rather than dot every 'i' and cross every 't'.

Of course there are some items that I have gone to town with more than others. For instance, my later constructions have tended to be more detailed by virtue of my time-improved skills and knowledge of materials, but the trains themselves and their operations are my number one points of focus.

Signals

Signal Construction

Signals have always meant a lot to me; 'And so they should!' I hear you cry.

But, let's face it, how many layouts don't seem to have any or, if they do, they don't work yet?

Maybe I had more money than sense when I started, but I bought quite a lot of those Hornby Dublo electrically operated ones with their exquisitely tiny mechanisms. I suppose they would cost the earth today and, perhaps, that is why they are not made any more. I consider then that they were an essential part of the scene and I still do.

(I have a similar 'hang-up' about lamps on locos and 'tail end charlies'.)

Having said all that, there are quite a lot of my

signals that 'don't work' and are there to 'complete the scene'.

Those of you with better memories than mine, may remember that I mentioned in earlier pages that I had removed the posts and arms from all the Dublo signals, and replaced them with more scale-like ones. That was after I made quite a number of non-operational signals, which gave me the feel of what was needed in a constructional sense.

I had always loved the sight of lattice signal posts and gantries, and I have tried various ways to achieve this effect.

The first was the gantry spanning the tracks at the west end of Aberford Central.

I fretworked the gantry lattice frames out of 1/16″ ply – it took simply ages to do, but it is still in position and holds up six signal posts.

I use the expression 'fretworked', but in actual fact I used my trusty piercing saw with its much finer blades.

Junction signal for down main line approach to Barrowby showing Peco point motors, wiring and linkages. 1991. (Photo KC)

Close-up of Barrowby down junction signal linkages. (Photo KC)

The signal posts themselves are ⅛″-square hardwood, and the arms (upper quadrant) are plasticard. I had my first experience of making guardrails for the catwalk using ½″ stationery pins for the posts to which I soldered thin soft wire for the handrails. I still use this method. It takes quite a time to get it all even and kink-free, but it is cheap and reliable.

This gantry actually has working guy ropes, because it is so long (12″) that it would twist without them.

It is this kind of structure that requires the services of a very soft long-bristled paint brush, when the time comes to remove accumulations of dust. Regard anything else as dangerous to the well-being of delicate parts.

Would you believe it, but my second 'home-made' signal was yet another gantry, this time within the loop lines of Barrowby station. I modelled it on a similar one that used to span the tracks at Bridlington (East Yorks) station. It also has six posts, again square.

This time I fretworked the frames out of plasticard, but never again; it is too much like hard work! As you saw away, the plastic keeps melting you know, and it melts to the saw blade.

It really is too much to cut out all these intricate parts with a knife, and anyway, there is a much better way to do it, as I subsequently found.

It was whilst completing this gantry that I 'discovered' how to make passable finials. Whilst not all that easy, and not as good as Derek Mundy's, they are most effective.

The routine is as follows:

1. Take a common or garden household steel pin and cut off the point about ½″ from the end – save it for later.
2. Tap the now pointless pin into a small block of wood, and with a brush, place a blob of liquid flux on the pinhead.
3. 'Tin' the pinhead with solder.
4. Place another blob of flux on the tinned pinhead and then solder yet another blob, but this time of low-melt solder, on to the pinhead.
5. Now pick up the pin point, by the point, and 'tin' the other end of it, first filing off any rough edges.
6. Place yet another blob of flux on the pinhead and, with the pin point firmly held in a pair of pliers, offer the base of the pin point to the fluxed pinhead and solder the two together.
7. With patience, plenty of flux and low-melt solder, keep touching the pinhead and base of the pin point with the soldering iron (no more than a 25-watter) until the solder forms itself into a neat little ball about ⅛″ diameter.

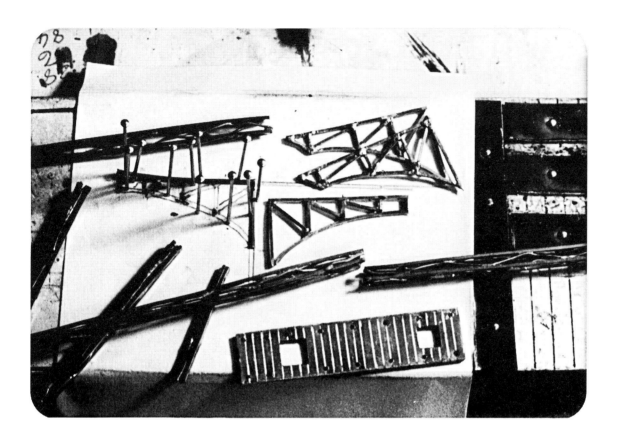

Construction details of lattice signals using ¹⁄₁₆ square brass wire. (Photo KC)

'Forest' of lattice signals for East Garforth, showing Hornby Dublo operating bases. (Photo KC)

Signal Gantry at Barrowby – using plasticard. Not so easy to make as the ¹⁄₁₆ square brass ones. 1986. (Photo KC)

8. When you think you have done it, blow on the solder to set it and then remove the iron from the pliers.
9. Check that the pinpoint is central and in line with the pinhead. If it isn't, take hold of the point again with the pliers and gently melt the solder with the iron to allow adjustment. You get quite good at it after a while.
10. When all is well, rinse the 'ball-point' pin in water to kill the flux.
11. Drill a pin-size hole through the cap at the top of the signal post, apply a tiny drop of adhesive to the base pin of the finial, drop it into position, paint it and that is the job finished.

A Valuable Visual Aid to Detailing

I nearly forgot to mention a most valuable visual aid tool that enables me to see tiny detail so easily. I have the kind of eyesight whereby I can see things, unaided, a long way off, but not close to. I think it's called long-sightedness. Therefore I need glasses of a magnifying nature to bring items within two or three feet into focus. They are all right until I want accurately to pick out small items like the pin-points referred to in finial construction.

There used to be an advertisement in the model railway press that said: 'You could make it if you could see it,' and it was placed by Mason & Gantlet, Optical Specialists, of Norwich, when drawing attention to their 'Binocular Magnifiers' known as 'Versator Plus'. They are rather like an extra pair of glasses, and can be worn for hours at a time if necessary, without eye-strain.

They are available in varying degrees of magnification, I think mine are 2½ times, anyway they make my thumbnail look the size of a sheet of newspaper at 3″ working distance.

Without these magnifiers I could never have undertaken a fraction of the detail work that I have done with them. In fact when I look at many of my lineside fittings from the normal viewing distance, I wonder how on earth I ever made them!

They don't come cheap, about £40.00 at today's prices, but what an investment!

Be careful who you let see you when you are wearing them – talk about looking like 'the mad professor'. You could positively frighten people. I am a very satisfied user indeed, and what now follows would not have been possible without them.

Constructing Signals – Using Plasticard

Years and years ago I made half a dozen North-Eastern slotted-post signals using plasticard. There is nothing very much I can say about the 'method', apart from saying that the simulated square timber posts were made of three thicknesses of plasticard glued together, with 'a bit missing' to provide 'the slot'.

I am not very happy about using plasticard for signals however, and this goes for the Ratio plastic kits, for the reason that they are all too easily broken.

Just think of it – signals are so often situated where there are points, and this is just where derailments are wont to occur. Re-railing a train in the proximity of plastic signals is asking for trouble, especially when the signals have sharp finials just dying to be caught up in one's sleeve.

Also, my plastic posts had a tendency to warp, so I must have done something wrong. I have subsequently remade them of square section hardwood from the local model aeroplane shop.

Constructing Signals – Using Wire and Solder

I referred, on page 58, to a much better way of doing things when it comes to making signals. I don't really remember what put me on to it, unless it was seeing some coils of $\frac{1}{16}''$ square brass wire in one of my local model shops.

You may remember me saying that I had always loved the sight of latticed signals, but how was I to go about it? Well, the $\frac{1}{16}''$ square brass wire provided the answer, and I have now signalled the remainder of my layout using this square wire together with narrow-gauge single core tinned wire.

Let us suppose that we are going to build a single, lattice post, 'Home' signal, 120mm (equivalent of 30 feet) from ground level to the top of the post – not including the finial.

What we are going to do is to draw out one side on to a piece of card as accurately as we can. Let us choose the side that will face an oncoming locomotive and call it 'the front' of the signal – and the other side 'the rear'.

And here is another of those 'but firsts'. It is always advisable to add, say, another 40mm to the length so as to allow for subsequent 'planting' in the baseboard when completed.

Let me suggest the following sequences of construction:

1. Draw a centre line from top to bottom on the piece of card. This will be the 'datum' line from which other measurements will be taken.
2. Draw a line representing the first 'upright' of the post, 2mm to the left of the datum line, and let the lower 40mm be vertical because it will be the part to be 'planted'. Then 'taper' the line 'upwards' towards the 120mm point at 1½mm to the left of the datum line. This is to suggest the taper of the real thing.

Barrowby down junction signal again.

3. Repeat all this for the right hand post.
4. Make a mark every 10mm up the line of the posts and, be careful here, join up the marks diagonally i.e., zig-zag fashion, side-to-side from top to bottom. Do not join up in cross-wise fashion for reasons that will become apparent as we progress.
5. Cut 4 × 160mm lengths of $\frac{1}{16}''$ square brass wire and straighten them carefully.

'Lattice' Signal Post
Constructional Detail Diagram

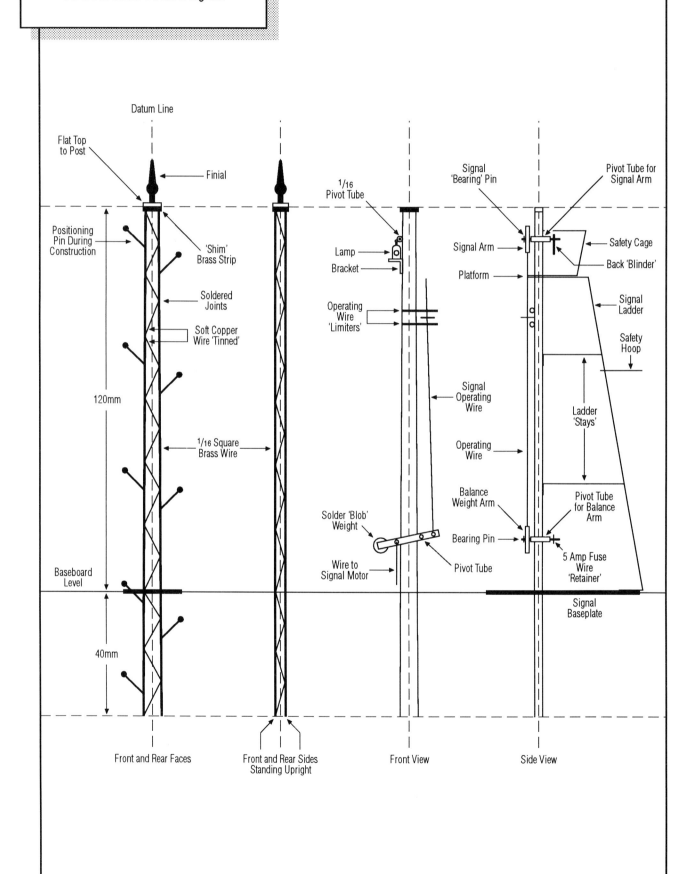

Datum Line

Flat Top to Post

Finial

Positioning Pin During Construction

'Shim' Brass Strip

Soldered Joints

Soft Copper Wire 'Tinned'

120mm

1/16 Square Brass Wire

Baseboard Level

40mm

Front and Rear Faces

Front and Rear Sides Standing Upright

1/16 Pivot Tube

Lamp

Bracket

Operating Wire 'Limiters'

Signal Operating Wire

Operating Wire

Solder 'Blob' Weight

Wire to Signal Motor

Pivot Tube

Front View

Signal 'Bearing' Pin

Signal Arm

Platform

Balance Weight Arm

Bearing Pin

Pivot Tube for Signal Arm

Safety Cage

Back 'Blinder'

Signal Ladder

Safety Hoop

Ladder 'Stays'

Pivot Tube for Balance Arm

5 Amp Fuse Wire 'Retainer'

Signal Baseplate

Side View

6. Clean with emery cloth; flux and 'tin' the 4 lengths – on all sides.

7. Put 2 lengths to one side for use later.

8. Lay 2 lengths on the drawing and secure in position with pins – not too many or they will get in the way.

9. Pin or glue down a piece of card across the bottom and top ends of the drawings, to act as 'stoppers' for the pieces of wire.

10. Strip the plastic coating from the fine-gauge wire and cut into 4 × 250mm lengths.

11. Flux and 'tin' these lengths of wire.

12. Using a 25-watt iron, and a sharp pointed craft knife to hold it in place, solder the first piece of wire to the first square brass 'post' – at an angle to correspond to the next soldering point on post 2.

13. Take the wire, diagonally, across to the 10mm mark on post 2 and hold it in position with the craft knife whilst you (a) bend it towards the next 10mm mark on post 1, and (b) whilst still holding the wire against the post with the craft knife, solder it to post 2, and so on until you reach the end of the post.

14. Trim off the end of the wire at the end of the post and carefully lift from the drawing.

You now have the complete 'front' face of the signal post. Really and truly, you don't need to solder wire across the first 40mm of the post because it will never be seen, but because this is perhaps your first experience it might well be easier so to do.

Hopefully, your drawing will not have burned away and you will still be able to see your lines. If in doubt, now is the time to touch them up, because you have to repeat items 8 – 14 to produce the 'rear' face of the signal, so go to it exactly as before with your post 1 and post 2 and fine wire zig-zag between them. Observe that the first soldered joint always seems to be the most difficult to get right.

You should now have two identical posts, so check that they match for size. If they don't, try squeezing them gently with the pliers.

The next stage is to make another drawing starting with a datum line, almost the same as the first but narrower – tapering from 3mm at ground level to 2mm at the top. You don't need to include the 10mm space marks this time.

Now take the 'front' face and the 'rear' face

posts and pin them upright along the lines of the drawing.

You may well observe that there is a 'front' and a 'back' to each post, and it is now that you use this to tremendous visual advantage and save yourself a lot of time and effort.

Look at the zig-zags. If you place the 'front face' post back-to-back on top of the 'rear face' post, you will notice that the zig-zags are opposed to one another and, from a distance, the zig-zags end up looking like criss-crosses – which is the essence of the 'lattice' post construction but with much less work.

So, happily, take the 'front' face and the 'rear' face posts and pin them upright, along the lines of the second drawing, and proceed as follows:

1. Take the third 200mm length of fine wire and solder, in our by now familiar zig-zag pattern, diagonally from base to top, thus joining 'front' face to 'rear' face and creating, effectively, a 'third' face.

   This is where you will acquire quite a lot of soldering skill, if you don't have it already, because you will have to be careful to flux and solder in such a way as not to melt the joints on the 'front' and 'rear' faces, so try and be as quick and certain as possible when you apply the iron.

   If you do melt joints accidentally, all is not lost – don't panic, just 'tease' the parts back into position with tweezers or pliers and re-solder. It's all part of the fun!!??

2. Having eventually 'wired-up' the third side, carefully remove the job from the drawing, turn it over and do a repeat on the opposite side, but this time, consciously oppose your zig-zags to create a visual 'lattice' effect.

3. All the time, try and keep the sides square to one another and don't forget the taper on all four sides.

4. When all is satisfactory, carefully remove from the drawing and start cleaning up.

   A really rough file is great for removing lumps of solder, but do not use your fine files because they will be ruined.

   If you have a nice mini-drill with some sort of a grindstone or milling cutter attachment, so much the better, but please be careful when you go near the fine wire. It would be a shame to grind through it; far better to clean off with a craft knife.

5. When all is cleaned off, cut a piece of shim brass 1mm wide and about 30mm long, and solder it round the top of the post. This looks nice and serves to hold the ends together.

6. Cut a small square of shim to the size of the top of the post and solder it there – carefully, then drill a hole in the centre to take the base pin of the finial that you are going to make.

So, there you are with a reasonably good-looking lattice signal post, and I hope it hasn't taken you too long.

Be sure that succeeding ones will be even better as you become more skilled and confident.

It now remains to add all the bits and pieces to make it work, and finally, to paint it.

Making the Signal Work

Here is where you need a visit to Eileen's Emporium, if you live in the north. This lovely lady visits most of the shows in our part of the world, along with Jim, her husband, who protects her from the amorous advances of we 'elderly geriatrics' (my sons' words, not mine).

Eileen sells bits and pieces, so valuable to DIY types like me who would rather 'chisel out of the solid' than go and buy the ready-made. By this I am referring to items like brass tubing, rod, sheet metal, wire of differing metals and gauges, solders, fluxes, nuts and bolts etc., plus tools of almost every make and description. She it is who takes more money from me than anyone else at the shows. May her shadow never grow less and may she live forever.

Enough of this eulogising, let's get on, now where were we? Oh yes, making the signal work. I remember –

1. An important raw material in signal making, after $\frac{1}{16}''$ square brass wire, is $\frac{1}{16}''$ brass tubing, which is just right for the pins that I use to hang the signal arms on. The pins are $\frac{1}{2}''$ steel stationery ones, which I also use as track pins and many other things.

2. A supply of $\frac{1}{2}''$ brass tubing will not come amiss whilst you are paying court to Eileen by the way.

3. Similarly, sheets of nickel silver, brass shim, wire, flux and solder.

4. Comet make some very nice etched brass signal arm frets, upper and lower quadrant.

Really, it is not worth making your own for the price they charge and the number you will need. Of course, if your penchant is for obscure types then Derek Mundy is your man.

5. A supply of 5 amp fuse wire, for use as directed later.

6. A length of brass signal laddering about 160mm.

So now you have all the raw materials to hand, let's get started.

1. Cut a 5mm length of $\frac{1}{16}''$ tubing and solder it on to the signal post about 10mm from the top – the side nearest the track. This will carry the signal arm to which you will have soldered one of the $\frac{1}{2}''$ pins.

2. Cut a piece of nickel silver sheet about 8mm × 4mm, and bend at a right angle in the middle. This is to form the lamp bracket that will be soldered in position below the signal arm bearing tube.

3. Cut a 4mm length of $\frac{1}{8}''$ tubing, and place in it a 6mm length of domestic pin – including the pin head – and solder the pin into the tube, leaving the head sticking out about 2mm. This will be the signal lamp, which in turn will be soldered on to the bracket mentioned in (2) above.

Bear in mind that the lamp has to 'shine' through the spectacle plates of the signal arm, so check that it is positioned correctly.

4. Somewhere between 10mm and 25mm above 'ground level', on the same face as the signal arm bearing, solder another 5mm length of $\frac{1}{16}''$ tube.

This will be the bearing for the 'balance weight arm', which also serves as a hooking-up point for the operating rod that goes to the signal arm and also for the rod that conducts the movement from whatever signal operating device you have decided upon, if any.

5. Fashion the balance weight arm from sheet metal, about 2mm × 20mm. This will have to have three pinholes drilled in it, as mentioned in (4) above – hole (a) for the signal operating device, hole (b) for the pivot bearing pin and hole (c) for the signal arm connecting rod.

I would suggest drilling hole (a) about 2mm from one end of the arm, hole (b) about

4mm from hole (a) and hole (c) about 6mm from hole (b).

As a final touch, melt a nice blob of solder at the far end of the arm to act as a balance weight.

6. Solder a ½″ pin through hole (a) and thread it through the lower bearing tube mentioned in (4).

Cut the pin so that it protrudes out of the tube by about 3mm, and taking the 5 amp fuse wire mentioned ages ago, solder a tiny length (about 3mm) near to the end of the pin. This will stop it coming out inadvertently, but will be easy to remove if necessary for subsequent adjustments.

7. Now take the signal arm and check that the bearing hole and the operating rod hole are clear to accept a ½″ pin. If not, then carefully ream out with the smallest of reamers. If you don't happen to have a reamer but do have a pin-vice, then cut the head off a ½″ pin and grip the pin in the pin-vice.

Now start to create a screwdriver-like spade-end to the pin on a sharpening stone, just the work of a couple of minutes, and use it to open out the holes in the signal arm.

This idea of using pins as drills and reamers comes in handy for fairly soft materials, but they are not hard enough for heavy duties.

Perhaps now the holes are large enough, so solder a ½″ pin through the bearing hole, with the pin head up against the face of the signal arm, and pass it through the bearing tube.

If your signal 'fret' has a 'back light blinder' included, then fit it on to the other end of the pin and trim the pin. Check that it is correctly positioned and lightly solder in place.

8. Take a 150mm length of fine-gauge nickel silver wire, about the same gauge as your ½″ pin, straighten it, and bend 4mm at a right angle at one end and thread it through hole 'b' in the balance weight arm. Then lift up the wire to correspond with its operating rod hole in the signal arm.

At this stage, may I suggest that you aim to have the balance weight arm just angled below horizontal when the signal arm is at 'danger', if your signal is to be 'upper quadrant'. If your choice is for 'lower quadrant', then I suggest the balance weight arm should

be inclined upwards to about 'ten past' when the signal arm is at 'danger'.

When decisions have been made and action taken accordingly, as just outlined, bend the end of the vertical operating rod through a right angle, towards the signal arm, and pass it through the appropriate hole in the arm.

Check to see that it works, and that the balance weight arm isn't falling to ground level, thus impeding its movement.

When all is satisfactory, solder a 3mm length of 5 amp fuse wire to the rod just behind the signal arm and cut off the surplus wire.

9. It may just be that a balance weight arm is not the best way to transmit movement, from your chosen signal operating device up the post to the signal arm. You may find that an 'angle crank' will be better suited to the task.

The market does not appear to cater very much for our need of small, strong, angle cranks, and so here is another item to make ourselves. Rather fiddly but not impossible. Proceed as follows:

(a) Mark out an 8mm square on a piece of nickel silver sheet.

(b) Counterpunch drilling points at three of the corners of the square with the point of a household pin, about 1½mm in from the edges, and drill holes to take ½″ pins.

(c) Emery-cloth the metal smooth where the holes have been drilled and mark out an L-shaped crank, arms about 1½mm wide, with a hole at each end and one in the middle, then cut out with a piercing saw.

Persevere with this fiddly job and you will learn a lot thereby about how to cut small bits of metal, and how to hold them whilst you cut them. You will also learn where to look for them when they jump out of your fingers. This is where it pays to have an old white sheet on the floor underneath your work area.

(d) When you have cut out the basic shape of the crank, file it smooth, perhaps even rounding off the corners and 'waisting' the arms between the holes, to give that 'professional' touch.

(e) Solder a ½″ pin into the centre hole of the crank and push the pin through the lower bearing tube of the signal post, solder a 3mm

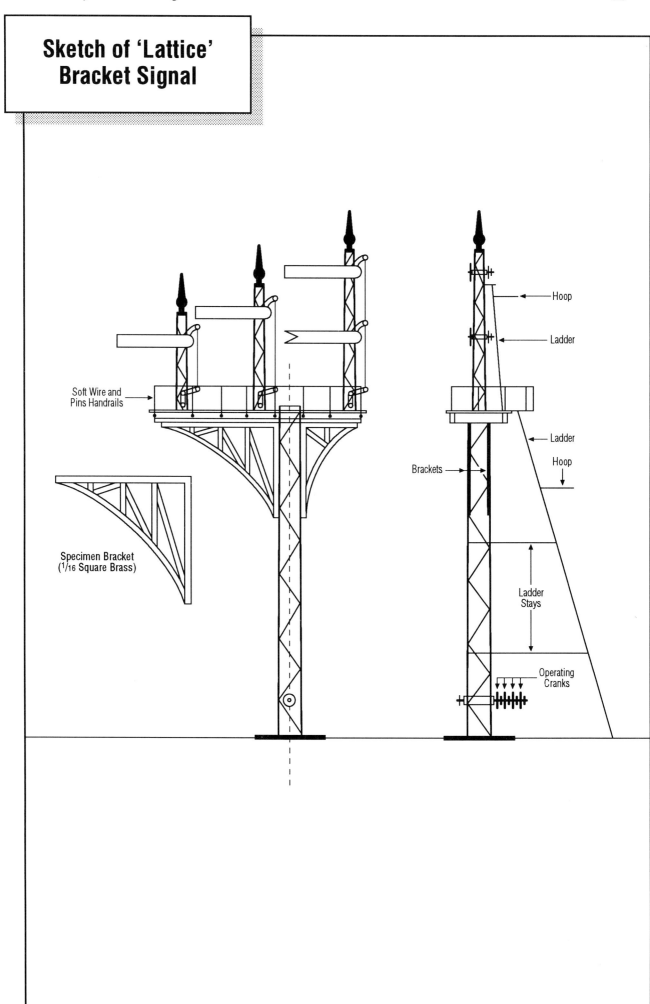

Sketch of 'Lattice' Bracket Signal

Soft Wire and Pins Handrails

Specimen Bracket (^{1}/$_{16}$ Square Brass)

Hoop

Ladder

Ladder

Hoop

Brackets

Ladder Stays

Operating Cranks

length of 5 amp fuse wire to the pin and cut off the surplus length of pin.

(f) Connect the signal arm connecting rod to the upper leg of the crank in the same way as with the balance weight arm, and secure it in position with soldered fusewire.

Endeavour to have the upper leg of the 'crank' at 'ten minutes past' when the 'upper quadrant' signal arm position is at 'danger'.

For 'lower quadrant' the upper leg will have to be at 'twenty-five minutes past' when the arm is at danger.

This is to reduce linkage problems when connecting the signal operating device.

10. Now is the time to cut the 'signal base plate' from nickel silver sheet (nickel silver takes paint better than brass).

(a) Cut a piece of sheet approximately 20mm × 50mm, and then cut a hole about 15mm from one end to the same measurements as the signal post.

(b) Push the signal post through until the lower 40mm part of the post is below the plate, then solder the post to the plate, making sure that it is vertical whichever way you look at it. The 'long' side of the plate is to give you somewhere to solder the ladder to, and should be towards the 'back face' of the post.

You may eventually decide that the 40mm is too long, in which case simply cut it to size.

11. Signal laddering comes next, so let's think about it.

The object of a signal ladder is to help the signal maintenance man reach all parts of the signal, especially the signal lamp. It is customary for the signal ladder to be attached to the rear face of the signal, so that the maintenance man will not have his back to on-coming trains whilst he is up the ladder.

The ladder angle must not be too steep, and for the purposes of our signal should start no less than 30mm away from the signal post, and be strengthened by side-stays about halfway up. These can be fashioned out of wire.

Look at any pictures of signal ladders that you can find, and you will see that every 10 feet or so there will be some sort of 'safety hoop' that a tired maintenance man can sit on, when going up the ladder, to

catch his breath. Again, this can be fashioned from wire. At the top of the ladder, where it joins up to the signal post, there is a small platform, roughly on a level with the lamp, and surrounded by a safety cage.

The platform can be fashioned from a small square of metal sheet, and the safety cage from wire.

Concerning 'our' signal, consider the following sequence for putting up the ladder:

(a) Bend back 5mm at the lower end of the ladder. This will provide something firm to solder the ladder to the baseplate with.

(b) Solder the lower end of the ladder to the baseplate about 30mm away from the post.

(c) Bend the ladder gently towards the post, to a point about 10mm below the lamp.

(d) Form a base for the platform by creating another bend in the ladder, so that the base will be about 10mm long. Allow a further 10mm and cut away the rungs from this additional 10mm. Bend the remaining sides to give a firm grip onto the signal post and solder to the post when you are satisfied with the positioning.

(e) Form the ladder side-stays by fashioning a length of soft wire into a 'U' shape. Solder the base of the 'U' to the ladder and the open ends to the sides of the signal post. For appearances' sake, position the arms of the side-stays so that they are horizontal.

(f) Form a safety hoop from wire, large enough for a scale 'man' to crawl through comfortably, and solder to the ladder immediately above the side-stays joint.

(g) Form the safety platform from a piece of sheet metal about 10mm × 6mm and solder on to the flat top of the ladder.

(h) Form the safety cage from wire. The main part will be a hoop-shaped horizontal handrail, held up by verticals soldered to the platform. The ends of the hoop can be soldered to the post.

12. Referring to the suggestions made on page 58, now make yourself a finial. When satisfied, solder it into the hole in the top plate of the signal post, making sure that is vertical from all viewing positions.

13 The time has now come for the final clean-up prior to painting, so 'disengage' the signal operating rod by first unsoldering the

tiny lengths of fuse wire holding it in position. Then withdraw the signal arm by first unsoldering the back blinder from the bearing pin.

'Clean-up' means getting rid of surplus solder from joints and surfaces, together with any other bits and fluff. Then give the whole 'job' a good brushing and soaking in washing-up liquid and hot water. I reserve an old toothbrush for this sort of operation. Leave at one side to dry thoroughly.

Painting the Signal

Paints Required:

Grey primer, Satin White, Satin Black, Signal Red (or Caution Yellow for a 'Distant' signal), Green for spectacle plate and Orange for the 'caution' indication if a 'distant' signal, Mid Brown for the 'platform'. Plus paint thinners and brush cleaner.

1. Grey primer is so easily applied by the car-spray variety that it is hardly worth the trouble of applying it by brush, so give all parts of the signal a 'quick burst'. Usually it will be dry enough to paint over within 10 minutes in a warm atmosphere.

2. Black paint – the lower 40mm and first 25mm above 'ground level' of the signal post, the baseplate, ladder, safety hoops, side-stays, balance weight arm (or crank) and bearing tube, signal back light blinder, signal operating rod, parts of signal arm.

3. White paint – the upper part of the signal post, lamp, signal bearing tube and finial, parts of signal arm.

    If you have a can of white car spray, you will find it will get into the nooks and crannies of the signal post 'filigree' much more effectively than a brush ever will. You can always cover up any oversprays quite easily if necessary.

The rest of the colours are best applied with good quality brushes.

Treat brushes as valuable tools. To this end I always have a box of small size tissues and three jam jars handy. One jar contains brush cleaner, one contains washing-up liquid and water, one contains fabric conditioner.

The uses of the first two are obvious, but the fabric conditioner is magic and restores life to tired bristles just as it does clothes. Try it and see. Wipe dry and reshape the bristles with a tissue.

Forget about cleaning brushes in white spirit, it always leaves a residue behind in the bristles.

The signal arms always take the longest to paint because of the sharp divisions of colours.

Before painting the arms, you might like to consider 'glazing' the 'spectacles' on the arms. It is a simple job and just requires cutting a small piece of thin glazing material and sticking it on the 'rear' side of the arm with super-glue, then trimming to size with a fine file. A touch of Humbrol metallic green and red (or orange for a 'distant' signal) will show up perfectly.

The 'front' face of a 'Home' signal is (yes I know you know) red and white. The 'front' face of a 'Distant' signal is caution yellow and black.

The 'rear' faces of both 'Home' and 'Distant' signals are white and black.

The colours of the 'front' faces are carried on to the upper and lower edges of the signal arms.

The area from the bearing shaft to the edge of the spectacles is black.

I suggest that you look at photographs to get the exact colour divisions but, in any case, they will depend on the actual size of your signal arm.

Roughly speaking, if you break the area to be painted into five parts, then, on the 'front' face of a 'Home' signal the 'outside' fifth will be red, the next fifth will be white and the remaining three fifths will be red.

On the 'rear' face of a 'Home' signal the 'outside' fifth will be white, the next fifth will be black and the remaining three fifths will be white.

The 'Distant' signal is much more difficult because of the 'V' cut at the end of the arm. This is a very 'hard act to follow', but is capable of being split into fifths as with the 'Home' signal as follows:

'Front' face outside fifth will be yellow, the second fifth will be a black 'V' and the remaining three fifths will be yellow.

'Rear' face outside fifth will be white, the second fifth will be a black 'V' and the remaining three fifths will be white.

The time taken over the painting is because of the need to let each colour dry before applying the adjoining one, to avoid runs.

I never find it easy to get the 'V's just right

on the 'Distant' signal arms. I think you must consider 'edging' it out in pencil first and then painting in the black with a number '00' brush – and a steady hand.

To complete the operation I like to give a final spray of Satin Varnish. This helps the colours to become more permanent.

When the varnish has hardened, in about 24 hours, refix the signal arm and back binder together with the signal operating rod, and touch up any blemishes thus incurred.

My word, I had no idea how much there was to it. No wonder signal making consumes a lot of time. The results are well worth the trouble though.

I suppose I ought to go into the subject of making 'bracket' or 'junction' signals, even gantries, but really, the principles are the same as those we have already considered, namely:

1. Create a working drawing round a datum line.
2. Use ¹⁄₁₆″ square brass wire for the support brackets and gantries, and also for the diagonals – narrow-gauge wire is too thin.
3. Make the support brackets separately from the posts and then solder them to the posts when the time comes.
4. Make liberal use of pins to hold parts in position whilst soldering.
5. The platform between signal 'dollies' (individual posts) is usually wooden planking in real life. This can be simulated by deeply scoring 'planks' into the metal platform with the reverse side of a cutting knife.
6. Handrails are soft wire soldered to ½″ pin verticals.

The platforms needs to be drilled to take the pins, the actual pinheads being positioned underneath the platform, and the points trimmed back to the height required – usually about 10mm.

This is where one of the excellent illustrated books on signals will be invaluable. I use A. A. MacLean's *LNER Constituent Signalling* (OPC).

Positioning of Signals

One very important consideration that has to be given, when positioning signals is: 'If it is at 'danger' (on 'ON' as the railway people say), will the driver be able to see the signal early enough to give him time to stop?'

This consideration leads to the existence of the large varieties of odd shapes, sizes and positioning of signals.

Before designing a signal for a particular location do try to get a driver's-eye view of the location, from at least an average train's length away, and see if the driver is going to be able to 'see' it. You might end up with a very tall signal, or a short one, or one on a left- or right-handed 'bracket', even perhaps a gantry.

Most signal posts are situated to the left-hand side of the track they are controlling but, occasionally and usually because of a curve in the track, they might be placed on the right-hand side of the track for better advance 'sighting'.

These are questions that only you will be able to answer, because of the design implications of your particular track layout.

Remote Control of Signals

Now then, even before we start on this section, I can see a 'long one' coming up, so be prepared.

It is all very well changing points and signals by hand, if the layout is rather small and there are not too many of them.

As a layout becomes larger and more complex, hand operation must surely become burdensome in the extreme because not only has 'the hand' got to change everything in the first place, but it also has to change everything back again.

In gauge '0' and larger, prototypical rods, wires, cranks and pulleys can be used to remotely-control points and signals to good effect.

My observations of layouts at exhibitions have led me to think that there are rather severe practical limitations to prototypical practice when it comes to the smaller gauges. I know it can be done, and done beautifully, by some of you out there; the model railway press details many instances, but I am lazy and time is short so I take the easy option and go for electro-magnetic operation.

I have made many references to the old Hornby Dublo electrically operated, remote controlled, signals and their wonderfully small, and simple, mechanisms: just two little solenoids per signal arm, with a tiny slotted iron armature sliding between them.

The lower arm of the signal operating crank simply dropped in to the armature slot, and that was it! The 'passing contact' switch did the rest i.e., it energised the solenoid connected to its respective contact in the switch.

Types of Switches

For the benefit of those who may not know about such things, may I explain the difference between a 'passing contact' switch and an 'on/off' switch.

An on/off switch has an 'input' and an 'output' terminal. It supplies either no power at all ('off'), or else it supplies continuous power ('on'). This is OK for lights, track sections, relays and the like; it is also known as a Single Pole Single Throw (SPST) switch.

A continuous supply of power to point and signal 'motor' solenoids, as supplied by ordinary on/off switches, would rapidly overheat and burn out the solenoids. Hence the need for passing contact switches.

A passing contact switch has an 'input' terminal and two 'output' terminals.

The interior mechanism of the switch consists of two 'wiper' contacts, electrically connected to the 'input' terminal, which 'pass' (or 'wipe') one of the contacts of the 'output' terminals when moved by the switch lever.

The 'wipers' do not dwell on the 'output' contacts but just make momentary contact with them; sufficient to send an electrical charge down the 'output' wire to energise, in our present case, one of the solenoids in the signal motor. They do need a microsecond or so of time for reliable operation however, so any temptation to 'flick' the levers should be resisted. Rather move them slowly.

Each of the 'output' terminals is electrically connected (by wire) to one or other of the two solenoids in, for the sake of this illustration, the signal motor.

Move the switch lever one way and the signal will move to 'line clear' (or, in railway parlance, 'Off'). Move the lever the other way and the signal will move to 'danger' (or 'On').

For many years, passing contact switches were the principal means of operating point and signal motors, but were becoming expensive, especially those as good as the Dublo ones.

They have now been superseded by other means of solenoid activating systems, such as the highly thought-of capacitor-discharge unit.

Capacitor-Discharge Unit (CDU)

The capacitor-discharge unit works on the ability of a thing called a 'capacitor' to store quite a hefty electrical charge from its 'input' source when its 'output' is not connected to something-or-other.

Connect its output to this something-or-other, say through an ordinary on/off switch and, whoosh! – the capacitor discharges itself in one hell of a rush, and becomes empty. (It can also give you quite a shock if your fingers happen to be in the way.)

The manufacturers liken its action to a bucket with a removable bottom; fill the bucket with water, then remove the bottom and, in an instant – no water left in the bucket! It all came out in a rush, as opposed to the controlled flow from a tap.

However, just as a bucket takes quite a time to refill from a tap, so a capacitor needs time to be recharged – about 2 seconds between 'bursts'. This is a handy protection device, because it means that the power supplied to point and signal motors can now be controlled by means of simple on/off switches if desired; if you forget to turn a switch off the capacitor will not recharge, so there is no fear of burning out a motor.

The main snag with on/off switches in this instance is that there may be lots of points and signals to control, and lots of switches to operate. As night follows day, one switch somewhere will be left on with the result that when the next point or signal operation needs to be performed, nothing will happen, because the capacitor has not been able to recharge.

Spring-Loaded Centre-Off Switches

The alternative to the simple on/off switch seems to be the spring-loaded 2-way 'centre-off' type of switch. A bit pricey perhaps, but they ensure that all switches automatically go to 'off' when you let go.

Press-To-Make Push-Button Switches

A further alternative is the 'press-to-make' push-button, which I bored you with in my rantings about 'Route Selection' way back on pages 33–43.

The 'Electric Pencil'

The last alternative switching method I will mention here is that of the 'electric pencil', where banks of twin terminals are set out on the control panel corresponding to the locations of points and signals. They are wired to the point and signal motors.

The 'electric pencil' is a sweet-sounding name for a short length of metal rod or wire, connected at one end to the capacitor-discharge unit output.

All that needs to be done to activate the motors is simply to touch their respective control panel terminals with the 'pencil' and, bingo, they be energised! The beauty of this alternative is that it is relatively foolproof, and cheap.

Maybe it's cussed of me, but I have left the best bit until last and that is:

Because of the high power and high speed of the discharge from the capacitor, the multiple operation of points and signals from single switches is now possible – up to 6 'motors' at a time is my experience.

Think of the cost saving on switches!

To the old 'Job's comforter' who says, 'What you save on one thing you only spend on another,' I say, 'If it helps bring about an improvement, do it. If it doesn't, then don't.'

Referring back to the section about 'Route Selection' on pages 33–43 will, I hope, have explained to your satisfaction and understanding, a well-tried and proven system of multiple operation of points and signals, using a variety of different types of switch together with the capacitor-discharge unit – often referred to nowadays as the 'CDU'.

All this cost me quite a packet in new switches when I made the changeover to my present control panel, although I did recoup some when I found a buyer for 24 Dublo passing contact switches.

What I have now is an infinitely better system that has excellently justified the cost and the effort involved.

Well, we have considered some of the various options open to us for supplying electrical power to signal, and point, motors. Perhaps now is the time to consider some of the types of motors available to us and how to connect them, physically, to the signals and points.

Signal Motors and Linkages

From the outset of this particular section I propose to deal solely with signal operation, rather than with points and signals. Some of what I have to say may well apply to points also, but that can be regarded as a bonus.

A signal 'motor' is the name given to two coils of wire, wound round a hollow tube or 'core tube', usually made of brass or similar non-magnetic material.

The basic effect of connecting the input wire and output wire of a coil to the 'output' and 'input' terminals, respectively, of a source of electrical energy (a battery or a power unit) is to create a magnetic field around the core tube, so that, when a small, loose, piece of ferrous (iron) material is placed within it, the piece of ferrous material will tend to move from one side of the core tube to the other. In other words, the coil becomes an electromagnet when you pass a current through it.

Now place two coils close to one another, end to end and, say, with a gap between them of about 10mm. Slide into their core tubes a loosely fitting piece of iron nail, about 18mm in length.

Connect the 'outside' wire of one coil to an electrical power source via a switch. Secondly, connect the 'outside' wire of the other coil to the power source via another switch – both switches to be in the 'off' position. Thirdly, connect the 'inside' wires of both coils together and connect them to the 'return' terminal of the power source.

Now change one of the switches to the 'on' position, and notice the iron nail move from one coil towards the other.

Return that switch to 'off' and the other switch to 'on', and notice that the iron nail moves back again -'or it did when we rehearsed it before the show' as the TV people say.

Now turn switch number 2 back to 'off' before you burn out the coil.

What I have been trying to describe is the principle and action of what is known as a 'double-acting solenoid' – or, a 'signal motor'.

In practice, the movement of the iron core is transmitted by some sort of 'linkage' to the outside world; in our case a signal. Apart from the Hornby Dublo signal motors, which have a slot in the middle of the iron core, most other makes

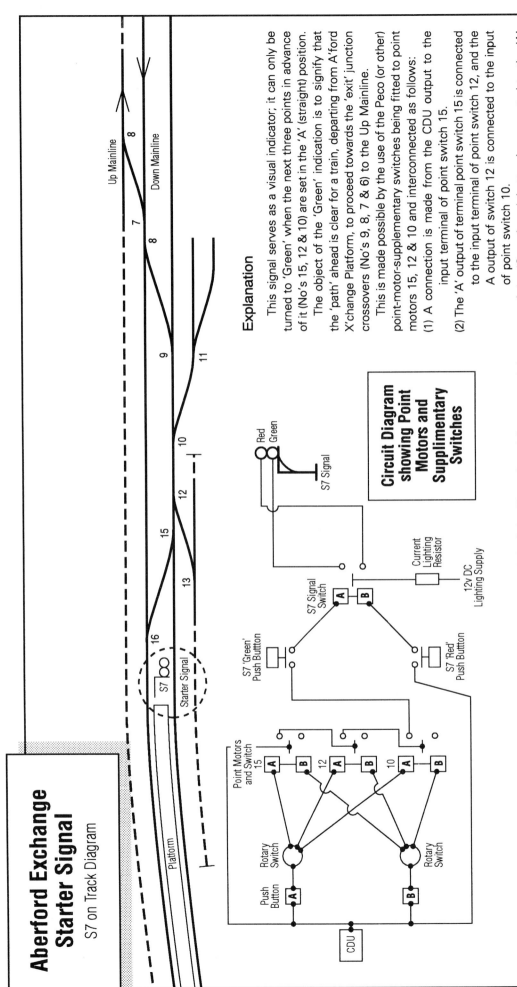

Aberford Exchange Starter Signal

S7 on Track Diagram

Up Mainline

Down Mainline

Platform

Starter Signal

Circuit Diagram showing Point Motors and Supplimentary Switches

Red
Green

S7 Signal

S7 Signal Switch

Current Lighting Resistor

12v DC Lighting Supply

S7 'Green' Push Button

S7 'Red' Push Buttton

Point Motors and Switch

Rotary Switch

Rotary Switch

Push Button

CDU

Explanation

This signal serves as a visual indicator; it can only be turned to 'Green' when the next three points in advance of it (No's 15, 12 & 10) are set in the 'A' (straight) position.

The object of the 'Green' indication is to signify that the 'path' ahead is clear for a train, departing from A'ford X'change Platform, to proceed towards the 'exit' junction crossovers (No's 9, 8, 7 & 6) to the Up Mainline.

This is made possible by the use of the Peco (or other) point-motor-supplementary switches being fitted to point motors 15, 12 & 10 and interconnected as follows:

(1) A connection is made from the CDU output to the input terminal of point switch 15.

(2) The 'A' output of terminal point switch 15 is connected to the input terminal of point switch 12, and the 'A' output of switch 12 is connected to the input of point switch 10.

(3) N.B. The output terminal of switch 10 is connected to the input terminal of the 'Green' push-button, and the output of the 'Green' push-button is connected to the 'A' terminal on 'point' motor S7. In other words switches 15, 12 & 10 act like a 'cascade'; if just one of them is not in the 'A' position then the 'Green' push-button can not activate 'point' motor S7 and cause the signal to show green. 'Point' motor S7 merely serves to activate the colour light switch.

(4) The 'feed' to the colour light bulbs is 12V DC (reduced to 9V, by a suitable resistor from Tandy to prolong the life of the bulbs) and is taken to the input of the switch S7.

(5) The 'Red' push-button is fed directly from the CDU output so that the 'B' solenoid and the 'Red' light can be activated at any time irrespective of the state of point motors 15, 12 & 10.

(6) The signal is not connected in any way to the track power circuits because of the amount of 'to-ing' & 'fro-ing' of trains in the vicinity; and to do so would, I feel, add unnecessary operational complexity to the system.

have a pin of sorts sticking out of the centre of the core. It is this pin which is connected to the linkage which takes the physical movement from the motor to the signal.

As I have said many times already, it is a constant cause for regret to me that present-day signal (and point) motors have to be so large, compared with the Hornby Dublo ones. I suppose the reason that will be offered will have to do with the extra 'punch' a larger motor is capable of giving.

Be that as it may, a signal motor takes some hiding or disguising if it is not to be in view. It is not always possible to mount them out of sight beneath the baseboard, and so some sort of disguise has to be attempted such as fitting a watchman's hut over them, or a piece of scenery.

The other alternative is to mount a relay directly underneath the signal, and connect the signal operating rod to the moving arm of the relay.

An important consideration that should be borne in mind is that relays require a constant power supply of direct current to activate them. This calls for, ideally, a power supply separate from that used for trains, point and signal motors and lighting.

On the other hand, 'double-acting' point and signal motors are quite happy to accept alternating current, if only because of the momentary nature of their power needs.

Linkages

Quite a lot of ingenuity is called for in linking up motors to signals, because nearly every location will have something unique about it.

The main consideration, as I see it, should be to avoid excessive distances between motors and signals, and also to keep the linkage in a straight line. Going round corners is all very clever but to do it requires the use of 'angle cranks' which can reduce the available amount of travel due to slack in the connections.

The most common form of linkage between motor and signal seems to be 26-gauge nickel silver or phosphor bronze wire, which is fairly stiff.

However, if the signal has a nice heavy balance weight arm, then there is no reason why very fine nylon fishing line should not be used instead of wire, so long as it can be kept tight enough to hold the signal indication against the counter-pull

of the balance weight arm. I have used nylon line linkage very successfully on the three-post junction signal controlling the 'down line' approach to Barrowby station, and it even goes round corners on tiny pulley wheels.

If the length of the linkage wire is more than 2 inches (50mm) then it will need to be restrained in some way to stop it 'whipping' or bending under load.

One way of achieving this is to thread one or two 15mm lengths of brass tubing along the linkage wire and solder the tubes to screws mounted on to the baseboard.

Somewhere near to the motor it is often desirable to bend what is known as an 'omega loop' in the wire, for the purpose of making slight adjustments to the length of the wire.

Aim at reducing linkage friction to a minimum, if only because the action of the motors is so quick that any undue 'binding' will restrict the short length of travel involved.

Finally, it sometimes happens that signal arms need some form of 'movement limiter' to stop them moving up, or down, too far.

This can be done fairly simply by soldering two small (10mm maximum) lengths of soft wire to the signal post, in close proximity to the signal operating rod, say about 5mm apart. Then solder another small piece of wire to the signal operating rod itself, in a position between the pieces soldered to the post.

Experiment with the positions of the small pieces of wire, relative to one another, until the desired signal arm positions are obtained, both 'up' and 'down', every time the signal is activated.

Operating Multiple-Post Signal Arms

We have been considering the construction and operation of a single arm signal, which rather begs the question of how to operate more than one arm on a signal, so let us see what is involved.

As far as I can see, there is no limit to the number of signal arms that can be operated, be they on one post or many posts as, for example, on a junction signal or signal gantry.

There is a problem however, and that concerns the 'disposal' or 'placing' of the signal motors, because, if all signal arms are to be operated individually, each one of them will need its own

Ultra close-up of signal posts on Barrowby Junction Signal. (Photo KC)

motor. So the problem is one of where to put the motors.

I referred earlier to the three-post junction signal controlling entry to the 'down' side of Barrowby Station.

This signal has no fewer than 5 motors operating 4 signal arms in the following way:

1. 'Panic' push-button No. 1 – all signal arms to 'On' (danger) and the 18-inch track section immediately preceding the signal to 'dead' (no current).

2. Push-button No. 2 – post No. 1 'Down Main Line' 'Home and Distant' to 'Off' (clear) and the 18-inch track section immediately preceding the signal to 'clear' (track current restored).

3. Push-button No. 3 – post No. 2 'Entry to Station Loop 15A' to 'Off' (clear).

4. Push-button No. 4 – post No. 3 'Entry to Station Loop 15B' to 'Off' (clear).

Note that to revert signal arms from the 'Off' (clear) indication back to 'On' (danger) all that has to be done is to press 'Panic' push-button No. 1.

The motors activating the crossover points that link section 15A with the Down main line, at the far end of the Barrowby station, are diode-linked

to the motor activating the 'Distant' signal arm on post No. 1, so that if the crossover is set 'against' the Down main line the 'Distant' arm on post No. 1 will go to 'On' (danger), indicating that the crossover-protection colour light signal might be 'On'.

This natty bit of circuitry (interlocking) ensures that the 'Distant' signal arm on post No. 1 can only indicate 'Off' (next 'Home' signal 'clear') if the succeeding crossover is set 'for' the main line.

One motor is used to activate an on/off section switch controlling the 18-inch track section immediately preceding the junction signal.

In this case the operating pin of the motor is connected to a 'slide bar', made from paxolin sheet, with a T-shaped wire contact at its far end. The track current is fed by wire to the slide bar and its end contact. When the motor is activated, the slide bar is pushed along a channel, made of two similar strips of paxolin sheet, and the 'T' contact will 'make' with a couple of short vertical contacts fixed to the motor baseboard, and electrically connected to the track.

So it can be seen that no fewer than 5 motors had to be accommodated in fairly close proximity to the signal.

As luck would have it, there was a narrow triangular-shaped area about 9 inches long × 2½ inches behind the junction signal, and it was into this space that I was able to place a piece of ⅛″ ply base onto which were mounted the 5 motors, and their accompanying circuitry, linkages and hand-cut angle cranks, not forgetting the junction signal itself.

I was able to make a cover over and around the motors out of stiff paper, surfaced with 'grass scatter' to make it resemble something like a grassy mound.

It should be possible to motorise a multi-post signal gantry using this method, the only hazard being what to do with the motors.

I must confess it took me a few weeks to make the junction signal and its appendages, and get it to work, but it does work and is most effective. The most difficult part of the operation was working in the dark; doing something that I had never heard or seen anyone else doing. Just like the original railway builders in a way, making progress through experience.

Making working signals has been, perhaps, the

most rewarding part of my layout assemblage. Not only are they lovely to look at, but they add an extra degree of operational interest that really keeps me 'on my toes'.

Obviously, signals are placed where they are for a purpose. They are mandatory warning signs which must be obeyed by locomotive crews for the safety of passengers and other trains.

The real railways are split up into operating sections, entrances to which are 'guarded' by a signal. Where two lines merge together, i.e., at a 'trailing junction', each line will have a 'Home' signal to 'guard' or protect the junction.

Where one line splits into two i.e., at a 'facing junction', the 'divergence' will be controlled by a two-post 'Junction' or 'Divergence' signal, one post for the 'left' and the other for the 'right' divergence. If one of the divergences is more important than the other then the post representing it will be taller than the post for the less important divergence.

Sometimes, where there are a number of divergences in rapid succession, there will be a multiple-post Junction signal, with the tallest post indicating the most important divergence, and the posts on either side of it indicating whether the divergences will be to the left or right of the most important one.

I have been talking all this time about 'semaphore' signals which, I suppose, betrays my age even though I make no secret of my great antiquity.

Colour light signals are the 'in thing' today of course, single aspect, twin aspect, three aspect and four aspect, not to mention 'splitting signals'.

Also many of the electrified lines are signalled for 'bi-directional' running, which all adds to the electronic complexity of their control systems.

The pity is that so few modellers seem to have a good understanding of signalling, and all I can say to them is neither did I, until I started with it. I picked up information as I went along, referring to books on the subject and trying to absorb it, in terms of modelling it.

Pause for Meditation

Having said what I have done about having a good understanding of signalling, I would also say that this is yet another instance where much tolerance is called for amongst modellers, be-

cause there is a limit to what an individual can take in about not only the 'real thing' but also the model.

Each of us has his or her special gifts, his or her particular likes and dislikes, and it simply does not do to highlight the shortcomings of others who do not see things through our eyes.

I can well imagine the 18-point-whatever chaps looking down their noses at my tawdry efforts in '00', but I ask them to bear in mind that, like them, I had to start 'somewhere', and that 'somewhere' was a long time ago, with limited knowledge, limited capabilities, and compared with today, limited product quality.

Not only was it a long time ago, but I have absolutely no training in wood or metal crafting – I was 'trained' in two things, music and salesmanship, neither of which did much for me as a railway modeller apart from providing the wherewithal to pay for the modelling.

I wonder what railway modellers will be up to in another 50 years' time, just what will be 'the state of the art' then?

Will modellers then be looking back on us and feeling sorry that we didn't have their facilities and the availability of perfect scale models, ready to run without the need for extra detail kits, wheels with the right number of spokes, perfect adhesion and frictionless motors?

Will there be 'out of this world' sophistication in control and operating systems?

Will there, in fact, be a need for model railways at all in 50 years' time?

I mean, will it not then be merely a question of designing a layout, with all its locomotives, rolling stock, signalling, buildings and scenery, and transferring all the information on to a computer disk, so that everything can be called up on a nice big screen, in beautiful 3-dimensional pinpoint detail, just awaiting our operational commands from a keyboard?

I think that could be very exciting indeed, from where I am sitting at my little word processor just a few yards away from my real-life model railway in the garage. It almost seems like having a model-of-a-model-railway, but with nothing I can hold in my hand and it can all appear or disappear at the touch of a key.

Will the days be then gone of creating something out of pieces of metal and wire and seeing it come 'to life', in 'the real'?

I just love model railways, and have done since before I can even remember – my parents told me so. Model railways are a part of my being and without them I would be like a man without a shadow. I have done the best I could with the knowledge that I had, then and now, and so, I hope, has everyone else. I mean, can you seriously imagine anyone deliberately making something badly?

So take heart those of you who feel you will never achieve a 'Norris' or a 'Pendon', or a write-up in a model magazine.

'Railway Modelling Is Where Mediocrity Can Flourish', and you don't have to account to anyone if you don't want to.

On the other hand, it is good to be able to discuss things with fellow enthusiasts now and then. This is how 'cross-fertilization' takes place and how we gain our new ideas and 'raise our sights'. Model Railway shows are good places to meet up with all classes of modellers – from the 'high and mighty know-it-alls-and-do-nowts', to the more retiring skilled craftsmen. Never be afraid of asking questions, that's how we learn. Very rarely, if ever, do I get a rebuff.

May I recommend that you always make out a shopping list before you go to a show to make sure you get what you really need; in fact it is a good idea to maintain an ongoing shopping list and to keep 'topping it up' as the need for something arises. Buying at shows can save a fortune in postage charges.

Try to resist those impulse or unplanned purchases that run away with a lot of cash and just end up in a drawer.

Be ruthless; if it's not on your list, don't buy it.

Feeding the Imagination

Three miles east of the city of Leeds, travelling the tracks of the Leeds to Selby railway, is the suburb of Crossgates. It was, until recently, the third station on the Leeds to Selby railway, the first two being Marsh Lane and Osmondthorpe, which were to either side of the Neville Hill loco sheds and carriage sidings.

From 1939 until 1943 I lived 400 yards to the south of this line, where the final half-mile approach to Crossgates station passed through a grassy cutting, bordered on either side with pleasant residential properties (houses).

Opposite our house was Valley Drive, a short cul-de-sac which approached the top of the cutting, at a right angle to it, and which provided we youthful train watchers with a first-class view, in those war-time days, of the very busy four-track main line. Note the expression 'train watchers'; 'train-spotting' was a term which came much later in history.

To our left, from this promontory, we could see two wooden-posted upper quadrant 'distant' (caution) signals, which afforded advance warning of the state of the Killingbeck crossovers half a mile downtrack; the signals were for the 'slow' and 'fast' lines into Leeds.

Immediately below us was an imposing lattice-posted, lower quadrant, 'distant' signal gantry spanning the 'fast' and 'slow' lines into Crossgates. The gantry's four posts were paired 'short' and 'tall', and gave advance warning of the state of the approaching 'facing' junction, just beyond the platform ends of Crossgates station, where the lines to Wetherby and Selby diverged, left and right. The 'short' signal posts on the gantry were 'for' the Wetherby line, and the 'tall' posts were 'for' the Selby/York line because it was classed as the 'main line'.

All 'stopping' trains used the 'slow' lines, because that is where the platforms were!

At Crossgates station itself, there were two wooden twin-posted, upper quadrant, 'home'

'splitting' or 'junction' signals, to protect the Wetherby and Selby junction. Again there were 'short' and 'tall' posts to indicate either Wetherby or the Selby/York routes. Beyond Crossgates station the number of tracks reduced from four to two; to both Wetherby and Selby/York.

Notice the variety of signal types in just three adjacent locations; wooden upper quadrant distants, metal lattice lower quadrant distants and wooden upper quadrant homes, not to mention the wooden lower quadrant starter signal at the end of the platform for the Leeds 'stoppers'. I suppose it kept the drivers on their toes.

Crossgates station, I should add, was also in a cutting and access to the platforms was gained down a fairly steeply sloped walkway.

Crossgates, in those days, could boast its own quite busy goods yard, but it was at the higher level of the rest of the township, overlooking the station.

The yard was approached and quitted, rather circuitously, by means of a set of 'trailing' points in the vicinity of the Barnbow Ordnance Factory complex, a mile or so along the Selby line. Trains requiring access to the yard would be required to reverse through the 'trailing' points and proceed up a gradient to rise over the Wetherby line and make the yard beyond an overbridge. Various representations of 'J' class 0–6–0 tank locomotives could be seen, savagely going forwards and backwards at great speed, shunting wagons with much smoke, steam, noise and clanking of buffers. Perhaps it was used as a training ground for would-be drivers.

Anyway, to return to our previously mentioned promontory at the top of the cutting/embankment half a mile west of the station.

It was a great place for us to make, because not only was the overall view excellent, but the signals gave us ample warning of trains coming in both directions and also if they were going to be 'fast' or 'slow'.

Unidentified B1 4-6-0 entering Crossgates station with Leeds-bound semi-fast. c.1955

Most often, trains signalled on the 'fast' lines were 'through' passengers, but 'goodsies' also used them, depending, so we supposed, on a 'path' being available.

To list the classes of locomotive we used to see in those days can be guaranteed to moisten the eyes of any LNER enthusiast today. I reckon, in order of class and frequency, the 'honours' would look something like:

D49, D20, J39, A8, V2, J21, G5, B16, C2, C3, C5, Sentinel Railcars, K3, V1/V3, D22, Q6, O2, J72, Q5, D21, A3 and A4, with the occasional LMS type 8F, class 5 and the odd 'Jubilee'.

Of all the types of locomotive, the D49s and C2 Ivat 'Atlantics' seemed to be best turned out in their green liveries. The rest were just plain filthy.

The line to Crossgates was on a rising gradient; not steep, but enough to require a locomotive to be 'worked'. The poor old G5s used to make the heaviest weather of it, with much explosive exhaust and clouds of steam leaking from every joint; a reflection perhaps of the deteriorating state of maintenance in those times.

On the lines into Leeds, being on a falling gradient, the crews' work was almost over and steam seemed to be shut off at the approach to Crossgates station, opposite the war-time ordnance factory at Barnbow. This was just as well because the complex junction, with the Wetherby line, was on a curve as it led into the station from the east, and many a speeding locomotive could be seen to rock most violently from side to side over the points in the most hair-raising fashion, if the crew had neglected to slow down soon enough.

A Night to Remember

Do you remember the little sentry-box-like watchmen's huts and braziers that Hornby used to make in the gauge '0' days? Just simple little lineside accessories, as they were called in the catalogues, and only cost about a shilling, but oh, how dramatic they could be under certain conditions in real life.

Probably the most poignant memory I have of my young days focuses on a watchman's hut and

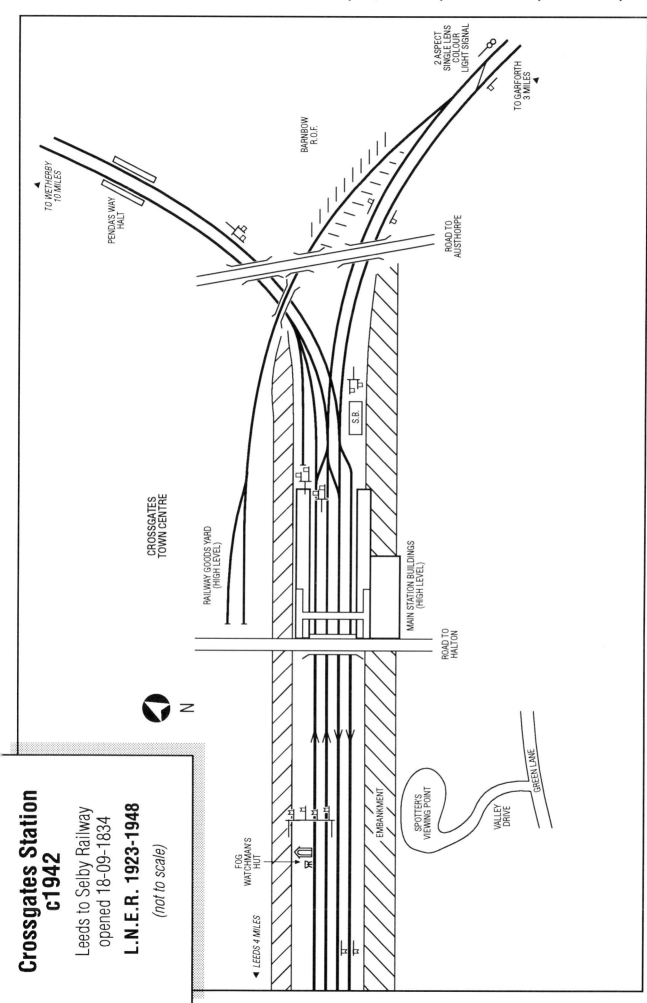

**Crossgates Station
c1942**

Leeds to Selby Railway
opened 18-09-1834

L.N.E.R. 1923-1948

(not to scale)

N

◄ LEEDS 4 MILES

FOG
WATCHMAN'S
HUT

EMBANKMENT

SPOTTER'S
VIEWING POINT

VALLEY
DRIVE

GREEN LANE

ROAD TO HALTON

MAIN STATION BUILDINGS
(HIGH LEVEL)

RAILWAY GOODS YARD
(HIGH LEVEL)

CROSSGATES
TOWN CENTRE

S.B.

ROAD TO
AUSTHORPE

BARNBOW
R.O.F.

PENDA'S WAY
HALT

TO WETHERBY
10 MILES ◄

2 ASPECT
SINGLE LENS
COLOUR
LIGHT SIGNAL

TO GARFORTH
3 MILES ◄

glowing brazier at the foot of the 'distant' signal gantry we were discussing earlier.

It was a mid-November night and there was a real old 'pea-souper' of a fog. Everything was quiet outside because what traffic there was had been brought almost to a standstill by the fog, but from our house I could hear mysterious bangings away in the mid distance. There wasn't an air raid in progress because the sirens hadn't sounded. It was too late for Guy Fawkes' night and, in any case, fireworks were banned during the war, so what was making the noise? It seemed to be coming from the railway.

My pal and I wrapped up and went to the top of the embankment, where we seemed to be getting closer to the sound. Remember it was foggy. All we could see of the railway was a ruddy glow coming from somewhere near the signal gantry.

Nothing daunted, we slithered down the embankment until we came to the railway fencing and there, 'before our very eyes', was the most mephistophelean sight that could ever be imagined!

Across the tracks, at the foot of the gantry, was a heavily overcoated watchman shovelling extra coals on to a brazier, placed in front of his watchman's hut, just like in the Hornby catalogue, but this time it was for real!

Well, I ask you, what with the pea-soup fog, the red glow of the coals in the fire and the smoke swirling up from them – it might have been Old Nick himself stoking up! Talk about spooky! To add to all the 'fug', the old watchman was smoking a pipe.

What was going on? Had there been a derailment? We were soon to find out, because the watchman moved towards a pair of lineside levers that we had never ever noticed before, and pulled one of them. We couldn't see what they were connected to until, slowly appearing out of the fog, like a furious smoke-belching dragon, there materialised an engine hauling a train of coal wagons.

Just as it drew alongside the watchman's hut there was an almighty BANG! Our insides turned to water with fright and it was all we could do not to turn and run for it, until we realised that what the watchman was doing with his levers was to place a detonator on the line to warn the locomotive driver that his signal on the gantry, which he could not see because of its height above the tracks, was at 'caution'. Phew!

The following day we went down to the trackside and saw for ourselves the hitherto unnoticed levers and the remains of the used detonators. The evening of that day turned out to be yet another pea-souper, so we went down again to observe the activities, this time with less apprehension than on the previous evening.

One Enchanted Evening

On a clear evening I could imagine nothing more enchanting than to stand on the station bridge and look down at the red, green and orange lights of the signals twinkling in the darkness. Oh, if only I could have a model railway with signals that lit up like that!

Two miles east of Crossgates used to be a small level crossing at Barrowby, where my pal Gordon Backhouse used to live in the adjacent gatehouse. I have a memory of walking out there on an early winter evening, in about 1935, the sky glowing red with sunset. We stood by the crossing gates to watch an oncoming Leeds express go past. Joy of joys, it was being hauled by a sparkling clean 'Hunt' class D49 4–4–0 – my favourite type of engine.

Hardly had the last Gresley varnished-teak-brake-3rd passed us when, on the other line, appeared a local passenger train hauled by a wheezing and grimy old G5 0–4–4 tank, belching smoke and cinders as it bellowed its way against the slight up gradient along the raised embankment into Garforth station a mile further on. Probably it was a stopping passenger on the 'Methley circle' route, turning right at Garforth junction for Kippax and Castleford.

All the colours took on a warm reddy-brown cast in the sunset glow, contrasting vividly with the white of condensing steam. And the smell – sulphur, steam and oil. It beat fish and chips any day.

Hot Summer Days

A hot summer's day and the mid-distance shimmers.

The grasses and wild plants are lushly fragrant, the buzz of a searching bee, the chirruping of a lark in the sky above. Yellow buttercups, the smell of a creosoted fence.

A tiny sound echoing through rails but a few

yards away, growing louder by the second until, out of the distant haze and betraying the merest wisp of exhaust, speeds the object of our attendance. A gleaming mechanical masterpiece, wheels and motion blurred by speed, followed by coach after coach in varnished splendour as the volume of their approach increases to a peak, and then changes tone to the familiar but, from that instant fading, clickety-click, clickety-click of wheels over rail joints until, in but a matter of seconds, silence returns and the colours and fragrances come back into focus.

Could not this be a scene in the life of a railside observer anywhere in the world? The locomotive power could just as well be electric, diesel or steam.

What a lovely way to spend a summer's day.

Not so very many years ago, nearly everyone would have such a scene virtually on his or her doorstep, as I had – and still have, even today, thank goodness.

The Fascination of Railways

In those early days, my particular railway colours were apple green and varnished teak – or black, mud and rust, depending on whether the train in sight was passenger or goods.

They still are today, as far as my model railway is concerned – apart from the mud and rust that is. In other words, the London and North Eastern Railway, with special emphasis on its North Eastern constituent.

Many are those who have tried to account for the fascination that railways have for them.

Some will say they thrill to the sight, sound and smell of huge mechanical creations at work and at speed. Others will, perhaps, react more to the sight of a dainty branch line train sedately winding its way through arcadian scenery.

All this applies to the railway modeller, with the additional aspect that he, or she, tries to re-create in model form what he or she has seen in real life.

The railway modeller observes in order to re-create (sounds like a good motto for someone to translate into Latin), and one also searches for those things that will reproduce well; almost like creating a photograph album that moves.

The railway modeller type produces an odd kind of individual who gains more by watching his railways from a well-chosen vantage point than actually travelling on them.

What I mean is, when one is travelling on a train one is primarily concerned with (a) how comfortable and clean it is and (b) how quickly one can arrive at one's destination. It matters little whether the coach in which one is travelling is vintage teak or HST.

If one is travelling at 100 m.p.h. it matters little what form the locomotive takes, be it an 0–6–0 tank or a class 91 electric. Rolling stock and haulage power are just a means to an end to the traveller, but to the railside observer and modeller they are of the very essence.

The railway modeller thrills to the sight of a train, regardless of the sweated labour of a fireman, or the sardine-packed passenger. The thrill, to the observing modeller, lies in the sight of movement amidst the colours and shapes of the landscape, or it might be the hustle and bustle of a busy station as trains arrive and depart to the accompaniment of the sounds of Tannoy messages, slamming doors and blowing whistles.

All these observations are stored in the memory banks of this peculiar individual, ready to be drawn, when the opportunity presents, on the modelling boards.

Youthful Observations of the LNER

I do not think I have made any secret of the fact that I have lived most of my life within sight and sound of the LNER.

My very earliest memories are of trains, and can remember being wheeled in my pram by my mother to the bridge over the Leeds to Selby line at East Garforth. I am told that my three earliest words were 'Puffer coming Mummy.' Would that my subsequent vocabulary were so pure!

I mentioned earlier that I was born at the same time as the D49 'Hunt' and 'Shire' class 4–4–0s first turned wheel, and grew up with them. I considered them the loveliest of all engines, and it was with some dismay that I was to learn, in later life, how little my enthusiasm was shared by those who had to drive them.

We later moved to Crossgates, about three miles east of Leeds, on the same line. Now this really was a train watcher's paradise, because of the sheer variety of loco power to be seen. You name it and it came through Crossgates!

The 4-track line carried the Hull and New-castle-Leeds-Liverpool expresses, and I have treasured memories of double-headed Ivat & Worsdell Atlantics belting in towards Leeds on the 5 p.m. mail train. It was a rare thing to see 'double heading' anywhere on the LNER, but this particular train seemed to be the exception. Sometimes it was even a pair of D49s.

Occasionally we would see an LMS 'Black 5' and Jubilee plus the odd A3 and A4.

From our house we could hear the chime of an A4 as it came towards us past Neville Hill loco sheds, two miles away, and it acted as a rallying cry for all we youngsters to drop our gang warfare and head for the trackside.

Having said this, I never remember seeing an A4 going into Leeds on these lines, only coming out.

Many years earlier, I can remember red and cream diesel railcars being tested on this line, but history shows they never came to anything. On the other hand, the green and cream Sentinel railcars were a regular sight, trundling along with their rapid but 'petite' exhaust rhythm. Local drivers referred to them as 'steam pigs', and young 'passed firemen' were often placed in charge of them. I don't think they ever reached 30 m.p.h. and seemed content to amble along as if there was no tomorrow. We schoolboys loved it when the 'school train' came into Crossgates station from Wetherby in the form of a railcar, because we had such a good view of things from the windows of the saloon-type layout inside. In those days, when train services seemed as frequent as the buses, I wouldn't mind hazarding a guess that the railcars slowed up the system more than somewhat.

4-4-0 locos abounded in the form of D20s, D22s and D49s and, I suppose, other D class variants as well. Many of them must have had Westinghouse brakes because you could hear the steam pumps going 'pu-pu' 'pu-pu' all the time they were standing in the stations. In the late 1930s and early '40s the old NER 4-4-0s were becoming run down and no longer painted green, more's the pity. It is only in retrospect that one appreciates the character of these mucky old engines, begrimed, bent and whitened with hard water lime deposits around the bases of their domes and chimneys.

From March until July 1939, I was sent away to school at Hornsea, on the east coast a few miles south of Bridlington. The great joys of that otherwise, for me, forlorn period were:

(a) the continuous sight and sound of RAF fighters and bombers (Harts, Furies, Battles, Hurricanes, Wellingtons) doing their bombing exercises in Bridlington Bay and practising mock dogfights right above us – the last few months before the outbreak of World War II.

(b) the opportunity of travelling, on my own, to and from school at the beginning and ending of each term, on the trains to Leeds.

The Hornsea Branch

Going to Leeds, one would walk along to Hornsea station, right on the edge of the sands, with its unique turntable at the end of the platform, on which incoming engines would uncouple, turn, and reverse via a loop line to gain the other end of the train ready for the return journey to Hull.

The engines were usually 0-6-0 J21s or the similar looking E class 2-4-0s and the odd 0-4-4 tank G5. You almost could have been forgiven for thinking that Wilson Worsdell had had some interest in the line at one time, but they always seemed to be in disgusting condition; what with accumulated soot, hard water limescale stains, not to mention seagull droppings!

The carriages weren't much better either, because if you patted the seats little mounds of soot would form on them.

To complete our 'cup of delight', the carriages were gaslit. And all this before the war had even started!

But there's more; wait until the train got the starting signal!

You never did see so much black smoke; it never let up until the train arrived at Hull Paragon station.

Some of the station names did nothing to inspire either – Sigglesthorne and Swine to name but a few.

The only attractive feature on the line was Hornsea Mere, just half a mile out of the station, and very good for coarse fishing. Yes, I think that would be quite apt. The rest of the countryside was almost dead flat and featureless.

I would say the journey took the best part of an hour, before passengers were dumped in some obscure bay at Hull Paragon, which was only a couple of shades cleaner than the rest of the branch and smelled to high heaven of fish.

The Hull to Leeds Journey

On arrival at Paragon station, I can remember humping my suitcase along what seemed miles of station platforms, until I gained the departure platform for the Leeds trains.

It was on this platform that the glory of the LNER hit one like a ray of sunshine after rain. There, awaiting our boarding, would be a train of those glistening varnished teak Gresley corridor coaches that I am always raving about. They looked simply luxurious from the outside, as well as the inside. No mounds of soot appeared on these seats when you patted them.

Bear in mind that most of the trains I had previously travelled on were 'stopping passengers', comprised of old stock with separate compartments each having a door on either side. In other words, no corridors, no toilets and stopping at every station.

Finding myself a seat 'up front' of the Leeds train and reserving it by leaving my case on it (no fears of having one's case stolen in those halcyon days of yore), I would soon be back on to the platform and walking up to see the engine. You could almost bet on it being a highly polished Darlington Apple Green D49 4–4–0 'Hunt' class, less than 10 years old and still in its prime.

They had the loveliest names like *The Bramham Moor*, *The Bedale*, *The Quorn*, *The Cottesmore*, etc., lovely sounding names of the even lovelier districts of the foxhunts they were named after.

The 'Hunts' had three features distinguishing them from their near neighbours the 'Shires':
1. Rotary valve gear with the distinctive rotating rods on the right-hand side.
2. Outside steam pipes to the cylinders.
3. A really thin eccentric rod cranked from the leading axle on the left-hand side which operated one of the lubricators.

The paintshop men who lined and lettered them did their job well.

Gold, red, white, brown and black letter and number transfers on buffer beams, cab and tender sides.

White-black-white lining for boiler bands, cab sides, tender sides and ends, and cylinders painted green to distinguish Darlington from Doncaster engine works, which were painted black.

Black and white edging round the red buffer beams.

Wheel centres, white around black centres.

I'm not certain about frame edges being lined red.

Back to the platform; a nice sunny day to add sparkle to all this mechanical artistry, the quiet background hum of superheating steam, the sound of the blower in the smokebox or the ear-splitting roar of Ross pop safety valves blowing off – a practice frowned upon by station authorities, but it was always happening.

The sound of the guard's warning whistle sent one hurrying back to one's carriage, a window seat facing the engine of course, the final slamming and clunking shut of doors, a waving of the guard's green flag acknowledged by a toot on the whistle and, we're off.

Slow puff, puff of the exhaust; clank, clank, of the Gresley steel coupling rods as the driver lets in the clutch and the train starts to move, smoothly at first until an oil spot on the rails encourages the engine to try and reach 60 m.p.h. in 5 seconds flat! Wheel slip, back with the regulator, start again. This time only a couple of suspicions of wheel slip before adhesion is positive, and we are on our way, non-stop, to Selby 30 miles away, along what used to be the longest dead straight, dead level, stretch of railway line in the country.

It isn't long before Hessle is passed at 50 m.p.h. plus. Then North Ferriby, Brough, all within occasional sight of the Humber; the Humber Bridge being merely a visionary's dream in those days. This long length of fast straight track was ideal for leaning out of the windows to watch the engine, and my word, those D49s were lively at speed. No doubt the crew would use a less complimentary word to describe the vertical top-to-bottom, side-to-side, front-to-rear 'bucking'. It was almost unbelievable and must have been a real trial to the fireman trying to aim his shovelfuls. I have heard it said that some crews volunteered for goods duties rather than drive a D49, so it looks as if the D49s were 'Beauty and the Beast' all rolled into one.

On a fine summer day, the scenery was pleasantly rural though flat, with the small villages and church spires passing by at a very satisfying pace. The horizons were low so there was always a lot of sky in view. This was the way to travel, I thought, and all paid for by Dad.

Forty-five minutes or so and we were slowing down for the junction with the East Coast main line and the famous, or infamous, swing bridge over the tidal River Ouse leading into Selby station. Most cross-country trains stopped at Selby and so did we for a couple of minutes or so.

This marked the end of the 'fast bit', and the rest of the journey to Leeds was at a more leisurely pace.

Departing from Selby station, a quick look to the right would reward the traveller with a glimpse of the imposing twin towers of Selby Abbey. It had to be a quick look because the line almost immediately ran under a large road bridge before it turned right, off the East Coast main line section, past the engine sheds and on to the line for Leeds via South Milford and Micklefield, where it met with the York, Church Fenton line curving in from the north in a chalky cutting.

By this time one was becoming aware of the northernmost edge of the great Yorkshire coalfield creeping into the picture. There seemed to be dozens of pits in those days, each with its pit-head winding wheels, sidings, hundreds of wagons and mineral engines not forgetting the mountainous pit heaps and their aerial tip-buckets. Not a pretty sight; all extremely important for the nation's wealth, but very dirty.

We were now approaching the area indicated by my model railway station names of Aberford, Barrowby, East Garforth, Bramham and Barwick-in-Elmet. Only East Garforth, in fact, ever had a railway in 'real life', but aren't they nice-sounding names?

Actually the villages are quite beautiful with lots of history attached to them, particularly during the Wars of the Roses. Cock Beck, at the battle of Saxton Moor, is said to have flowed red with the blood of the fallen.

The next station to be passed was Garforth with its extensive coal refuge sidings, and then along the lengthy embankment past the gasworks to Barrowby Crossing. On the north side of the line just here there were left-overs of a World War I munitions factory together with rusting bits of old railway track and point levers, all very derelict but a great adventure playground for we youngsters. I suppose that is how the Barrowby

level crossing and gatekeeper's house came to be there in the first place, but in my young days the road had become merely an unmade track leading off Barrowby Lane.

A little bit further along was rather a unique colour light signal on the opposite track; it was single aspect but could show red or green.

Passing Crossgates station we were nearing journey's end, but it was nice to have the satisfaction of passing through one's local station on the 'through' line.

The approach to Leeds City station, after Osmondthorpe station and the Neville Hill engine sheds and carriage sidings, was firstly through very high brick-faced cuttings and bridges in the Richmond Hill area, before passing Marsh Lane goods and passenger station, and then on to the final cemetery embankment past Leeds Parish Church, and the many 'sweatshop'-type premises in the upper storeys of buildings in which one could see dozens of women sitting at sewing machines stitching clothes. Of course Leeds was the home of the ready-made clothing industry in those days.

Finally, we drew slowly into the murk of gaslit Leeds City station, an extremely busy place with no time to allow trains to hang about. Mum and Dad were waiting for their starry-eyed soot-smutted offspring, but not before I had had another quick look at our D49 and the sight of those varnished teak coaches.

Reunion conversation, on the way home, was not about school and how I had missed them, but about the engines I had seen, the speeds we had travelled at, but most of all – those lovely D49s.

What transport of delight, what memories!

Hitchin Station, 1938

Mother's sister, Auntie Elsie, was matron of the Letchworth Garden City's Isolation Hospital in 1938; a beautiful place. She it was who invited us to spend our two-week summer holiday with some friends who lived in nearby Hitchin, about 3 miles away.

I was ten years old at the time, not knowing much about our railway system, only that I liked trains.

Almost as a matter of course it wasn't long before I found my way to Hitchin station and there, oh boy, did I see something to fill my memory banks (things not talked about in those days).

Hitchin station, as everyone but me knew, was on the LNER (Great Northern division) East Coast main line, some 34 miles north of King's Cross. It was a four-track station, with platforms serving the two outer tracks for the stopping trains. Hitchin was the junction station for the Baldock, Royston and Cambridge branch.

May I remind you of the date again: August 1938, a time when the LNER was at its most glamorous.

For almost two weeks the LNER put on a spectacular show for my benefit, the like of which I have never seen since.

Its full armoury of engines and rolling stock was brought out in rapid succession every day. I was spellbound and Mum and Dad had to come and collect me every teatime, otherwise I would probably have stayed there until nightfall.

This was the time when the A4 streamliners were brand new and the *Mallard* had just gained the world speed record for steam.

What beautiful things they were with their sloping fronts and chime whistles, painted garter blue with dark red wheels, tearing past at all of 90 m.p.h.

The trains they were hauling were all the prestige ones such as 'Flying Scotsman', 'Queen of Scots Pullman' and 'Yorkshire Pullman', but the two we loved best were the 'Coronation' and 'West Riding Limited' which were painted two shades of blue, Garter & Marlborough, to match the engines. As if that wasn't enough, the 'Coronation' sported a 'beaver-tail' observation coach at the back, a lovely sight.

Their design concept, like that of the earlier 'Silver Jubilee', was one of aerodynamic type smoothness; matching the streamlining of the A4s that hauled them.

The space under the solebars, between the bogie frames, was valanced almost down to track level and painted black.

The space in between the ends of the coaches was filled in with a rubberised fairing painted to match the two blues of the sides and the light grey of the roof.

Also like the 'Silver Jubilee', the 'Coronation' and 'West Riding Limited' coaches were 'articulated', whereby the inside ends of each pair of coaches just sat on one bogie. There were four pairs of articulated coaches to each set, plus the beaver-tail on the 'Coronation'.

West end of East Garforth Station – warts 'n all. (Photo KC)

The real 'Dominion of Canada' BR 600010, observing the speed restriction through Durham Station with the up Tyne/Tees Pullman in 1957. (Photo KC)

The interiors of the coaches were sumptuously furnished and decorated in two shades of green, with individual swivel armchairs in the first class. Not that I ever travelled on it; I just picked up the information in a book.

The 'Coronation' train was inaugurated to celebrate the coronation of Their Majesties King George VI and Queen Elizabeth in 1937. To go with such an historic event, even the engines had imperious names like *Dominion of Canada, Commonwealth of Australia, Dominion of New Zealand, Empire of India* and *Union of South Africa*. The *Dominion of Canada* had a silver bell fitted in front of the chimney and whistle which was the gift of the Canadian Pacific Railway, and you could hear it too, occasionally.

I have always been surprised that, until very recently, no enterprising manufacturer ever saw fit to produce a model of the 'Coronation' train and observation car. Perhaps it was because so very few people, relatively speaking, ever saw it, as it didn't depart from King's Cross, and Edinburgh, until 4 o'clock in the afternoon, a time when most people were at work.

The observation cars were put into storage when the war broke out in '39, and the rest of the coaches along with those of the 'West Riding Limited' were, I believe, painted 'simulated teak' and absorbed into 'the system', where they lasted well into BR days after the war.

I have seen pictures of the observation cars painted BR maroon and they saw some service on the scenic lines in Scotland, but my impression was that they had had their unique beaver-tails

modified to something more angular and easier to repair when necessary.

Anyway, I, for one, saw the 'Coronation' and 'West Riding Limited', in their original splendid condition, almost every day for that never-to-be-forgotten two weeks of August 1938.

I lost count of all the other A4s I saw except one that stuck in my mind particularly, but for no special reason other than I saw it almost every day, and that was *Sea Eagle*. Its name was subsequently transferred to a Peppercorn A1, which was a worthy recipient.

All the other main line engines seen were A1s or A3s, *Flying Scotsman* and *Papyrus* amongst them, always spotlessly turned out of course.

I must have seen some mineral and freight trains, but I have no memory of them.

The local passenger trains, and 'stoppers' to King's Cross, were dealt with by the small-boilered Ivatt Atlantic 4–4–2 C1s (Henry Oakley type) and the Ivatt C12 4–4–2 tanks, plus many variants of the N class 0–6–2 tanks. Needless to say these were not kept in the same pristine condition as their express bedfellows.

Oh, those A4 chime whistles, was ever there a sound more thrilling? I only hope Mum and Dad enjoyed their holiday as much as I did.

Journeys from Leeds to Blackpool

How difficult it was, and possibly still is, to find a train running directly to Blackpool (noted for fresh-air-and-fun) from anywhere outside Lancashire, except on summer Saturdays. Certainly there were no through trains from Leeds in my young days, and one always had to change at Manchester or Preston.

I travelled regularly between Leeds and Blackpool between 1944 and 1949 – a period which included war-time and post-war travel, not that I noticed much difference in the timings.

Reference to railway maps will show the prolific accumulation of seemingly superfluous mileage involved.

Because of its trans-Pennine nature, it was never a route for high speeds, but, if one scoured the timetables with assiduity, one could find a 3-hour train leaving Blackpool North about 8.10 a.m. and Leeds Central about 3.50 p.m. – 3 hours for 80 road miles!

The evening train travelled over what I suspect

were GN metals to Halifax via Low Moor and Laisterdyke (there's a name for you), then Sowerby Bridge and Todmorden before going on to Manchester Victoria (or was it Exchange?). Passengers relied on this train keeping time into Manchester in order to meet a connection, from I don't know where, but which came in within 10 minutes of our arrival and got us to Blackpool, via Preston, at 7 p.m. or so.

Nothing very remarkable about the journey I suppose, except perhaps the race out of Manchester with a Southport-bound train on an adjacent track. I have memories of this particular train being hauled by LMS class 2–6–4 tank engines, and one could gain an excellent side-on view of a loco hard at work trying to keep up with ours.

I have no idea what form our hauling power took to Manchester, but I seem to remember scruffy old Claughtons as I walked off the platform at Blackpool.

The coaching stock was similarly uninspiring and, if one was not careful, quite a number of coaches were non-corridor. To spend a penny involved letting the guard know where one was going immediately the train stopped at a station. They were duty-bound, in those days, to hold up the train for one's basic needs. I know, because I often was 'in need'.

So, scruffy engines, scruffy coaches, scruffy stations and uninspiring industrial scenery.

Perhaps the scenery was a touch more interesting on the Leeds, Dewsbury, Huddersfield, Stalybridge route to Manchester, but usually involved a much longer wait of anything up to an hour at Manchester.

Cross-country trains, even to this day, do not seem to carry the glamour of the London expresses and there seems to be a notable lack of urgency about them.

Wath Hump

My family stems from that salubrious South Yorkshire watering place of Wath-upon-Dearne. The River Dearne is a tributary of the River Don which giveth its name to Doncaster. I suppose the word 'river' ought to be in parenthesis because I remember it as a mucky beck, the waters of which no doubt helped keep up the levels of the numerous 'cuts' or canals in the vicinity. No doubt the cuts existed before the railways and were used for the transport of coal.

At the time my memories commence the whole area was a spider-web of railway lines interconnecting everything with everything else. There were literally acres of railway marshalling and colliery sidings as far as the eye could see, and beyond, separated by further acres of flat waterlogged land, which used to flood at the first sign of rain. Add to that the overall pall of smoke and smell of sulphurous gases emanating from the collieries and coking plants and you have an area of unmitigated industrial ugliness.

But, let's face it, memories are not merely the consist of pleasant happenings or scenes; we have to take the rough with the smooth.

It was in the centre of all this hive of coal mining activity that Wath Hump was situated. The term 'hump' referred to the top of a gradient up which coal wagons were pushed, and which were then required to freewheel downhill into one or other of the multitude of sorting sidings on the other side. There, pointsmen would hand-change the points as required whilst nimble-footed shunters would use their shunting poles to knock down the brake levers. The wear and tear on wagons must have been enormous, but no one appeared to care. As labour was cheap and plentiful in those days, maybe new wagons were as well.

Before World War II the area abounded in collieries – Wath Main, Manvers Main, Corton Wood, Elsecar, Wombwell and Wentworth to name but a few, all interconnected with the vast network of railway lines focusing on Wath Hump marshalling yard.

Wath, in those days, boasted no fewer than three railway stations: Midland, Lancashire & Yorkshire, and Great Central, each providing ready outlets for the coal traffic.

The principal type of locomotive that I used to see trundling around the colliery lines, at a walking pace, were the Robinson ex-GCR O2 2–8–0s; whilst on the 'Hump' itself one could see the unique 0–8–4 'Wath tanks' with 'booster' drive to the rear bogie wheels. The maximum speed of locomotives in this neck of the woods seemed to be no more than 10 m.p.h.

In the world of model railways, there is nothing more eye-catching than a train of colourful, dainty, private owner coal wagons. In real life they would be lucky to remain like that for a fortnight, especially at Wath.

Five miles or so to the north west of Wath yard was the Worsborough incline for which the solitary Gresley 2–8–0 0–8–2 Garrat locomotive was designed to push long and heavily loaded coal trains up the 'bank' towards Penistone and Woodhead, thence into Lancashire. This locomotive was a regular sight at the Hump yard.

Latterly of course, this line was electrified and E1 Bo-Bos took on a big share of the traffic. The 'posts' went up in 1938–9, but progress was shelved until after the war ended in 1945.

Sadly, from a railway enthusiast's point of view, the whole of the electrified line from Sheffield to Manchester has now been lifted. Most of the collieries themselves are now but a memory and England's green and pleasant land is, at long last, taking the place of the dark satanic mills of yesteryear.

Early Post-War Impressions

There came a period of nearly twelve months, between 1952–53, when my job took me into the south of England, and I would travel on the midday 'Queen of Scots' Pullman from King's Cross to Leeds almost every Friday.

This was luxury and the lunches superb and reasonably priced at 7s. 6d. (37½p) plus the 4s. (20p) Pullman supplementary charge, a meal at every table.

One really felt one was travelling on that prestigious train. My amateurish attempts at train-timings regularly came up with 90 m.p.h. by the time Hitchin and Sandy were reached.

The Peppercorn A1s were almost 'run-in' by this time and made child's play of the relatively lightweight 10-coach Pullman. Nevertheless, the A4s still couldn't be beaten for maximum speeds. The 168 miles to Leeds Central was reached comfortably in 3 hours, including the stop at Wakefield where the Bradford portion was split off.

I think my best Friday 'marathon' was in February 1953 when I left Cowes, Isle of Wight, by the 7.30 a.m. ferry to Southampton and still made King's Cross in time for the Pullman after belting up the Southern main line to Waterloo hauled by a rebuilt Merchant Navy Pacific.

It's rather a funny thing, but I can never remember running late on the Southern main line, either the Southampton or the Bournemouth routes, even as long ago as 1947. Could it be that their timetablings were more realistic than those of other regions?

Of course, what I have been doing here – as I am sure you have gathered – is to record railway impressions.

I had a job far removed from railway operation, and even though I travelled a great deal by rail, I had little time, or energy, to explore much in the way of detail. Mostly I caught the trains by the skin of my teeth.

What I was doing was to add to my store of impressions against the day, if it was ever to come – and it did – when I could restart railway modelling in earnest.

The Commencement of the Present

After four pleasant years living back in Leeds, the requirements of my job brought about my next domiciliary move, which has lasted to this day.

My company asked me if I would represent them in south-west Durham and North Yorkshire in the August of 1953. I viewed the move with more than a little trepidation because I had never been further north than Scotch Corner. Also I knew the scenic deprivations of the South Yorkshire coalfields and I had visions of mile upon mile of unbroken industrial gloom being repeated for me in the North-East.

I chose to settle in Bishop Auckland, a market town in S.W. Durham and a pleasant, busy, natural commercial centre for the surrounding area, with much historical, ecclesiastical and Roman heritage. So much so that it is difficult to dig the garden without unearthing some old Roman stone.

Whilst collieries were still highly active throughout the county, there was far more in the way of green fields and really beautiful countryside between them than in South Yorkshire. In fact a 'little voice' told me that I was going to like it here – and it has proved to be so.

To study the history of County Durham is to study the history of railways. This is where it all started – immediately around Bishop Auckland!

The Stockton & Darlington Railway started at Witton Park Iron Works, just up the road, rope-hauled up Brussleton Incline and then down into

Shildon, where Timothy Hackworth's 'new-fangled' steam engines took over at Mason's Arms Crossing, which formed the entrance to the now-closed Shildon Wagon Works.

And so I was to see out the steam era on British Railways in the area in which it started. Gone now are the local Q6s and 7s, the J21s and 27s, J39s, K1s, A8s, A5s, G5s, V1s and L1s and the assorted BR 2–6–0s.

The East Coast main line is a mere 5 miles away at Aycliffe and my job, as a sales representative, took me within sight of it nearly every day somewhere between Thirsk and Newcastle.

Mind you, the main line up here does get a bit boring after a while because it is all express traffic.

In the steam days of the 1950s and 60s almost every engine was a Pacific, A1, A2, A3 or A4. It came as welcome relief to see a freight or mineral train hauled by a V2, B1, Q6 or a 9F 2–10–0.

Then came the diesel English Electric class 40s ('Whistlers'), class 45s (noisy brutes), class 47s, followed by the Deltics, followed by the HSTs, now followed by the Class 91 electrics.

South of Northallerton one could see more variety because of the industrial and freight trains to and from Teesside, which leave and join the main line there. I used to look forward to catching a glimpse of the 'Tyne-Tees' Pullman between 9 and 9.30 a.m. just south of Durham, depending where I happened to be at the time, usually hauled by a 'Streak' A4 in steam days.

One of my first sights of a Deltic was at North Cowton on an autumn morning in 1961. Its two-tone green livery, in my opinion, looked very tasteful at the head of the brown and cream 'Tyne-Tees' Pullman coaches. Luckily for me I had my cine camera with me at the time, so was able to record the event in full scenic splendour.

Father-in-Law

Yes, you guessed it, I got married.

But what hand of destiny decreed that Cupid's arrow should land in the heart of an engine-driver's daughter? May she ever be blessed amongst women.

Father-in-law, may he also rest in peace, spent his service life with the LNER, betwixt and between Kirkby Stephen, Darlington, Selby, Hull

Dear old father-in-law, John Alexander Forbes (3rd from left) at a ceremony in West Auckland Shed. Date and photographer unknown.

and West Auckland. He was 'passed' to drive between Tyneside, York, Selby, Hull, Darlington, Teesside, Wearside, Richmond, Hawes Junction, Barnard Castle, Stainmore and Tebay. What more 'freedom of the lines' could a man want?

Of course, he didn't look at it quite like that when he had to leave a warm bed at some unearthly hour in the middle of a foul night in midwinter, to lead a coke train from West Auckland to Tebay, over the intimidating Stainmore line (he was once marooned at Belah for two days in the 1947 snows).

Because of the loading limitations of the slender Belah viaduct, on the descent to Kirkby Stephen, engine power was limited, but 'two at the front and one at the rear' was a common sight.

Father-in-law seemed to have one favourite class of engine above all others, and that was the Vincent Raven class Q6 0–8–0. Very often he would trot out his complimentary 'They were grand mineral engines, them!'

For local passenger work he had a soft spot for the Vincent Raven A8 4–6–2 Tankers, rebuilt from their original 4–4–4 configuration. They carried the nickname of 'Teddy Bears', why I don't know, unless it was because they were big, cumbersome and tended to roll. They were not exactly A4s in elegance, but they could produce a sometimes alarming turn of speed on the sinuous down grades from Barnard Castle to Bishop Auckland.

This happened once when mother-in-law was on the train returning from 'Barny' and, on arrival at Bishop Auckland station, was soon on her way 'up front' to give the driver a piece of her mind. Imagine the scene when she found the driver to be none other than, yes you guessed it, dear old father-in-law. I would like to lay odds that he is still hearing about it to this day.

Most of his life was spent 'leading' mineral trains, and leading them to the Teesside railway complexes was certainly not his favourite way of spending a working day.

Situations would regularly occur similar to the way aircraft are 'stacked' over busy air terminals.

Laden (or unladen – depending whether they were going to or returning from Teesside) mineral trains, on some lines, worked something called a 'lock and block' system, which allowed one train to be held at a signal and then succeeding trains would be allowed to close up to them. This could, and often did, entail a wait of hours. It wasn't unknown for a driver to reach the end of his shift in charge of one of these static trains. The driver would telephone control and tell them to send a replacement driver because he was 'Gan Yam' (going home). I was never quite sure how they did get home on these occasions; probably 'thumbed' a lift on another slow-moving train going in the opposite direction.

It was very sad to see one line and then another closed from the late 1950s onwards, first to passenger traffic and then to goods. There were many heavily attended public meetings held in Middlesbrough about the proposed closure of the Stainmore line, which was considered by many, then and now, to be of vital strategic importance, because it provided a relatively short connection between the North-East and the North-West; not so much for passenger traffic but as an alternative route for almost everything else. As it turned out, closure went ahead as intended and now the A68 road over Stainmore has become a nose-to-tail affair due to ever-increasing volume of traffic.

Father-in-law again (in cap at right) with last passenger-train to use the Weardale branch. 29 June 1953. (Photographer unknown)

In his last years before retirement, father-in-law received training on the new diesels; first DMUs and then type 2s and 3s, as they were called then. It was amusing to hear his comments on DMU gearboxes, because he never did learn to drive a car. It must have been quite a change after a lifetime of 'notching up' reversing gears. He 'passed' on the diesels without too much trouble, but I can remember him spending a lot of time at home studying the training manuals.

It was in the late 1960s that a big new cement works was built at Eastgate-in-Weardale, right out in the sticks. A 'merry-go-round' system of loading was introduced and he was involved in leading trains of loaded wagons to Heaton yards at Newcastle and bringing back the empties. On one of his return trips an empty presflo wagon became derailed and peeled all the rest of the wagons down the embankment at Birtley, just south of Gateshead on the main line. Luckily no one was hurt, but there was a court of inquiry held. Thankfully, father-in-law was completely cleared.

Before a driver can be allowed to drive a route on his own he must 'pass the route'. Father-in-law's method of learning the route was to stick endless pieces of paper together and then, from memory, he would draw in the tracks, points, signals, signal boxes etc., all the way from start to finish. I don't know if all drivers were so conscientious but I always had the feeling that, if they were, safety on the railways was in very good hands.

The object of recording these memories of my father-in-law at work has been to show an aspect of railway operation divested of some of its glamour and as a profession requiring much training, a high degree of intelligence and a lot of brute force, grit and determination.

Engine drivers, as a class in society, were highly skilled men belonging to an exclusive club, but they would not thank you for saying so.

The Coming of the Diesels to the North-East

Now firmly ensconced in the North-Eastern scene, I saw in 1960 the first appearance of what I call the second generation of diesel locomotives.

As far as the North-East main line was concerned however they were the first generation.

I refer to the Class 40s or English Electric 'Whistlers'.

As stated earlier I tried to make a point of being by the railside about 9.10 a.m. in order to see the southbound 'Tyne-Tees' Pullman coming out of Durham, formerly in the care of streamlined A4s. The brand new and sparkling green D200s made their debut at the head of this Pullman. They were good-looking and of pleasing proportions, even when their noses became covered in bright yellow paint. Their exhaust noise was even pleasant-sounding, so they must breed 'thoroughbreds' at English Electric.

About this time, English Electric had pulled another rabbit out of the hat which was to set the standard for main line diesel haulage the world over – the Deltic class 55s.

My first sighting of one was from a friend's garden by the railside at Chester-le-Street (I pick my friends carefully). My friend Stuart had told me that a late afternoon southbound express was being hauled regularly by a Deltic, so I arranged a visit to coincide. Sure enough, at the appointed time, the calm of the afternoon began to resonate to the new and hitherto unheard sound of a Deltic engine, under load and at speed, approaching from Birtley.

All too soon it was on and passed us, but not quick enough to prevent a mental snapshot of a blinking warning light and two-tone green livery all included in a shape of considerable artistic proportions.

With 22 of them on the East Coast main line, it was not surprising that we began to see a lot of them, but one never heard the comment 'oh, its just another Deltic.' They were always a thrill – to ride behind, to watch from the railside or to stand beside on a station platform. The engines (two per loco) always seemed to 'tick over' at a remarkably high speed, which turned to a positive roar when they set off.

The late 1960s and early '70s saw a proliferation of new designs amongst the diesel fraternity. I use the word 'design' with some reluctance because, to me, so many of them appeared aesthetically unsatisfying and mechanically unreliable.

BR 61448 B16/2 4-6-0. Gresley rebuild of Raven B16 (S3) at Darlington. Date unknown. (Photo N. Stead)

I suppose it was the old old story happening all over, just like houses-for-the-masses, whereby quality and appearance were sacrificed for quantity and quick delivery.

In my eyes, the ultimate in functionalism without any pretence to aesthetic appeal were the Derby Sulzer class 45s and 46s. They were ugly snub-nosed affairs with an equally ugly sound to them. Many of their drivers seemed unable to avoid violent stops and restarts, much to the discomfort of passengers. I experienced this for myself on many occasions and was appalled by it.

My interest in diesel power reached its nadir at this time only to be revived in the 1980s with the introduction of the HSTs. Now they were – and still are – something to be wondered at.

The HSTs are aesthetically pleasing, superb to ride in and, up to press, relatively safe when derailed. There are so many of them now that they have become quite commonplace, even on cross-country expresses.

When one has to go from, say, Darlington to King's Cross, one has no regrets for the passing of steam and the old 60ft rail joints. Instead, one sits back comfortably, amidst air conditioning, and revels in the thrill of smooth safe speed along long-welded rail.

Now in the 'evening' of my young life, I only have occasion to travel by rail very infrequently, but I am impressed by the design of the East Coast main line Class 91 electrics and Class IV coaches, also the latest breed of multiple units.

Who, I ask, is going to be the Nigel Gresley-of-the-electric-locomotive for the new millennium?

Four Locomotive Portraits

The Worsdell G5 0–4–4 Tank

Built by Wilson Worsdell between 1894 and 1901 as NER Class 0, there was a total of 110 of them busily occupied on branch lines throughout the NER system. The last to be condemned was BR 67280 on 22nd December 1958.

I suppose at one time there must have been some clean ones, but like their tenderised counterparts the J21s, they were usually dirty in the extreme and, I venture to suggest, left to the tender mercies of the less experienced crews.

Nevertheless, they had character; tall tapering

Nu-cast Raven Q6 0–8–0. (Photo KC)

chimneys, huge domes and very prominent, voluptuously curved, outside vacuum ejector steam pipes running from cab to smoke box on the right hand side.

They used to make a brave sight during World War II as they battled their way out of Leeds with a six-coach train to Harrogate or Wetherby – issuing smoke and steam from every joint, and what noise!

Any railway modeller seeking inspiration for 'weathering' need look no further for a subject; a muddy brown-black with a surface like sandpaper, highlighted by white streaks from hard water leaks and, wait for it, bird droppings, especially seagulls.

Strangely enough, the appearance of these lovely old engines was never better than in British Railways days when their paintwork became fully lined-out. They must have been good to remain in service until the last days of steam, bless 'em.

Worsdell Clan GS (NER Class 0) 0–4–4T No. 2097. Location not known. (Photo J W Armstrong)

Another G5 0-4-4T. (Photo J W Armstrong)

The Raven B16 4-6-0s

Introduced in 1919 as NER Class S3, the 70 locomotives of this class were probably the most successful and hard-worked of any of NER's mixed traffic engines. With their 5ft 8ins coupled wheels they could plod along steadily with 70-wagon freight trains, and yet could maintain a good turn of speed on passenger trains when required, usually on excursions, duplicates, horse-box specials and the like. Quickly identifiable by their squat chimneys (in LNER days), long boiler and high pitched cab.

Gresley fitted Walscheart valve gear to seven of them, which became known as B16/2s. Drivers spoke well of them however and they were often to be seen hauling 12-coach holiday excursion trains out of Leeds to the seaside resorts of Scarborough and Bridlington.

The Raven Q6 0-8-0s

The first of the NER Class T2 engines was built at Darlington in 1912 and altogether 120 were built, proving to be one of Raven's best designs and for more than 50 years they were the mainstay of the mineral traffic in the North-East.

Identifiable by a long tapered chimney, long boiler, carbuncular dome and what seemed like a long way between the leading driving wheels and the front buffer beam.

Under pressure of a heavy load and adverse gradient the 'bark' of their exhaust could be quite frightening. Father-in-law's epitaph of the Q6s was; 'They were grand mineral engines them.'

Again, they were always dirty. So much so, that the preserved one on the North Yorkshire

Moors Railway doesn't look 'quite right' in its lined-out shiny black.

The Sentinel-Cammell Railcars

A fleet of nearly 90 of these attractive steam-driven railcars used to grace Great Northern, Great Central and North-Eastern low-revenue local passenger services from 1927 until 1948.

To all intents and purposes they were a saloon coach with a boiler 'up front' and were carried on two four-wheel bogies, one of which – the one underneath the boiler – was the powered one.

The seats had backs that could be moved to enable passengers to face the direction of travel; rather like the trams that hummed and rumbled through the city streets of yesteryear.

Their apple green and cream colour scheme made pleasant contrast to the otherwise normal, rather grimy, teak suburban coaching stock.

We schoolboys of those days loved any opportunity that presented itself of travelling in one, because of the almost uninterrupted views to the right and left through their many-windowed sides; even forward if the boiler end was at the back.

I suppose they must have been double-manned, otherwise who would have stoked the boiler when they were running in reverse i.e., boiler at the back?

The boilers were small and vertical; being contained within one of the end 'compartments'. I had the impression that firing was done with a hand shovel similar to the ones we used at home.

Judging by the apparent youthfulness of the drivers, they must have been in the charge of 'passed firemen'.

They had a characteristically rapid 'phut, phut, phut, phut, phut' type exhaust sound, due no doubt to the small but high-speed cylinders which drove the wheels of the 'power bogie' by means of gears and chains.

Their top speed, in calm weather, would be about 30 m.p.h. as they pursued their gentle paths, regardless of traffic building up behind them if ever they got on to a main line.

There were no concessions made towards streamlining in their design, merely a slab-sided coach with a dished roof and lots of window space. Just the job for the rustic scene, and journeys through the dales must have been lovely for those passengers not in a hurry.

Just occasionally one would be seen with a goods van tacked on at the back. This was the most they were capable of pulling when they had anything like their full complement of 30 passengers.

Sadly they were not a great financial or mechanical success and therefore had a relatively short life, but those of us who remember them do so with great affection.

Summary

These then have been my reasons for choosing the London and North Eastern Railway as the subject for my railway modelling.

It is the region that I know best. You might say it is the only region I know, but that would not be strictly true because I have seen, and travelled over, most of the country's lines at one time or another.

I know the attractions of the GWR, the Kings & Castles, the Dukedogs and the little 0–4–2 tanks, the Brown & Creams, the dainty little branch lines like the Chippenham to Calne when I was in the RAF down there.

I know what it is like to spend the night in Templecombe station waiting room, waiting for the first train out of Shillingstone at 6.30 in the morning; all because there was no local train to connect with the 8 p.m. from Waterloo.

I know the LMS main line from Euston to Blackpool and the 'Irish Mail' to Crewe.

I know the St Pancras to Leeds and the 'Pines Express' from Bournemouth to Leeds via the Somerset & Dorset.

But it was always to the North Eastern Railway that I returned; no Belpare fireboxes, no copper-topped chimneys, no Malachite green 'Spamcans', just Worsdells, Ravens and Gresleys – what more can a fellow want?

My two sons 'knew not' this period, except from my models and the accumulation of railway albums collected over the years. Hence the 'intrusion' into 'our' model railway of a limited amount of diesel power – limited in the respect that they had to 'belong' to this region. Let's face it, these are what the boys knew in their formative years just as the 'steamers' were what I knew in mine.

Having said that, I can still take much pleasure in the sight of a clean diesel locomotive and train, although some of the colour variants, these days, leave me speechless.

In the areas around Leeds in which I lived we were surrounded by railways. It was difficult to escape from them in any direction, even if one had wanted to – which one did not.

They were exciting things, they made exciting noises, they made exciting smells and they made exciting sights.

Leeds was the centre of a star from whence radiated railways in every direction. Here was the confluence of NER, GNR, LMR and LNWR.

'My' side of Leeds was NER of course; the Leeds to Selby Railway to be precise.

Model railways and I grew up together, Binns Road, Liverpool 13 was one of the first addresses I knew off by heart.

Life 'was' Hornby trains, Dinky toys and Meccano; nothing in life could compare. Remember the excitement of Christmas Eve? Remember waking up on Christmas morning to see what Santa had brought (hopefully from Binns Road)?

Clockwork came first, then electric. Remember the 20-volt a.c. engines with the electric bulbs in the middle of the smoke box doors? I never did fathom out the reason for their presence.

Remember the six-step transformer controllers where the full speed position was next to stop; as quick switch from one to the other activated the automatic reverse. Remember also the smell of a transformer burn-out through overheating?

Really, I suppose, those lovely old Hornby engines were nothing like the 'real thing', but then again, yes they were. Each of them encapsulated features that could be related to the real ones in some way, when we used our imaginations.

I would like to hazard a guess that people, in criticising Hornby trains as being nothing like the 'real thing', are in danger of overlooking the one most important ingredient that was abundantly present in those days, which was, namely – imagination!

Your oval of track, your lithographed tinplate bridge and station platform, your signal, your little 0–4–0 engine – was your British Isles, and you could travel the length and breadth of the country with those little trains, in your imagination. It was something akin to being in fairyland.

Perhaps too little is left to the imagination these days; we can have detail right down to the last rivet head reproduced with photographic

Hornby/Gresley A1 4-6-2 No. 2559 ascends Brussleton Bank over river Eyewater. 1986. (Photo KC)

precision. We can now model anything and everything regardless of scale. Look at the wonders of N gauge/2mm scale for example; I never cease to be amazed how they do it. But yet there is something missing.

In those days of yore, we stretched out on the floor with our tracks under beds, tables, wardrobes, sideboards, even on the lawn in summer. Very few of us had more than one engine and a couple of sidings at any one time, but most of us ran 'main lines' and travelled from city to city, day after day, in our imagination.

Then would come adolescence and the realisation that perhaps our trains were a little short on detail when compared with the 'real thing' as seen at the railway side, and so we would add a few details of our own (such as replacing the smokebox bulb with a black-painted cork).

We would also begin to hear of Bassett Lowke, Leeds Model Company, Milbro of Sheffield and others who made 'scale'-like models. We would also note their prices and run a mile. For instance a Hornby E220 Special LNER D49 Hunt Class 4-4-0 and tender cost 67s. 6d. (£3.37½) in 1939. The same thing from Milbro was about £20, and pro-rata for coaches and wagons, not to mention

brass track on wooden sleepers with cast chairs. I suppose this was when many of us had to prepare ourselves for getting a very well paid job when we grew up, or 'come into a fortune'.

In the meantime we did the best we could with what we had whilst we could, because now there was a war on and supplies were running out. This interim period was used by many of us for the purpose of fixing in our mind what railway region and period we were going to model.

In my case I wanted a model railway that said 'LNER', North Eastern Region, period 1935–1939.

Quite a simple object you might say, but it was enough to keep me 'on the right lines' and prevent me frittering away my slender resources on a lovely 'Castle' or 'Duchess' as they were introduced ready-to-run or in kit form after the war came to an end.

Lucky for me that I knew enough about 'the system' to form a 'vision' early on in life.

Feel sorry for those coming new to the hobby these days after buying their youngest his or her first train set for Christmas. Look at it through their eyes – a lifetime without any particular interest in railways maybe. Where does one start?

The field is limitless and almost as large as life itself when one considers the sheer number of products and systems that there are to choose from. It is of no use telling people to ask themselves what they want, because they simply will not know.

So what's wrong with telling them, simply, to enjoy the experience of 'playing trains' and buy whatever suits them? Let their imaginations run riot! Surely this is what most of the rest of us did in the first place. Just caution them about buying too much and getting indigestion, then perhaps they will find out:

(a) if model railways are for them.

(b) how to design a layout.

(c) how to get things going and keep them going.

That should be enough for starters. Time will tell if any particular preference is beginning to manifest itself, i.e., steam/electric/diesel, region, main line or branch line, 'continuous' or 'end-to-end' etc.

If they have looked after their equipment and have not 'modified' it too much, they will not find it too difficult to trade in when they want to update or make a change.

Most great layout/systems do not happen at one stroke. They develop as opportunities are recognised and exploited.

Model railways are fairly demanding on time, not to mention money and space. Also, one overlooks one's accountability to wife and family at one's peril.

As Sam Goldwyn is again quoted as having said – 'If at first you don't succeed, give up. It's no use making a damn fool of yourself.'

Taking that peculiar and questionable philosophy a stage further, one is bound to make mistakes and false starts. Learn to profit by the mistakes and not to be too reluctant to make a fresh start.

Think of we blokes who had to change from gauge '0' to '00', then from 3-rail to 2-rail etc.

Now the choice is between '00' and Scalefour gauge and, much as I admire all that Scalefour stands for, I am now too old and too committed to '00' for the change to be practicable.

There will not be much of what has been done that is not capable of being undone, but for the pocket's sake if for no other reason, do resist the temptation to change for change's sake.

Perhaps this is the real 'me' talking here, because, for myself, I try to build 'for keeps' and unless a new idea or product will fit in with what has been tried and proved successful over the years, I have to shelve it.

The same is true of 'the schedule'; to keep it on two sides of A4-size paper is very good discipline. Over the years, it has become a major item for consideration to come up with a new operating sequence that constitutes a real improvement on the existing ones, and which does not add unnecessary complexities to the system.

I therefore 'rest my case' and crave the reader's indulgence. We have been 'treading the waters' of decision making to some extent, and every man/woman must be accorded the right to make his/her own decisions, be they right or wrong in our eyes. Otherwise where would be the future for originality?

Furthermore

Useful Ideas and Worthwhile Tips

I offer the following ideas and tips for what they are worth, in the hope that they will help someone, somewhere, sometime. I make no claim to great originality, but it does seem a pity to me that many of us find novel ways of doing things quite independently of one another, and yet they never get written down. So I thought I would list a few of mine whilst the opportunity presents itself in the form of this dissertation.

1. Plasticine.

   Use as a filler for small cracks and gaps in joints. Takes paint perfectly. Apply with the tip of a find pointed craft knife and 'tamp' into place. Gently scrape away surplus and paint. Roll with finger, along a piece of card, into 1mm diameter lengths before applying. Will not blemish delicate paintwork.

2. Tin lids and small bottle tops.

   To save paint and thinners drying out in their containers whilst in use, pour very small quantities onto the tops of upturned lids and work from there instead of the paint tin. Heinz tomato ketchup bottle tops ideal for this.

3. 'Old-fashioned' pen nibs.

   For easier 'fine-lining' and lettering, try using a old-time 'school' pen and nib. I think it is still possible to buy them. Using the inverted ketchup bottle lid referred to above, to hold a mere 'meniscus' of 50/50 paint and thinners, dip just the point of the nib in the paint and apply to the workpiece. It is not possible to load the nib to give a line longer than 20mm without losing control of the thinness of the line, so much patience and endurance is called for, but the results are good.

   Obviously a 'fine' nib will create a finer line than a 'broad' nib.

   Note that use of enamel paints, suitably thinned, is quite practicable; try it.

   Lining around awkward shapes is best done by 'spotting' with the nib rather than 'drawing'.

   As the lining process tends to take up a lot of time, the paint will become too thick in a rather short time, so keep an eye-dropper handy with which to drop a minute amount of thinners on the edge of the 'meniscus' of paint, as and when required. Keep a supply of small tissues handy on which to wipe the nib from time to time.

4. Eye-droppers.

   The type of eye-dropper that I have in mind comes with the small bottles of nasal inhaler drops. Fenox is the name of one make. These are very useful for dispensing very small quantities of many liquids, such as paint thinners, liquid fluxes, oils etc.

5. Brush rests.

   What to do with brushes when you need a rest? – use something heavy with a hole down the middle to place them in, such as a coil of solder.

6. Cleaning and conditioning of brushes.

   As with the rest of one's tools, brushes last longer and work better when kept in good condition.

   Requirements – 3 jam jars containing:

   (a) Brush restorer (Polyclens, Nitromors etc.) about ½″ depth.

   (b) Water + washing-up liquid – full.

   (c) Fabric conditioner (Comfort, Lenor etc.) ½ full.

   Method – dip brushes, successively, in jars (1), (2) and (3) and wipe between each.

   Replenish jar (2) fairly frequently because residual brush restorer tends to make wash-up liquid go stringy.

   This 'discipline', if rigorously observed, will keep bristles clean and pliable and also help to maintain their shape. A real money-saver.

7. A hardwood 'pencil'.
   Sharpen a piece of 5mm hardwood dowelling into a 'pencil' point, and use to 'prise' or 'poke' bits of glue or excess paint from delicate surfaces likely to show up scratch marks.

8. Looking after superglue.
   Whatever you do with this stuff, it will beat you in the end, but try and delay the need to spend money more often than necessary on replacements by adopting the following 'disciplines':

   (1) Never, repeat never, let the bottle (or tube) lie flat, always keep it nozzle up, in something like a 35mm film can.

   (2) Maintain a 1-inch panel pin in the nozzle and do not replace the cap, even if this means using a pair of pliers to remove the pin.

   (3) Rather than risk flooding a workpiece with superglue, simply dispense a drop on to a ketchup lid and apply with a knife point where needed.

   (4) Immediately the glue is dispensed, stand the dispenser upright – it doesn't matter about putting the pin back in immediately, in fact a slight delay will allow the glue to return to the bottom of the nozzle before it hardens.

   (5) Wipe the top of the nozzle before replacing the pin and, if there seems to be a build-up of glue in the hole, clear it with an old $\frac{1}{16}''$ drill.

   (6) If you have used a knife blade to apply the glue, just give it a few strokes on a sharpening stone to clean off.

   With a bit of luck you might get to use up all the glue in the bottle before it gums itself up, thus saving lots of useful money at the glue maker's expense. Remember what they used to say about Colman's Mustard? 'Mr Colman didn't make his money from the mustard people ate, but from what they left upon their plate.' So don't give 'em 'money on a plate'.

   The main thing is to treat your glue dispensers as you do your favourite brushes – keep them clean, clear and vertical.

9. Most used colours.
   Black, white, grey, red, yellow, brown, green, flesh, blue.

10. Economical use of Evostik.

I always use the small tubes of Evostik – when I can persuade the local shop that I don't want it for glue sniffing, although I must in fact sniff quite a lot of it.

I find that I can control the flow from the small tubes better than I can from the large tubes and tins, but there are one or two prior provisions that can be made to assist its successful and economical use:

(1) As with superglue, keep the tube vertical in a small glass jar and keep the jar near to hand when using.

(2) Squeeze gently, but from the bottom only and gradually flatten the lower part of the tube, without twisting or kinking it. If you fold the tube as you go along, it will get lost in the jar as it gets shorter.

(3) By keeping the tube vertical when not in use, and provided you have not squeezed it too hard, the glue will drop back into the tube rather than continue to ooze out.

(4) Wipe the nozzle frequently.

(5) Make use of a 1-inch panel pin as a stopper when not in use.

11. Assembling Iain Kirk plastic bogies.
    I have heard a number of criticisms of Iain Kirk bogies not being up to the work they have to do, and yet I have had rakes of coaches running satisfactorily on them for years.

    Perhaps the secret is to use Evostik (small tubes remember) and make up the bogies before commencing the rest of a kit.

    In this way the glue will have a few days (weeks?) to set solid. Even stick in the brass bearing cups with Evostik.

    Need I mention the need to ensure the wheel axles run at right angles to the track?

    Check the assembled bogies on a small mirror to make certain all wheels are touching, in other words check the assembly is square. If it isn't, try giving it a gentle twist to 'even up'.

12. Maintenance of craft knife blades.
    I only seem to use three types of blade – the sharp pointed one, the one like an angled chisel and the Stanley knife type. However, as they do not remain sharp forever, a 6 × 2 inch combination stone (smooth one side, rough the other) makes a good investment. Keep it always to hand to freshen up tired edges.

13. Plasticard and general plastic cutting.

Rather than waste away your precious knife edges, try using the reverse side as a 'scraper'.

'Scrape' away until you have scored a line deep enough to allow bending and breaking away to take place.

14. Painting lots of 'little people'

Roll out ½″ diameter lengths of Plasticine (not Blu-tack because it sticks to the models) and cut them into 3-inch pieces. Press the rolls on to your work surface and then, taking each 'little person' in turn, press their feet into the Plasticine, just far enough to secure them. And there you have it – paint away in comfort. You can even lift up your roll of 'peopled-Plasticine' to make painting easier if you wish.

When you have painted the top parts, turn the people over head first into the Plasticine and paint the feet.

15. Airbrush painting.

If ever cleanliness and a dust-free atmosphere were critical, then this is it.

It helps if the atmosphere is warm because the paint dries quicker and doesn't form moisture bubbles, as it tends to do if the paint is colder (or warmer) than the surrounding air. Obtain a pair of discarded, but washed, ladies' tights and cut off a couple of inches. Divide this into two.

One piece of tight, thus formed, becomes a filter through which to strain your paint or varnish into the paint jars or reservoirs. Gets rid of all the little bits.

16. Making a paint stirrer for the mini-drill.

If I can do it so can you. No great engineering experience necessary.

Obtain a 2½″ length of ⅛″ brass rod and, holding it in the vice, cut a ⅛″deep slot in one end with a mini-hacksaw. Then cut a piece of nickel silver (or brass) sheet approximately ¾″ long × ¼″ wide and solder the centre into the slot. With a small grindstone in the mini-drill, round off the ends and grind down the centre until it is flush with the end of the rod.

Finally, put a 'twist' into the rounded ends after the style of a aircraft propeller, and there you have it, a paint-'paddle'-cum-stirrer.

Once you have made this 'paddle' never, ever again, shake your paint tins. In this way you will maintain your paint tin lids and edges clean and free from paint build-up.

To clean the paddle after use, keep a small jar of white spirit handy, and simply operate the paddle in it until it 'comes clean', then wipe dry with a tissue.

17. Warming paint tins and paint jars before using.

Don't larf, but what's wrong with putting them in your trouser pocket for five minutes? Just make sure the lids are on tightly. It's a bit cold at first in winter, but soon warms up.

Don't forget they are there however, or at least don't hold me responsible if you do. These are only suggestions you know.

18. Use of scissors in modelling.

I am the possessor of two pairs of quality Wilkinson scissors; a general household pair and a needlework pair with very fine points.

I have also managed to come across a Wilkinsons Scissor Sharpener, with which I can maintain a good edge.

The large pair will cut most of the normal-gauge metal sheets we railway modellers use, as well as plastics and fabrics, especially if they have been 'scored' first. I wouldn't be without them.

19. A glass cradle.

Use a large pickle jar (140 × 90mm) as a loco/coach cradle. Place an inch or so of foam padding at the bottom to protect delicate lamps and couplings.

This way, you can work on, or paint, the front (or rear) of a loco, or a coach end, using the jar to keep the item vertical and steady.

20. Making your own metal strip.

Or how to make narrow metal strip without cutting from sheet metal.

Take a length of single-core wire, not steel, and remove the plastic sheathing.

Straighten and lay the bare wire on a heavy metal surface, like a bench vice, and tap with a flat-head hammer until the wire is flat and about the width you want. It doesn't take long. Practice will make perfect. Obviously the width of the strip will primarily depend on the gauge of the wire, but if you want very thin strip then tap a little more with the hammer.

21. The need for a vacuum cleaner.

Nearly everything a modeller does makes dust of some sort. Sawdust, metal dust, tobacco dust, airborne dust and cobwebs. Just moving about creates dust crying out for a cylinder-type vacuum cleaner to remove it.

No matter how we try to 'clean up as we go', dust will always beat us and dirty up our treasures with its specks.

Assist your vacuum cleaner with (a) a very soft camel-hair brush and (b) a soft 1-inch paintbrush.

Use the brushes to flick away small specks and to loosen dust around delicate parts, so that, for example, if any of your 'little people' have come unstuck then at least you will have a chance to lift them out of the way before they get sucked into the vacuum tube.

Think of the times you sprinkle scatter material on your scenery, or ballast a new length of track. With care, you can vacuum the surplus into a clean bag/cylinder, and re-use it.

After 30 years or so you will be pleased you bought one. You can also use it on the car.

22. The value of a finishing list.

When you buy a kit, or decide to build something 'from scratch', I imagine you will want to lay out all the bits and pieces and check the instructions before you commence construction. You may even do a 'dry run'.

In other words you want to make sure that you have all the parts you are going to need, and the knowledge of how to fit them together and in what order, rather than find out later that something is missing, or you have forgotten to fit an important bit.

This is a good discipline, or method; a 'starting list' in fact. So, as the final addition to this list of ideas and tips, may I recommend that you consider the importance of making out a 'finishing list' as you approach the end of a piece of work? Really it is the opposite of the 'starting list' you had at the beginning.

As one comes near to finishing construction, lots of ' things to be done' come to mind that are not necessarily in the instructions but are nevertheless very important to the finished product.

Now, I suggest, is the time to keep a notepad handy and write down these items before one forgets them.

Before long it may become quite lengthy and include such things as 'remember to paint

the chassis before fitting the wheels', or 'solder on the lamp irons before painting', or 'remember to paint the black and white line around the buffer beam before varnishing'.

There is a very real danger that one will say 'oh, I will do that later' – and it never ever gets done, perhaps to the detriment of an otherwise first-class piece of work.

There is a real art in 'finishing' a job completely and it takes some working at. It also takes time when one's inclination is to get on with something else, but years after, when all the trials and tribulations are over, one is glad one made the effort to 'finish off the job'.

As a parting word on this subject, I am reminded of a prayer that Sir Francis Drake is purported to have offered on the eve of the Spanish Armada, '. . . when Thou givest to Thy servants to endeavour any great matter, grant us to know that it is not the beginning but the continuing of the same unto the end, until it be thoroughly finished, which yieldeth the true glory . . .'

Modelling the LNER 'Coronation' Train

In 1991 I became intrigued by advertisements in the modelling press by an organisation calling itself 'Mailcoach'.

The adverts were announcing the introduction of their plastic kits to make up into replicas of the pre-World War II LNER 'Silver Jubilee' and 'Coronation' coaches.

South-west corner of layout at Aberford, showing 'Coronation' train being loaded in to storage cassette. (Photo KC)

The only snag, as far as I could see, was that there was no mention of the Coronation's Observation Coach, so I decided to wait until there was.

Sure enough, in 1992, it appeared in their lists, so I ordered one from them.

This, I thought, was just what I had been waiting for all these years and I could, at long last, see the 'end of the line' as far as my shopping list for LNER was concerned. If the observation coach was 'as required', then I could go ahead and make myself a 'Coronation' train to go behind my Hornby A4 'Seagull'.

The kit duly arrived in its little postal jiffy bag after a short wait, and I soon had the contents laid out in front of me.

No secret was made of the fact that Ian Kirk's manufactury was involved, but that was all to the good as far as I was concerned. The main departure from normal practice was that the coach sides were made from clear, yes clear, plastic. This was the result of a high-level decision to try and achieve the 'flush' glazing associated with the sheet metal coach bodies on the real thing. One thing that was very certain, was that those windows had to be kept scratch-free at all times, so much care was to be called for. Now, there is a lot of stainless steel lining to be reproduced on the 'Coronation' coaches, and my question to myself was, could I do it with Humbrol silver? I wasn't sure at that stage, but made a start on the construction nevertheless.

My thoughts on the subject were, if I couldn't achieve a satisfactory finish on the most important part of the train – the observation coach – then I would go no further as far as the remaining coaches were concerned.

My first job was to assemble the bogies – with Evostik – and let them harden; a fairly straightforward task.

Next came the floor, interior seats and partitions, which I painted in the recommended colours: green carpet, green swivel armchairs and white partitions; before gluing them carefully in place in relation to where the windows were to be.

Then came 'the test', could I paint the sides carefully enough to avoid getting any onto the windows?

Thankfully, I had some good masking tape, and first cut squares to fit over the window frames, then a strip to mask the lower half. The upper half is painted Marlborough Blue – a very pale blue arrived at by mixing drops of Garter Blue into a tin of satin white until the right shade is achieved. I sprayed this on with the airbrush and 'saw that it was good'.

Then I cut another length of masking tape to cover the entire upper half, removed the lower half masking and sprayed it Garter Blue. This also came good, and when I judged it to have dried thoroughly (24 hours) I removed all the masking tape. Success! The windows were perfectly clean.

My final 'act' was to replace the masking tape on the windows and give the whole side two sprays of satin varnish.

Having satisfied myself thus far, I turned to the inside face of the sides and brush painted them the recommended Pale Green, in the same proportions as the Marlborough Blue mix, and then picked out the window frames in Mid-Brown. This detail shows up in some of the interior photographs I have in my albums.

I then got out my trusted ketchup lid, along with my school pen and nib, and placed on it a couple of drops of silver paint ready for the silver lining-ing.

Luckily, for most of us, the kits' doors and windows have been given a certain amount of raised edging which makes lining easier, so this was no real problem. However, I took the silver lining right to the very edges of the window panes and that occupied a lot of time. The toplights had to be picked out also, on all faces. It needed careful scrutiny at all times to make sure nothing had been missed.

The real test was the waist line and the lower body line, because too much paint on the nib would cause it to run.

There is no way that a pen nib can draw a continuous paint line for more than an inch at a time, and I had to be very careful when recharging the nib and to make sure the paint was sufficiently fluid.

This is where the eye- (or nose-) dropper comes in with the thinners; a single drop every five minutes or so on the edge of the paint meniscus seems to be sufficient. It is advisable to wipe the tip of the nib on a tissue before each recharge.

It is also useful to fix the coach sides, with a small piece of plasticine at each end, to a clean piece of card before commencing the lining. It

'Beaver-tail' Observation Coach of 'Coronation' train on up-mainline passing East Garforth goods yard. 1993.
(Photo KC)

will allow for a ruler to be used to guide the pen, but do remember only to allow paint on to the lower ⅛″ of the nib.

Remember also that I am no Rembrandt, and what is most important when it comes to lining, is to get the lines the same width and the same constancy of colour all along. That is why I use a pen nib more than, say a '00' brush.

I also realise that there must be better ways of doing it and that there are many who can do a better job of it than I can, but what I do know is that there are a lot of 'liners' who have jibbed at lining a set of these 'Coronation' coaches. So, once again, it was a job 'that had to be done', and I found a way that I could do it.

What I would like to see is a transfer producer bring out some 'chromium'-cum-stainless steel linings in ¼mm and ½mm; the 'market' needs them. There are two good reasons for this, namely (a) silver paint only 'simulates' chrome lining and (b) silver paint tends to run when sprayed with varnish, which is ruinous and causes much 'touching up' to take place.

Luckily for all of us, the firm of Woodhead have produced some 'chrome'-cum-stainless steel lettering and numbering masterpieces in the way of

press-on transfers for the 'Coronation' and the 'Silver Jubilee' coach sets. Without them, for me, the job would have been impossible to complete.

They need much care in their application, so don't stint yourself. Buy two sets at a time rather than one. In fact, for the whole set of 'Coronation' coaches I 'dipped into' no less than four sets of transfers. Blow the expense!

The next item in the construction of the observation coach is, possibly, the most critical to the success of the venture, i.e., the curved, and sloping, rear end of the coach.

It is produced, like the sides, in clear plastic, and needs to be thought about very carefully:
1. Does it fit?
2. How much 'flash' needs to be removed to make it fit?
3. How is it going to 'fair in' with the sides?
4. How is it going to 'fair in' with the roof?
5. How is it going to 'fair in' with the buffer beam?

There must be no sharp edges, everything must be rounded off, as per the 'Bugatti' racing car influence on Sir Nigel.

This is where the judicious use of the tiny

rolled lengths of plasticine, that I talked about earlier, come into their own to fill in gaps at joints. Press them well in with a 'sharpened' length of dowelling rod, and smooth over with a small brush loaded with paint thinners (not cellulose!).

Use Evostik as the adhesive, but be careful not to allow it on to the windows.

When satisfied that the thing is going to fit, put to one side and consider that, on the 'real thing', there is what can best be described as a 'window ledge' stretching across the width of the coach behind the rear-end window, about 2 feet deep from front to back, and raised above floor level to the level of the lower edge of the bowed window.

This is not provided for in the kit, but can be made simply from a piece of plasticard. There will have to be a vertical piece made to act as support in the form of 'cupboard doors'. I suggest these items be painted a pale brown to simulate light oak panelling or whatever.

I picked this detail up from one of the photographs I saw.

Mention of 'not provided for in the kit' reminds me that the plastic buffer heads, as provided, are very poor and should be discarded in favour of metal ones. I was able, with a bit of jiggery-pokery, to adapt a pair of sprung buffers to fit, and work, within the confines of the kit's moulded buffer 'shanks' – at the 'observation' end. The other end just has straightforward non-working metal replacement buffer heads inserted into the shanks, but keep the shanks on the short side to allow close coupling.

Other small items not provided are, (1) steam heating pipe, (2) vacuum brake pipe, (3) scale screw coupling, (4) two rear lamps and 'lamp irons'. All these items show up very prominently on the photographs. (Ref: illustrations in *East Coast Pacifics At Work*, by P. N. Townend, pub. Ian Allen; and 'A History of the LNER', volume 2, *The Age of the Steamliners, 1934–39*, by Michael R. Bonavia, pub. Allen & Unwin.)

Mentioning rear lamps and loco lamps in general, I always 'go' for the Kenline series with their tiny 'brilliants'.

With a tiny drill held in a pin vice, it is possible to drill through the small 'stem' on the upper part of the lamps, from front to back, and insert a short length of 'tinned' 5-amp fuse wire to form into a

'carrying handle' loop, using low-melt solder to join the ends together. It's a bit fiddly, but the results are worthwhile; try it. Scrape the lens sockets clean of paint before supergluing in the 'brilliants' and apply the glue with a knife tip.

Loco lamps, if not securely mounted, tend to come off and get lost in the track surrounds, never to be seen again. In an effort to avoid this happening, carefully low-melt solder them to their lamp irons and either (a) solder the lamp irons into holes drilled in the metal or (b) superglue them into holes drilled in the plastic, but do be careful with them because they are so tiny and time-consuming to prepare. Having said that, loco and coach lamps were so much a necessary part of railway life that their presence is quite critical.

Mounting the bogies

Mailcoach, bless them, have endowed the undersides of the coach floors with much detail in the way of struts and bracing appropriate to the 'real thing', but it does tend to get in the way of the wheel flanges on curves of less than 6ft radius (of which I have more than my fair share). There's only one thing for it and that is to grind off the bits that get in the way. They will not be seen anyway, plus they will be painted black.

I am also not happy about the central 'boss' mounting assembly, so I prefer to 'heat-melt' a $\frac{1}{2}''$ steel rivetting washer on to the base of the bogie boss underneath the coach, and smooth off the corresponding area on the top face of the bogie. This has the beneficial effect of (a) cutting down unwanted side-to-side 'wobble' whilst the coach is on the move and, (b) raising the coach body a shade higher over the wheels. I also place a small quantity of petroleum jelly between the bogie and the steel washer as a form of lubricating grease.

Before fitting the roof

Before fitting the roof in place, consider adding some 'passengers'. The observation coach was the first time I had tried this and I have been very pleased with the effect.

I also noticed, from the aforementioned photographs, that there is an interior handrail, running about halfway up the windows. On the left-hand side of the coach ('beaver-tail' to the right), the rail commences along the window next to the door and continues until the final 'sloping' panel of the 'beaver-tail', which is left plain. On the right-hand side the rail commences after the 'mail compartment' and continues as far as the 'beaver-tail', which is left plain again.

Finally, check that all the passengers and their seats are well and truly glued in position – and also the other bits and pieces such as partition walls and corner seat.

When satisfied, apply the Evostik to the roof and side edges and press together.

The beauty of Evostik is that you can take the roof off again, if you have to, without too much disfigurement.

It is now that some judicious sanding is going to be needed i.e., the joint between the white plastic roof piece and the clear plastic of the 'beaver-tail' portion requires to appear seamless.

Any gaps between roof pieces and body shell should now be filled with rolled plasticine and smoothed over.

The main roof is recommended to be painted a light grey; remembering that within a couple of weeks it would turn black in 'real life'. The edges of the 'beaver-tail' window panels need to be picked out carefully in silver.

The corridor gangway to be painted black.

Transfers

Refer to photographs for accurate positioning and remember that the numbers go to the right side and LNER to the left, as you look at the coach.

The whole word 'Coronation', across the rear end of the 'beaver-tail', does fit if you are very careful, so stick the coach in your large pickle jar to hold it steady, and have a go. Faint heart ne'er won fair maid.

The Woodhead transfers are not of the easiest to deal with and there seem to be no short-cuts, but they are excellent in all other respects. The numbers are, perhaps, the most tricky to apply, especially when they have to be applied individually.

When satisfied, one or two light sprays of satin varnish should secure them, but do remember to shield the windows again.

The rest of the 'Coronation' train

There were eight coaches altogether plus the 'beaver-tail' comprising the 'Coronation' trains,

but as my layout is not quite large enough I compromised with six.

The 'cute' innovation here is the use of 'articulation' in the centre of pairs of coaches, which means balancing the ends of two adjacent coaches on one bogie, thus utilising three bogies for two coaches instead of four.

No great problem here except for the gap between the coach ends. The gap has to be long enough to keep the corners of the coach ends from touching each other ('binding') when negotiating the less-than-scale-like curves of the model railway. This calls for the bogie mounting holes for the 'spigots' on the coach ends to be slightly elongated towards the couplings.

When the ideal position is ascertained, may I suggest that the newly positioned holes be 'bushed' with a short length of ⅛″-bore brass tubing, firmly glued in place?

To be strictly accurate, there should be a flexible fabric 'fairing' fitted between all coach ends to assist airflow. I tried all sorts of ways of effecting this desirable feature but, no matter what I tried, the coaches became derailed on curves of less than 6ft radius due to the resistance of the fairing material. I very much regret to say that I have had to forego these desirable details – and it hurts! So, until some one comes along with some gossamer-thin material, my 'Coronation' train will have to remain 'fairing-less'.

For the rest of the coaches, as with the 'Observation Coach', I made up the bogies first and set them to one side to dry and harden. I have had no running problems with them whatsoever and they are beautifully solid.

The coaches went together quite straightforwardly; the only slight problems were the occasional gaps between roof and sides, and roof and ends, but these were filled with Plasticine and have painted up perfectly well.

By the time they are all assembled I became quite proficient at making seats and tables; there are dozens of them. I also had to paint about sixty seated passengers, and provide them with things like newspapers and drinking glasses. Well, it all adds variety does it not?

Couplings

For appearances' sake I wanted to couple the coaches as closely together as the prototype but circumstances militated against me, namely, radius of curves insufficient and rather steep downhill gradients, both of which tend to create buffer-locking problems.

At this stage in the construction of the train, Christmas was drawing near and I was going to be needing time for things unconnected with the railway, so I settled for modified tension-lock (Hornby) couplings until I could come up with something better.

Now commenced a period of trial-and-error adjustment, until the day came when I could journey the train around the layout, in any direction, without derailments occurring due to buffer lock or 'binding' of the coach ends. The coaches are very much closer together than any of my others had ever been, so much so that I have subsequently gone through most of the rest of my rolling stock and brought them closer together in a similar way.

The 'Coronation' Engine

I had long since decided that I wanted A4 No. 4489 *Dominion of Canada*, to haul my 'Coronation' train, if I was ever to have one, so proceedings were taken to bring this to effect, as follows:

1. I already had the Hornby valanced A4 'Seagull', closely coupled to the tender, Jackson wheels on the front bogie, together with vacuum pipe, train heating pipe, screw coupling, steel buffer heads, lamp irons and lamps. I had also incorporated what I call 'bogie side-play limiters' which have the effect of steering the loco into curves and reducing 'hunting' from side to side on straight track. In other words I had a loco in first-class running and electrical condition, which was good.

2. 'The Bell', was the item that bothered me most, but 'it had to be done', so I did it.

    Aided by my bench-mounted Black & Decker drill and a 'pin' from an old-type 5-amp plug, for the first time in my life I 'turned' that pin into a perfect little scale-size bell – using my 'East Coast Pacifics at Work' book as benchside aide-memoire. It is only 4mm long but even has a clapper and, what is just as important, it hangs in a correctly detailed and proportioned 'cradle'. I am really proud of it, even if it doesn't clang!

3. Thanks to the Woodhead transfers, I had a supply of 'stainless steel' LNER letters and numbers, but first I had to remove the Hornby ones, and they don't half stick 'em on. I didn't want a major repaint job on my hands, so I very carefully erased them with a glass fibre brush and gently rubbed down the surrounding paintwork. There were slight traces of letters and numbers left but this helped subsequent positioning of the new transfers, but first I masked off locomotive and tender and gave a couple of sprays of Garter Blue. This was highly effective and it wasn't long before the new letters and numbers were in place, including the No. 4489 between the buffers. Finally the new nameplate was added and the whole sprayed with two coats of satin varnish.

    Cab window frames, handrails etc., were picked out in silver after the varnishing, rather than risk the silver 'running'.

All in all then, a very satisfying conclusion to 14 weeks' work and my sincere compliments to Mailcoach for having had the courage to produce the kits.

Need I add that the 'Coronation' train is 'pride of fleet' on the Aberford, Barrowby and East Garforth Railway, and inspires the picnicking trainspotters, crowding the vantage viewing points, temporarily to cease their munchings in respectful admiration as the train streaks past them.

Day-by-Day Model Locomotive Maintenance

Way back on page 22 I quoted from a book on gardening where it said 'a garden should be rather small, 'else you'll have no fun at all.'

Now, the last thing I would wish to imply is that you will get no fun at all from maintaining your stock; it's just that the more of it you have, the more of it there is to look after and it takes time.

I am going to assume that you are like most of the rest of us, in that you do not have unlimited access to uncountable wealth.

Whilst I am at it, assuming I mean, I am also going to assume that you are again like most of the rest of us, in that you do not have the benefit of unlimited time to do with what you will.

So I am back on my old hobby horse of 'making the best use of time' by developing some sort of a method when it comes to looking after all our bits and pieces.

F'rinstance, I find the best time to overhaul an engine, or an item of rolling stock, is when it comes in at the end of its 'journey'. It is then that whatever needs doing is at the forefront of my mind.

If I leave it until that item is due to be used again, I may either forget, or I may be a bit pushed for time, with the result that it doesn't get done at all.

In other words, 'there's no time like the present', so get out your little craft knife and scrape the lumps of whatever it is from the treads of your wheels, refix that lamp, adjust a coupling, touch up a scratch mark etc., so that, when next you come to use the item there it is – all ready to go.

Of course there will be a bit more to it than that, but I think you will have got the message by now.

Some hints for improved running on RTRs

Howling motors

- or is it only me that gets this phenomena? Any which way it usually indicates that one or other of the motor shaft bearings needs a drop of oil on it. Just be careful not to get any on to the carbon brushes or commutator.

The most common motor-type for this kind of noise, on my layout, seems to be the 'ringfield'.

Motors 'going slow'

This is, sadly, an indication that a new armature is going to be needed shortly. This seems to be a particular problem with the early Mainline motors and the only answer, I'm afraid, is to write to the makers and ask for a replacement. You'll have to pay for it of course. Lima and Hornby armatures can usually be obtained, and fitted, at local stockists – if they have the 'approved' boxes of spares. 'Quality' motors such as the old MRRC & Bulldog together with the newer Mashima and Sagami don't seem to have this problem, but think twice about the 'Coreless' motors if, like me, you have 'compensated closed loop feedback' type of controllers. These expensive motors can come to

a rapid demise unless you use the more traditional type of controller.

Improving Current Collection on motor units with traction tyres

It's a bit fiddly, but pays rich dividends in smooth running ever after, if you fit nickel silver current collector wires to all non-tyred wheel treads.

I emphasise wheel treads as distinct from wheel-backs, for the simple reason that the wires will help keep the wheel treads clean. Now there is no need to go mad and fit heavy-gauge wires; nice thin ones about 30 swg seem to do the trick quite nicely.

Taking a typical Hornby steam outline like the LNER 'Flying Scotsman', go about it as follows:
1. Remove loco chassis from its body and note that, on one side of the chassis, there are two vertical phosphor bronze collectors with wires going to the loco-to-tender coupling. They will be on the same side as the tyred-wheels of the tender drive unit.

   It is the other side to which I want you to give your attention, at this stage, and eventually fit a second set of collectors.

   This other side could be called the 'live' side, because the wheels and axles take current from the rails and pass it through the metal parts of the chassis on to the motor, or at least they are supposed to.

   My contention is that this does not always happen, hence the need for the extra pick-ups.
2. Take a length of 26–30 swg wire, form a tiny circle at one end and, with the soldering iron, fill it in with a small blob of solder.
3. Now measure the wire along the top faces of the wheel treads from the leading driving wheel to the rearmost driving wheel, allowing about ½ an inch at each end to 'curve' down to the contours of the wheels, then, when satisfied you have the length about right, cut the wire and form yet another tiny circle at the second end and fill it with solder. This is to be your pick-up.
4. What you have to do now is to mount it securely so as to press gently, but positively, on the wheel treads.

   This is sometimes easier said than done because the kind of metal Hornby's use for the chassis does not take solder, so any kind of securing device will have to be 'anchored' in some of the plastic fittings on the top of the chassis.

I tend to use more of the same wire that I made the pick-up from and gently 'heat sink' it into a conveniently placed bit of plastic with a soldering iron. Don't overdo the heat, and as soon as the wire starts to go into the plastic remove the iron. A couple of seconds wait and the plastic will harden around the wire giving a firm mounting – try it. If you don't get it in just the right position first go, simply apply the iron gently again and adjust.

5. It is not possible to say exactly what shape the pick-up securing device will take, because its shape depends entirely on where it is to be anchored. Look at it this way; all it has to do is to hold the pick-up in contact with the wheel treads. The pick-up has to be flexible enough to 'give' with the movement of the wheels, so anything rigid will be out of the question.

6. I now suggest drilling a short ⅛″ diameter hole in the chassis in which to introduce a small self-tapping screw.

The idea of this is to gain a positive electrical entry into the chassis metal, via the screw.

7. The screw head should now be 'tinned', because to it will be soldered two lengths of lightweight flexible insulated wire. One, about 2 inches long, will be (lightly) soldered to the pick-up. The second, about 9 inches in length, will extend through the loco firebox and into the tender, where it will eventually be soldered to the 'live' terminal of the motor. But more of that later.

8. The time has now arrived to 'tweak' the solder-blobbed contact ends of the pick-up to ensure that they bear, continuously, on to the wheel treads both forwards and in reverse, and also when the wheels move up and down in their bearings. I find that a pair of sharp-nosed pliers do this 'tweaking' best.

Another reason for using light-gauge wire is that too much pick-up resistance will inhibit the lovely free movement of the wheels.

9. Now look at the loco body and see if there is a hole through the firebox into the cab somewhere. If there isn't, then drill a ⅛″ hole just underneath the firebox door.

This is to pass the 9-inch wire through on its way to the tender, just check to see that the hole you are about to drill will not cause the wire to be trapped by the chassis. If it seems likely to then drill the hole in a different position.

10. Fit the chassis and the body together again; first guiding the 9-inch wire through the hole 'near' the firebox door. Replace any body-securing screws.

11. It is not intended that the 9-inch wire should be permanently connected to the motor drive in the tender, but rather that it should be 'interrupted' at a point about 2 inches from the firebox. It is at this stage that a half-inch length of 1⁄16″ brass tubing will come in handy, to solder the wire from the firebox to. Now find a half-inch length of wire or rod that will give a fairly tight fit into the brass tube. To the end of this half-inch rod solder the spare bit of wire just cut off the nine inch length.

This then is the 'interruption' that I referred to earlier. It is obviously going to be necessary when it is required to separate the loco and tender.

12. The Tender.
Using a small screwdriver, gently prise off the tender superstructure from the chassis and place to one side.

Turn the chassis so that the non-tyred wheels are facing you.

13. Using another length of 25–30 swg nickel silver (or phosphor bronze)wire, 'create' another pick-up for the 'outside' wheels by first forming a tiny circle to be filled with solder. Then measure along the top of the wheel treads to the wheel at the opposite end, allowing for a 5mm downwards curve at each end plus a further 4mm for the 'tiny circle'. Cut the wire and form the circle.

14. As with the loco chassis, somewhere has to be found to anchor the pick-up support. Whilst it is a bit 'hairy', there are one or two points near the base of the motors where there is some substantial plastic, suitable for 'heat sinking' a couple of pre-tinned Bambi staples. Once these are in position, it is a fairly simple matter to 'angle' the pick-up wire so as to allow it to be spot soldered to the staples.

15. Once again the time as come to 'tweak' the

end circles of the pick-ups to ensure continuous contact with the wheel treads.

16. Taking a 3-inch length of lightweight insulated wire, solder one end to the pick-up and the other end to the unattached end of what was left of the 9-inch wire from the loco. Then solder the joined up wires to the chassis terminal tag on the motor, if there is one. If not, then very carefully spot solder to the appropriate carbon brush spring retaining arm on the motor.

17. Now guide the length of the 9-inch wire round the side of the motor, using small pieces of plasticine, until it will come out on to the footplate alongside the wire from the insulated motor terminal.

18. 'Plug' the tender wire into the brass tube of the loco wire and couple the loco to the tender.

    Check that the wire between tender and loco is just long enough to be flexible. If it is tight in anyway it will restrict flexibility between loco and tender. On the other hand, if it is too long it may push the tender out of alignment with the loco.

    If you have got it right, congratulations, the job is finished apart from painting the wire some sort of neutral colour to camouflage it.

19. The time has now come for track testing – what could possibly go wrong? Let me suggest a few things:

(a) Loco driving wheels don't go round – tension of pick-ups too strong so ease them off a shade.

(b) Short circuit light comes on at the controller – check to see if you have connected the tender wire to the wrong brush on the motor. If that isn't the cause, then trace the 9-inch wire right back to the self-tapping screw on the loco chassis to see if some part of the wire has become 'bared' and is touching some of the wiring on the 'insulated' side of the loco or tender.

(c) Tender derails on corners – wire too short.

(d) Tender, or loco, derails on the straights – wire too long and is creating a conflicting 'bias' between loco and tender. This may also happen if the wire is too heavy gauge.

20. This procedure can be adapted to all known (to me) types of tender drive locomotives with traction tyres; it will just be a case of making adjustments according to the designs of the models.

It can also be applied to Diesel outline power units to similar advantage, because the main object of the exercise is to increase the number of power pick-up points and thus do away with those annoying hesitations due to track irregularities, dirt on the rails and/or dirt on the wheel-treads. Think about it.

Electronic track cleaners even recommend clean wheels and track, and who am I to disagree?

Strange as it may seem, even Bachmann/Mainline locos respond well to at least one extra wheel-tread pick-up per side as I found to my advantage recently. Just a trace of oil on one axle can play havoc with current conductivity when the current has to be passed through the frame, especially on starting.

So, in other words, slow starts and slow running become very much more certain. Need I say more?

Weighting of locomotives and power units

To me, one of the joys of the beautiful little tyre-assisted traction units available to us today, is the comparative lightness of the chassis and superstructure of the locomotives, be they steam outline or diesel; gone are the days when all the neighbourhood's lights went dim when I chose to run a long heavy train. The little tyres are to thank for it, and long may they continue.

I know that this renders me a heretic in the eyes of many, but I was always a nonconformist when it came to adopting majority opinions. However, even the best of the tyre-assisted traction units benefit from a modicum of judiciously-placed lumps of lead, for example:

1. Tender drives – there is usually a space of about 20 × 10mm behind the motor where one or two carefully cut pieces of lead sheet can be secured. The locomotives do not need weighting very much at all.

2. Diesel outlines – I know there is usually a hefty piece of iron in the centre of the chassis, but try and find space directly above the motor for some of our carefully cut pieces of lead sheet. Fix to the bodywork with Blu-tack. If the model has a 'bonnet' or 'nose',

try and put some there, but only at the motor end.

3. Mainline & Bachmann steam outlines – I know it is a shame to cover up all the lovely firebox detail, but these beautiful engines do tend to slip a lot and filling the whole cab with lead can add a couple of coaches to a train.

   With the LNER V2s and their wonderfully sprung bogies and pony trucks, tiny adjustments to the spring tensions can effect a marvellous balancing of the overall weight dispersal to excellent effect – in addition to a cabful of lead.

4. The only locomotives that I have not found the need to add extra lead to have been the Mainline/Bachmann J72s and the B1s. The latter, of course, has tyres on the rear drivers.

5. Kit-built locos – every one I have ever made needs every possible space packing with lead. No wonder the motors run warm!

Cleaning Motors

Up to going to press I have yet to find anything better than methylated spirits for cleaning muck out of electric motors. I know it pongs a bit, but not for long.

Ideally, if you can take the motor away from its gear trains etc., put it in a small stoppered jar containing meths, and then 'swirl' it round for a minute, you will be pleasantly surprised by the dirt that comes away. Just be careful how you remove the motor from the jar afterwards to ensure that you do not re-deposit the dirt. Don't try to be economical with the dirty meths – soak it up with a tissue or two and dispose of.

Cautionary points:

1. the meths may degrease the motor bearings and metal gears. In which case, be prepared to lightly re-oil.

2. certain plastics do not 'respond' to meths very favourably so, as a general rule, keep meths away from all plastics.

3. Remember that methylated spirits are inflammable – and how! No naked lights please.

General Cleaning of Rolling Stock

Under this heading I include the use of a soft

brush to remove fluff and hairs etc. from mechanisms, between wheels and chassis, axles, valve gear and bearings – regularly.

'Warming-up' times for electric motors

I have noticed over the years that electric motors work better when they get 'warmed up'; not hot, but warm. Even in real life a cold engine tends to be rather sluggish, be it steam, electric, petrol or diesel.

What I am suggesting is to be gentle on the accelerator following a cold start; give the motor time to warm up. It will pay dividends. In this respect our little electrical power plants are like us in that they appreciate being allowed time to get into their stride.

Ideally I suppose, we ought to devise some sort of 'warming-up' device for engines before sending them out on journey. Like letting them run under power, on rollers, for a minute or two. There's a project for some enterprising inventor to work on for you – if I don't get there first!

'Cooling-down' times for overheated electric motors

Just the opposite of the above, except that a 'hot' motor usually indicates that something is wrong somewhere.

It may be stiffness in the gearing and wheels, too heavy a load, insufficient motor ventilation, or quite simply an inadequate motor. Under the latter heading I include the DS10s. Half a dozen circuits of the layout and the locos will hardly pull their own tenders; they are all right on the level, but give them an uphill gradient or two and you are in trouble.

Again, they are all right when being driven flat out; but that is no use for my dainty J21 and its 2 ancient clerestories 'gently plying between the country stations'.

Until I find a better alternative motor of similar dimensions, I am simply having to restrict D10-driven locos to a maximum of 10 circuits before giving them an hour or so to cool down.

Shortening the gap between locos and tenders

Once you leave the realms of 15- and 18-inch

radius curves, I think you will be quite pleased to find how much closer together you can afford to run your locos and tenders, and how much better they look for so doing.

Nothing very clever about this, so long as you think about it first.

Certain points need to be considered, not the least being where the actual power unit is i.e., is it in the loco or in the tender?

If the power unit is in the loco then it is recommended practice to bring the weight of the tender to bear on to the 'drawbar' of the loco so as to assist its back end to bear down on the track, for adhesion purposes.

If the power unit is in the tender then it does not matter too much and all that is needed here is to concentrate on the 'gap'.

I prefer to do away with 'what is provided' in the way of loco-to-tender couplings and to fabricate my own, as follows:

1. Take a 2-inch length of copper wire, about $\frac{1}{16}''$ diameter, and lay it on the top of the vice. Then simply tap it with a hammer until it becomes flat.

2. Grip the first 10mm of the flattened wire in the pliers and then bend into a shallow 'D'-shaped curve about 20mm in length, returning to the datum line opposite the end being held in the pliers. Bend the next 10mm so that it is in line with the first 10mm end and cut off the remainder.

3. Place the two end 10mm lengths, flat, on the bench, and the curved bit should leave a gap between its inside face and the bench of no more than 3mm.

   Let us call this workpiece 'the loop'.

4. Now take a 1-inch length of the original, unflattened, wire and flatten the first 8mm of it.

5. Hold this 8mm in the pliers and bend it at a right angle to the rest.

6. Very carefully, and with a pair of sharp-nosed pliers, bend downwards the remainder of the wire another 90 degrees, so that the gap between it and the 'flat bit' is no more than 2mm.

   Let us call this piece 'the pin'.

7. If the superstructure of the loco and tender are plastic, then 'heat sink' the flat ends of the loop centrally on the front beam of the tender so that the down-pointing bit is opposite the centre of the loco-mounted loop.

9. Offer the loco to the tender, on a length of track, and see if the two items match and note what the gap between them is. There should be no more than 2mm free play on straight track.

10. Now test on the tightest curve of your layout and see if the loco and tender will go round it without binding. Hopefully they won't, but if they do then simply 'unheat' the pin from the tender and re-bend to allow for an extra 1mm gap, and re-try.

11. When the results of the tests have proved satisfactory, the final adjustment will be to the pin, to see that the horizontal part at the top just rests on the loop when the loco and tender are on the track, regardless of whether the power unit is in the tender or the loco.

12. If the loco and tender are metal kit-builts, use low-melt solder where the expression 'heat-sink' has been used.

Of course, epoxy or superglue can be used as alternatives to the 'heat' methods.

Close Coupling of Coaches and Wagons

Once you have got the feel of shortening the loco-tender couplings, why not have a go at your coach and wagon couplings, particularly the tension lock types?

The main objective will be (a) to bring the crossbars back until they lie just a shade in front of the buffers, and then (b) shorten the coupling hooks until they just allow about 2mm 'slack' when coupled.

In both instances some cutting will be required, as follows:

Metal tension lock types

1. Using side cutters, cut each of the side arms about half way along their length.

   Clean up the cut edges with a file or mini-drill grindwheel and remove the paint for about 5mm from the cut edges. 'Tin' these cleaned up edges and solder the side arms back in place, but this time – as stated earlier, position them so that the crossbar is just a shade in front of the buffer heads.

2. Again with the side cutters, cut the coupling hook about half way along its length and

clean up as with the crossbar side arms. Then 'tin' both sides and solder together again, positioning the hook until it just allows about 2mm of 'slack' when coupled.

3. Rinse soldered areas and dry, prior to repainting – otherwise they will corrode or, at best, go very rusty.

Plastic tension lock types

Now these can present a problem unless you are prepared to 'heat-sink', because whilst the operation is similar to the metal version, the reinstatement of the plastic parts is not strong enough to be reliable in operation. A different approach needs to be made, as follows: (read first before trying)

1. Take a 12-inch length of $\frac{1}{16}''$ copper or brass wire and hammer it flat on the vice throughout its length. Then 'tin' it throughout its length.

2. Cut off the plastic crossbar and some of the side arms to a point just underneath the buffers.

3. Taking the tinned and flattened wire in sharp-nosed pliers, twist and then bend the first 3mm at right angles.

   Then, at a point equal to the length of the previous crossbar, twist and bend a second 3mm at right angles. Cut away from the main length of wire and you have now prefabricated a new crossbar.

4. Carefully holding the crossbar in the pliers, and finding a means to steady the hand, offer one of the small side arm pieces to the plastic 'stumps' of the old side arms. Holding a soldering iron in the other hand, place the iron gently on to the metal side arm to heat it. It will quickly become hot enough for you to 'heat-sink' it into the plastic 'stump'. Remove the iron and blow on the side arm to dissipate some of the heat, but don't move the crossbar until it has set. It will only take about 10 seconds.

5. Repeat with the other side arm.

6. Hopefully you will have remembered to ensure that the newly fitted crossbar is positioned just a tiny bit in front of the buffer heads.

7. Try and 'tweak' the shallowest curve into the crossbars, so that when they rub together

whilst being propelled round bends, they will not bind.

You might not like this but,

8. Cut off the plastic coupling hook at a point just behind the new crossbar.

9. Cut and 'tin' a 20mm length of $\frac{1}{16}''$ copper or brass wire and bend at right angles in the middle.

10. Holding one end of the above piece of bent wire in the pliers, 'heat-sink' the other end into the plastic 'stump' of the previous coupling hook, endeavouring at the same time to let the new hook overlap the new crossbar by about 2mm.

I said you might not like it because you have now lost your 'automatic coupling'.

In my case all but one of my trains are run in 'rakes' and are only uncoupled in emergency, derailment, or, in the case of the front and rear wagon or coach, for uncoupling from or coupling up to the hauling locomotive. My need for automatic couplings is, therefore, nil.

Another feature of running 'rakes' is that only one 'hook' per vehicle is necessary and the 'bent pin' type of hook described in (9) and (10) above seems to have done away with 'train divided' situations on my layout. It seems such a simple expedient that I have at times wondered why we have needed to complicate couplings so much. It is only when I remember those modellers who love marshalling and shunting trains that I appreciate their need for automatic couplers and un-couplers. I guess it is another instance of 'live and let live' and 'horses for courses'.

I find it very satisfying to view my now very much closer coupled rolling stock trundling round the circuits, but there are two limiting factors to getting them as closely coupled as in real life, namely buffers and track curvature.

Buffers tend to 'lock' together on curves when they are too close coupled, especially when a train is coasting downhill and the couplings are slack. At such a time the vehicles are in a 'propelling' situation, so the buffers need to be kept slightly apart by the crossbars of the couplings and the distance apart depends, as I said, on the diameter of the curves and the length of the buffers.

You would be quite correct to observe, by the way, that I do not use 3-link couplings, Alex Jacksons, Spratt & Winkle, Kaydee – yet!

Valve Gear Improvements to Hornby Locomotives

1. The one outstanding shortcoming of the Hornby Walshearts valve gear, as fitted to their LNER engines, is the angle of the 'eccentric crank' when the wheels are at 'bottom dead centre'.

   Hornby have the crank leaning towards the back of the engine, which is correct for the LMS whereas for the LNER it should lean towards the front. In other words it needs changing by 45 degrees.

   A little bit of filing in the fixing slot will effect this quite simply.

2. The big 'knuckle' joints on the 'combination lever' and 'union link' are a bit of an eyesore to me. Some careful attention from a mini-drill with grinding stone attachment will pare them down a bit.

3. Another thing that irritates me is the excessive downward slope of the union link on some engines. This can be levelled off by increasing the amount of kink in the combination lever (put there by Hornby so as to give clearance to the 'crosshead'). Do this carefully with the sharp-nosed pliers.

Front Bogie improvements to Hornby Locomotives

1. I wish everything was as simple as this, but it improves the front end appearance no end if the Hornby bogie wheels are changed for Jackson wheels of the correct diameter (check your reference books first).

   Reduce the 'sideplay' of the wheels to a minimum by fitting the small Peco fibre washers on both sides. This will encourage the bogie to 'steer' the engine.

2. It will further encourage the front bogie to steer the engine if the almost unlimited sideplay of the whole bogie is limited to a minimum, by the creating and installation of 'bogie sideplay limiters'.

Each engine type has to be dealt with individually but, in general, the idea is to form a length of $\frac{1}{16}''$ copper wire into a flat based 'U' and superglue the flat base to the loco chassis, laterally, so that the 'legs' of the 'U' are positioned to either side of the bogie, equidistant between the wheel axle positions.

Allow a sideplay clearance on each side of no more than 3mm, and cut the 'legs' in line with the bottom of the bogie frame when the engine is on the track.

All the engines to which I have fitted limiters have shows a remarkable and gratifying increase in lateral stability.

Lap Counters for Continuous Layouts

On continuous layouts, trains run round, sometimes, for hours on end without any notice being taken of how far they have actually travelled.

So what, you might say, isn't the basic idea of continuous layouts to do with 'tail-chasing' and all that sort of thing?

Well, that might be the case, to a degree, because I do admit to like watching my trains go round and getting some exercise.

However the thought came to me one day that it might be possible to add another dimension to the operation of 'the schedule' if I could introduce some sort of time or distance recorder to the layout. Perhaps I was being got at by some vestigial memory of my boyhood days when Leeds to King's Cross was represented by 200 circuits of my layout and so on.

Anyway a chance visit to a local Tandy brought to my attention an electromagnetically triggered counter, operating on 12 volts; 0–10,000 being shown in the style of a mileometer, and with a zeroing button.

Cutting a long story short, I bought two – one to record laps on the Up main line and one for the Down main line; great.

A subsequent visit to the Harrogate Model Railway Show at Easter that year resulted in the purchase of 24 small circular magnets and a dozen ¾″ reed switches.

I mounted the 'lap counters' in a display panel above the main control panel and wired them into the 12-volt d.c. circuitry, with their 'feed' wires going first through the reed switches.

I decided the place to put the reed switches was right opposite the control panel – in between the running rails of the main lines going through Barrowby station. I couldn't have chosen a better spot.

As with everything I ever do, there was a problem viz., the reed switches were being activated twice; once when the magnet passed over the entry wire to the reed, and again when it passed over the exit wire. Perhaps I should have bought smaller reed switches and placed them across the track instead of placing them longitudinally.

My way out of this one, found by experiment, was to use the 'entry wire' to the reed as the 'sensor' on the sleepers, and have the reed itself disappear vertically down a hole through the baseboard. This has had the added advantage of protecting the delicate little 'glass bottle' from nasty knocks. With a bit of careful wire-bending I now have a half-inch of 'sensor' wire lying on the sleepers soldered to the 'feed' wire from the 12v d.c. source, brought up through another hole in the baseboard.

The sensor wire at the other end of the reed hangs nicely through the baseboard and is, in turn, soldered to a further wire which is soldered to the 'input' terminal of the 'lap-counter', thus completing the circuitry because the 'output' terminal is connected back to the 12v d.c. source.

The last hurdle to be overcome was where to put the magnets. My first thoughts were the engines, until I realised that I had more engines than magnets, so I decided to mount one on each 'train', be it coaching stock, goods vehicles or DMUs. It was just a matter of making a mount for them somewhere along the underside centre-line of whichever vehicle, to give a height above track of 1mm.

This consideration, in turn, led me to put some plasticard packing under the 'sensor' wire to lift it just sufficiently to be physically 'cleared' by such things as bogie-mounting screws and low-hanging couplings.

For added protection I have placed a plasticard 'ramp' over the 'sensor' itself and secured it with a track pin at each end.

I have been recommended to include a diode in the feed wire between the reed switch and the lap-counter, but I haven't got round to it yet.

All I can say is that it works most satisfactorily, and once I get back to the layout after completing this tome (let it be soon) I shall be actively considering ways of making much practical use of the facility of 'lap-counters'.

A useful indicator

There are some very useful flashing LEDs (or Light-Emitting-Diodes) on the market nowadays which can be used to good effect as 'polarity indicators' around the layout, particularly on buffer stops but also on arrival platforms. The idea is this:

Wire a red flashing LED across the tracks leading up to the buffer stops at a terminus, in such a way that, when the section is powered to accept an incoming locomotive, the red light will flash. If it doesn't flash when you turn on the power, and the locomotive is moving towards the buffers, turn the LED round the other way.

When you have got it right, remember that when you reverse the locomotive away from the buffers the LED will not light because the polarity is wrong way round in that direction.

Also, it is wise to fit a current-limiting resistor between the rail and the LED, to avoid overloading it. Flashing LEDs seem happiest operating on between 6 and 9 volts d.c.

This flashing light will serve two useful purposes:
(1) To indicate where the buffers are and
(2) To indicate that you have selected the correct polarity to accept an incoming train.

The second type of flashing diode I have found useful is the yellow one to use as a 'train arrival indicator' for platforms approached from the main lines.

I suggest making up a small ⅛″ brass tube post about 60mm high, like a colour light signal post, and placing in an easily visible position on the appropriate platform. The LED can be placed on top of the post, surrounded by a suitable shade. The wires can go down the tube and be connected to the running rails for the platform.

As with the red diodes to the buffer stops, it will indicate that the polarity is correct for an incoming train and also serve as a warning that the section is under power.

I hope you will find this as useful as I have. There must be many ways of adapting the idea to further advantage.

'Time present and time past
Are both perhaps present in time future,
And time future contained in time past.'

What Then of the Future?

Prior thoughts

As we commence this, the final part of our conversation about the history of the whys and wherefores of the Aberford, Barrowby and East Garforth Railway, I am concerned lest I should be considered to have been a bit too pedantic in what I have been writing. I apologise to anyone who has gained that impression and ask them to blame it on my enthusiasm getting the better of me.

The older one gets the more there seems to be to learn and, in my opinion, it is very ill-advised of anyone, young or ancient, to take the stance that there is only one point of view or only one way of doing anything.

I have yet to find something that I can do that someone else can not do better.

My little pocket Oxford dictionary defines the noun *hobby* as being 'a favourite occupation not one's main business'.

I'll go along with that and simply add that a hobby gives the hobbyist something to look forward to every day; the thoughts of it lift up the heart when life gets wearisome. I'll go further, a hobby actually gives some people something to live for.

No two of us will ever see things in quite the same way; f'rinstance, did you ever find two women agree on how to bring up babies or about which was the best washing powder?

Mind you, there is no one who is too old to learn; it's just that it takes longer to sink in.

Many of our hobby's greatest advocates will concede that they don't do so many new things as they get older; but they do the old things so much better because they have done them so often.

Two things are certain in this life: one being that you can't do everything. I mean by this, for example, that a skilled engineer, whose rolling stock leaves us breathless with wonder and admiration, may be quite inadequate when it comes to making or devising scenery: and vice versa. This is how I came by the expression 'where mediocrity can flourish'. So very many of us work on our own and do the very best we can with the skills and tools we have, yet have to leave it to others to do for us what we can't do ourselves. If it were not so then RTR manufacturers, manufacturers of electrical components and the like would have had a very lean time of it.

The other certainty in this life is that 'you can't take it with you', and I would like to see someone, much better versed in the subject than myself, take up the subject, on our behalf, of what should happen to our model railway treasures when we depart this mortal coil, and what sort of preparations we can make ourselves to relieve our dependants of the possible problems of disposal. Certainly some consideration needs to be given to the disposal of a valuable layout in the event of one's demise, otherwise there is a grave danger of much of it 'going to a song' to the first bidder, or simply being thrown away as scrap.

The vultures are always hovering in wait for easy pickings.

Anyway, back to more immediate (I hope) things.

On the grounds that 'a cat can look at a queen', I still like to hear, read and see the best that is taking place in the world of model railways because it helps me raise my sights.

Whilst I shall never achieve the great skills of the contributors to such learned periodicals as the *Model Railway Journal*, it is from such periodicals that I am so often inspired to do 'my own things' just that little bit better.

Having said all this, if I did not enjoy model railwaying I fail to see how I could spend all those hours in sub-zero temperatures, sitting at a workbench headbanded with my 'mad professor' binocular magnifiers, chipping away at a speck of metal the size of a full stop.

If ever there was a saying relevant to the hobby on this point I think the honours would go to whoever it was that said, 'the ends justify the means'.

It must be our vision of the end product that keeps us at it despite the difficulties and frustrations; and off-days when nothing goes right and when the 'little bits' we have been labouring over for ages suddenly go 'ping' and shoot off in all directions, never to be seen again.

As year succeeds to year and one looks at one's achievements in baseboards, track, wiring, rolling stock and scenery, despite all their many shortcomings, one gets a feeling of justification and satisfaction in that almost every spare minute of one's life can be accounted for. Either that or the feeling 'I must be crackers and should have my head examined!'

Actions

Up to now, modelling time seems to have been apportioned roughly ninety per cent construction and 10 per cent running, and that 10 per cent mainly to see if what I had made did, in fact, work; because it would then be back to the bench to tackle the next item on the agenda, which had a weird knack of coming into the mind just about the time when the previous item was in the process of being finished.

So now, after spending all these years building myself a model railway system, and having 'completed my agenda', I am having to learn how to run it! It is a peculiar experience and one, I freely confess, that I completely failed to anticipate. I had just assumed that, when 'the day' came, all I would have to do would be to switch on and start running for ever and ever.

In actual fact what has happened is that I have often had to spend hours on track alignments, re-wheeling to improve consistency in running, finding out causes for derailments, sorting out peculiar characteristics and mannerisms of engines and rolling stock etc. etc., in my quest for smooth and reliable running.

I have had to acquire familiarity so as to operate the controls with 'finesse'. I have had to become familiar with the route selectors, the 'polarity changers', the signalling and, most important of all 'the schedule', with the objective of 'not getting into a knot' more often than just now and again.

Add to that, the working out of a system for storing the 'train cassettes' off the layout, in such a way that the next cassette required is not always at the bottom of the pile.

Now that all the major items of the agenda have been completed and shortcomings caught up with, it is becoming more and more possible to get down to some real running sessions and see 'the plan coming together'. It is with a real sense of achievement that I come to the end of an occasional incident-free session.

I will return to the household 'walking on air', feeling that perhaps it has all been worth while after all.

Of course, the next time I do in, everything will go wrong that could possibly go wrong – the typical banana-skin situation: 'after the rise, the fall'. I ought to be used to it by now.

Nothing lasts forever though, and some of my early scenery and buildings are getting a bit shabby and are in need either of replacement or 'prettying up'. Well, this is where some of my acquired skills might help me bring about some real improvements.

The backscenes could also do with a lift, and I have in mind to 'hinge' the coupling rods on my six-(and eight-)coupled kit-built engines so as to allow me to introduce a modicum of compensation. Of course they were built before compensation was thought of, but now everybody does it, even Hornby and Bachmann, which is good.

Having a railway in a garage tempts the household to use the areas under the baseboards for storage, which is all right to a point, but if I want to 'pretty up' the railway I think I am going to have to start by disguising the 'builder's yard' appearance under the boards.

Also there is the cat's cradle of wiring all over the place. I have tried to be as tidy as possible and staple wires or bind them into cables with tape, but there is so much of it!

There is the question of what to do with the boxes that RTRs and other things come in.

I had a clear out of old boxes many years ago – and wish I hadn't. The boxes are now worth as much as what came in them, especially the old Hornby Dublo stock. So now I keep 'em all, but what a pile there is and something else that has to be covered up.

Are there any swap meets just for empty boxes I wonder?

I have the feeling I am going to be involved in some curtain hanging ere long. Nothing jazzy of course, but who on earth sells 'drab brown'?

The railway itself is tidy inasmuch as everything is in its rightful place and there are no extraneous bits and pieces lying around the tracks. In other words the railway is sacred to everything but dust: for dust knoweth no master.

Nothing is allowed on the railway that does not belong there, not even dust (when I can get round to Hoovering it up).

My workbenches, on the other hand, are an offence to the eye, because everything needs to be within easy reach.

Everything seems to be the operative word because everything seems to be there; all my tools, mini-drills, knives, brushes, paints.

I have bottles, containers and jars for every-thing, not just for liquids but for screws, small files, lengths of wire, metal strip, plastic strip. There's no way I can see of making it look tidy because it is in continuous use. Let's face it, this is where all the work is done.

Have you noticed that no matter how large the bench, the available workspace always seems to whittle itself down to 12 inches square?

Recent articles in the modelling press have been concerned with lighting and presentation of layouts, which has set me thinking.

Over the years I have gravitated towards fluorescent lighting because of its evenness and reduction of hard shadows. It also has an effect on the colours one chooses. No doubt my electricity bill has gone up accordingly, but I hate working in gloom.

I intend to give much thought to lighting canopies. Whilst I have shielded most of my 'tubes' from direct view, I am sure I can do much better to show the layout in the best light.

And so, back to the trains. Thank you for your company; perhaps we shall meet again, who knows?

Finale.
Nu-cast/Sentinel Railcar No. 2133 climbs to Brusselton Summit (1370 ft) on the last train of the day. (Photo KC)

Locomotive and Rolling Stock Inventory

Steam Outline

1. Mainline J72 0–6–0T No. 581 in factory finish green, with added lamps, vac. pipes and exhaust ejector pipe. Now, alas, running very slowly.

2. Mainline J72 0–6–0T No. 509 resprayed 'mucky' unlined black, with added details as per No. 581. Very lively and additional pick-ups to wheels have improved performance considerably. Spends its life as the 'Barrowby Shunter'.

3. Mainline J72 0–6–0T *Joem* (I love these little locos), in factory-finished NER green, and numbered No. 510, detailed as 581 and 509 above. Quite lively. 'Doubles up' with the class 03 diesel shunter as Aberford Exchange station pilot.

4. Wills/Triang chassis X04 motor J39 0–6–0 No. 2995, unlined black with Romford wheels, will pull anything on the layout.

5. Wills/Triang chassis MRRC 5-pole motor J38 0–6–0 No. 1443, unlined black with Romford wheels. Good hauler – does not seem to miss the old 'magnadhesion' system.

6. Nucast 0–6–0 J21 No. 996, with DS10 motor, unlined black, – gets hot and loses power after half a dozen circuits (typical DS10 fault).

7. Nucast 0–6–0 J27 No. 2340, with DS10 motor, unlined black – same performance characteristics as the J21.

8. Nucast Sentinel-Cammell steam railcar No. 2133 *Cleveland*, in Apple Green and Cream. The power unit is a Hornby HST power bogie with the Nucast bogie sides 'elongated'. No one has ever noticed and it runs perfectly with pick-ups on all non-tyred wheels.

9. Nucase 0–8–0 Q6 No. 2235, with MRRC motor, in unlined black. One of the first batch ever made and with a number of shortcomings, not the least being gear-stripping.

10. Nucast 0–4–4T G5 No. 1920, with Triang X04 motor, in 'mucky, unlined black. Needs brakegear to complete. Will pull 4 coaches fairly contentedly.

11. Nucast 2–6–2T V3 No. 391, with Mashima can motor and compensated, in lined black. A lovely performer and very smooth. Made just 12 months before Bachmann brought out theirs.

12. K's 4–4–2 GN C2 Atlantic No. 4423, with Romford wheels and X04 motor, in lined LNER green. Crossheads require improvement to stop them coming out of the slide bars.

13. DJH 4–4–0 D20 No. 2109 with Romford Bulldog motor in lined LNER green. A gear-stripper. Not one of DJH's best.

14. DJH 4–6–0 B16/1 No. 2381 with MRRC motor in unlined black. Another gearstripper and not one of DJH's best.

15. DJH 4–6–2T A8 *Teddy Bear* No. 1501 with Mashima can motor and compensated. A very smooth runner but oh, does it roll! The castings needed a lot of cleaning up and I wish DJH would re-tool all their ex NER locos to bring them into line with their latest productions.

16. Gem 4–4–0 D21 No. 1239 on Triang M7 chassis and X04 motor in lined LNER green. Now with Romford wheels. The most trouble-free kit I ever assembled.

17. Jameson 'handbuilt' kit 4–4–0 D49 Hunt class *The Craven* No. 274 in lined LNER green, and with 'mock' rotary valve gear and the tiny lubricating eccentric rod. My first ever kit-built loco (what a way to start!) and took 1½ years to complete. Now powered by a Hornby tender drive unit.

18. Mainline 4–6–0 LMS Jubilee *Leander* No. 5690, in LMS maroon (they were to be seen

quite regularly on NER metals) – rechassised by Bachmann after it 'went slow' on me. Needs a cabful of lead to help it grip the track. A real good-looker.

19. Replica 4–6–0 B1 *Springbok* No. 1000, in lined LNER green. A real good-looker, and, thanks to its rubber tyres, grips the track beautifully. It stripped its gear on one occasion necessitating a replacement chassis.

20. Hornby 4–4–0 D49 Shire class *Yorkshire* No. 234 in lined LNER green. A real beauty with a number of refinements including lamps, vac. and steam heating pipes, screw coupling. Extra pickups on all non-tyred wheel treads and two wire leads from loco to tender give almost perfect pick-up. Bogie 'sideplay limiters' also contribute to smooth running and make the bogies steer the engine round curves.

21. Hornby 4–4–0 D49 Shire class *Cheshire* No. 2753 in lined LNER green. Another real beauty with the same detailing as the *Yorkshire*.

22. Hornby 4–4–0 SR Schools class *Charterhouse* No. 903 in lined SR green. I just could not resist this one, and, after all, we do have *Repton* on the North Yorkshire Moors Railway occasionally.

23. Triang 4–6–0 B12 No. 8522 in lined LNER green, with MRRC motor and Romford wheels. Now very elderly.

24. Hornby 4–6–0 B17 No. 2848 in lined LNER green, detailed as with the D49s above. Will do anything asked of it.

25. Hornby 2–8–0 LMS 8F No. 8193 in unlined black (well, you did see them all over the country). Detailed as with the D49s.

26. Hornby 4–6–2 A3 *The Tetrach* No. 2559 in lined LNER green, detailed as with the D49s plus a D&S Great Northern coalrail tender and more scale-like combination lever. There is nothing this loco cannot deal with – even, on occasion, 15 corridors coaches.

27. Hornby valanced 4–6–2 A4 *Dominion of Canada* No. 4489 in Garter Blue, detailed as with the D49s plus the commemorative bell.

28. 2–6–2 V2 *Durham School* No. 4831 in lined LNER green. Our latest acquisition and a real beauty. A good runner now that we have filled the cab with lead and adjusted the tension on the leading pony truck and trailing bogie springs. Fitted with a scale metal chimney.

A total of 14 kit-builts and 14 RTRs.

Locomotive and Rolling Stock Inventory

Diesel Outline

1. Bachmann Class 03 shunter No. D2012, in BR green with 'wasp' warning stripes. A rarity – nothing to add, just as it came out of the box, perfect.
2. Hornby Class 08 shunter No. 13012, in BR green with 'wasp' stripes painted by me. Not in very good condition.
3. Hornby HST 125 in original blue, plus non-powered car. Extra pick-ups on all non-tyred wheels. A better performer than the Lima version.
4. Hornby 3-coach DMU in white and blue – very smart. Extra pick-ups.
5. Hornby 2-coach 'Pacer' in dual blue – not very inspiring.
6. Lima 2-coach 'Super Sprinter' in blue and off white – not very inspiring.
7. Lima Class 20 No. 20215, in grey. Very smooth and reliable at low speeds.
8. Lima Class 31 No. 31327 'Phillips Imperial' in grey. Bought by No. 2 son at a time of weakness. A good performer though.
9. Lima Class 31 No. 31283 in BR blue. Comments as for No. 8.
10. Lima Class 37 No. 37012 *Loch Rannoch* in BR blue, resprayed and reliveried, with extra front end detail added plus front and rear lights. A very reliable performer and most realistic-looking.
11. Lima Class 40 No. D261 in BR green with extra front end detail added plus front and rear lights. Very smart and most reliable, especially when compared with a previously owned Jouef version.
12. Lima Class 47 No. 47705 in Scotrail livery with front and rear lights. Very smart and reliable.
13. Lima Class 47 No. 47522 *Doncaster Enterprise* in LNER lined green. Very smart and a good performer.
14. Lima Class 55 Deltic No. D9008 *The Green Howards* in original 2-tone green, with added front end detail and front and rear lights, plus extra pick-ups to non-tyred wheels. Even sounds like the real thing.
15. Lima HST 125 *City of Humberside* in 'Executive' livery plus non-powered car *Edinburgh Military Tattoo*. Extra pick-ups on non-tyred wheels, plus a lot of extra weight to increase adhesion.
16. Mainline Class 45 No. 45060 *Sherwood Forester* in BR blue. Completely resprayed and re-transferred. Extra front end detail plus lights. New transmission gears. Almost too powerful.
17. Mainline Class 56 No. 56079 in BR blue. A good performer but drab. Extra pick-ups.

All diesel units are RTR.

Appendix III

Passenger and Parcel Vehicles

1. 6 P C Gresley Corridors in teak. Quite elderly now but superb runners.
2. 5 Ian Kirk Gresley Corridors in teak, of much more recent vintage than the P C ones.
3. 5 Dublo Pullmans plus 1 Triang (current type). Always kept clean and well touched-up.
4. 2 Triang Clerestories painted teak – and hand numbered and lettered.
5. 4 Triang Clerestories (including 1 ex-GWR corridor) all painted teak and re-transferred.
6. 5 coach 'mixed' LNER Gresleys in teak, comprising 2 Dublo tinplates, 2 Kirk suburbans and 1 Kemilway etched brass 'Lav/compo' (my first venture in etched, so a few shortcomings may become apparent if inspected too closely).
7. 6 coach 'parcels', comprising 3 Lima Palethorpes Sausage bogies (to go with the Pork Pie factory), Dublo 6-wheel passenger brake van in BR maroon with central wheel-set removed, 1 D & S etched 4-wheel Pigeon Van in teak, and 1 Triang Hornby LMS clerestory (scale length) corridor in maroon.
8. 5 Triang Hornby BR Mks 1 and 3 in blue.
9. 5 Lima BR Mk 3s in 'raspberry ripple' livery – HST 125 set.
10. 5 Lima BR Mk 2s in 'Transpennine' livery – very smart.
11. Triang Hornby 3-car DMU in white.
12. Triang Hornby 2-car 'Pacer' in dual blue.
13. Lima 2-car 'Super Sprinter' in blue and white/grey.
14. 6 Bachmann Thompson corridors in maroon – for 'preservation specials'. Heavy but smart.
15. 6 Mailcoach articulated 'Coronation' corridors plus beaver-tail observation coach in Garter & Marlbrough Blue, complete with seated passengers. Constructed in 1992 and the pride of the layout.

Total 65 (non-powered) coaches, 21 of them kit-built.

Note – to avoid the sometimes unavoidable 'daylight' showing between corridor coaches, try making some black paper 'spacers, approx 25mm high × 20mm wide and folded 5mm from each end, one of which is glued to the centre of a corridor vestibule door. With a bit of luck, these spacers will 'give' with the movement of the coaches and should not present any problems with stability on the tracks. Try it anyway, won't cost much.

Goods Vehicles

1. Express freight ('fitted') comprising 16 assorted, and I do mean assorted, vans by Dublo, Airfix (kits) and RTRs, Mainline plus Mainline LNER 20-ton brake van at each end – with lamps! Total 18 vehicles.

2. Pick-up goods comprising 5 assorted open wagons with loads – some sheeted, 6 vans and a Crosfields tanker by Dublo, Peco, Mainline & Airfix, plus a Slater's kit-built 'Birdcage' brake van. Makes a very interesting train to look at. Total 13 vehicles.

3. Tanker train comprising 10 assorted tankers by Dublo, Airfix (kits – poor) and Mainline, together with statutory open wagon at each end by Parkside (kit-built) and a Dublo LNER 20-ton brake van. Total 13 vehicles.

4. 'Bogie bolster' train comprising 4 bolsters and 4 Welltroll, with loads, by Mainline, together with Mainline NER Brakevan in maroon and a Triang ditto in grey. A very sensitive train highly susceptible to derailments. Needs a very smooth and slow-running loco 'up front' such as the V3 or the A8, with their Mashima motors. With the right engine it will run perfectly all day. I have not yet fathomed out the answer to the sensitivity problem; wheels are all Jackson's and the couplings modified to bring the vehicles closer together. If I ever write a sequel to this book, I promise to let you know what the solution proved to be. Total 10 vehicles.

5. Coal train comprising ancient Dublo tinplates and more recent plastic ones all different shapes and sizes, plus 4 Airfix RTR 21-ton hoppers, with a Dublo ex-LMS 'veranda' brake (tinplate) in grey at one end, and a Dublo plastic ex-GWR 'toad' in grey at t'other. All vehicles fitted with 'loads' and Jackson wheels. It must be quite a heavy train judging by the way many locos 'jib' at it on the up gradients. The Hornby 8F 2–8–0 usually hauls it, but gets warm after about half an hour. The best engines for the coal train have been the J39s, but they look too small at the head of it. Total 16 vehicles.

Total 62 vehicles plus 8 brake vans, all RTR except for 7 kit-builts.

End of Locomotive and Rolling Stock Inventory (as at 11.11.93).